"Here comes trouble," said Naomi.

I craned my neck to catch a glimpse of a Park Avenue sophisticate as she darted around one of the security guards and stepped between Philomena and the camera. The woman wore a Hermes scarf stylishly draped around her neck and secured with a large sapphire brooch that mirrored the midnight blue anger in her eyes. "Isn't that—?"

"Oh yeah," said Janice. "It most definitely is."

"Cut!" yelled the *E!* producer. "What the hell do you think you're doing, grandma? We're taping an interview here."

Grandma? I pegged her at late-forties, early-fifties at the most, but I suppose to a twenty-something, that's ancient.

"Nice suit," said Tessa. "Classic Armani. Who is she?"

"Sylvia Gruenwald," several of us said in unison.

"Hell hath no fury like a trophy wife scorned," said Naomi.

W9-BYK-854

Acclaim for the Anastasia Pollack Crafting Mysteries

Assault with a Deadly Glue Gun

"Crafty cozies don't get any better than this hilarious confection...Anastasia is as deadpan droll as Tina Fey's Liz Lemon, and readers can't help cheering as she copes with caring for a host of colorful characters." – *Publishers Weekly* (starred review)

"Winston has hit a homerun with this hilarious, laugh-until-your-sides-hurt tale. Oddball characters, uproariously funny situations, and a heroine with a strong sense of irony will delight fans of Janet Evanovich, Jess Lourey, and Kathleen Bacus. May this be the first of many in Winston's Anastasia Pollack Crafting Mystery series." – *Booklist* (starred review)

"A comic tour de force...Lovers of funny mysteries, outrageous puns, self-deprecating humor, and light romance will all find something here." – *ForeWord Magazine* (Book-of-the-Year nominee)

"North Jersey's more mature answer to Stephanie Plum. Funny, gutsy, and determined, Anastasia has a bright future in the planned series." – *Kirkus Reviews*

"...a delightful romp through the halls of who-done-it." – *The Star-Ledger*

"Make way for Lois Winston's promising new series...I'll be eagerly awaiting the next installment in this thoroughly delightful series." – *Mystery Scene Magazine*

"...once you read the first few pages of Lois Winston's first-in-series whodunit, you're hooked for the duration..." – *Bookpage*

"...madcap but tough-as-nails, no holds barred plot and main character...a step above the usual crafty cozy." – *The Mystery Reader*

"...Anastasia is, above all, a JERSEY girl..., and never, ever mess with one of them. I can't wait 'til the next book in this series..." – *Suspense Magazine*

"Anastasia is as crafty as Martha Stewart, as feisty as Stephanie Plum, and as resourceful as Kinsey Millhone." – Mary Kennedy, author of the Talk Radio Mysteries

"Fans of Stephanie Plum will love Lois Winston's cast of quirky, laughable, and loveable characters. *Assault with a Deadly Glue Gun* is clever and thoroughly entertaining—a must read!" – Brenda Novak, *New York Times* best-selling author

"What a treat—I can't stop laughing! Witty, wise, and delightfully clever, Anastasia is going to be your new best friend. Her mysterious adventures are irresistible—you'll be glued to the page!" – Hank Phillippi Ryan, Agatha, Anthony, and Macavity award-winning author

"You think you've got trouble? Say hello to Anastasia Pollack, who also happens to be queen of the one-liners. Funny, funny, funny—this is a series you don't want to miss!" – Kasey Michaels, *USA Today* best-selling author

Death by Killer Mop Doll
"Anastasia is a crafting Stephanie Plum, surrounded by characters sure to bring chuckles as she careens through the narrative, crossing paths with the detectives assigned to the case and snooping around to solve it." – *Booklist*

"Several crafts projects, oodles of laughs and an older, more centered version of Stephanie Plum." – *Kirkus Reviews*

"In Winston's droll second cozy featuring crafts magazine editor Anastasia Pollack...readers who relish the offbeat will be rewarded." – *Publishers Weekly*

"...a *30 Rock* vibe...Winston turns out another lighthearted amateur sleuth investigation. Laden with one-liners, Anastasia's second outing (after *Assault With a Deadly Glue Gun*) points to another successful series in the works." – *Library Journal*

"Winston...plays for plenty of laughs...while letting Anastasia shine as a risk-taking investigator who doesn't always know when to quit." – *Alfred Hitchcock Mystery Magazine*

Revenge of the Crafty Corpse

"Winston peppers the twisty and slightly edgy plot with humor and plenty of craft patterns. Fans of craft mysteries will like this, of course, but so will those who enjoy the smart and snarky humor of Janet Evanovich, Laura Levine, and Laura DeSilverio." – *Booklist*

"Winston's entertaining third cozy plunges Anastasia into a surprisingly fraught stew of jealousy, greed, and sex..." and a "Sopranos-worthy lineup of eccentric character..." – *Publishers Weekly*

"Winston provides a long-suffering heroine, amusing characters, a...good mystery and a series of crafting projects featuring cloth yo-yos." – *Kirkus Reviews*

"A fun addition to a series that keeps getting stronger." – *Romantic Times Magazine*

"Chuckles begin on page one and the steady humor sustains a comedic crafts cozy, the third (after *Death by Killer Mop Doll*)... Recommend for Chris Grabenstein ("John Ceepak" series) and Jess Lourey readers." – *Library Journal*

"You'll be both surprised and entertained by this terrific mystery. I can't wait to see what happens in the Pollack household next." – *Suspense Magazine*

"The book has what a mystery should...It moves along at a good pace...Like all good sleuths, Anastasia pieces together what others don't...The book has a fun twist...and it's clear that Anastasia, the everyday woman who loves crafts and desserts, and has a complete hottie in pursuit, will return to solve another murder and offer more crafts tips..." – *Star-Ledger*

Decoupage Can Be Deadly
"*Decoupage Can Be Deadly* is the fourth in the Anastasia Pollock Crafting Mysteries by Lois Winston. And it's the best one yet. More, please!" – *Suspense Magazine*

"What a great cozy mystery series. One of the reasons this series stands out for me as a great one is the absolutely great cast of characters. Every single character in these books is awesomely quirky and downright hilarious. This series is a true laugh out loud read!" – Books Are Life–Vita Libri

"This is one of these series that no matter what, I'm going to be laughing my way through a comedy of errors as our reluctant heroine sets a course of action to find a killer while contending with her eccentrically dysfunctional family. This adventure grabs you immediately delivering a fast-paced and action-filled drama that doesn't let up from the first page to the surprising conclusion." – Dru's Book Musings

"Lois Winston's reluctant amateur sleuth Anastasia Pollack is back in another wild romp." – The Book Breeze

A Stitch to Die For
"*A Stitch to Die For* is the fifth in the *Anastasia Pollack Crafting Mysteries* by Lois Winston. If you're a reader who enjoys a well-

plotted mystery and loves to laugh, don't miss this one!" – *Suspense Magazine*

Scrapbook of Murder

"This is one of the best books in this delightfully entertaining whodunit and I hope there are more stories in the future." – Dru's Book Musings

"*Scrapbook of Murder* is a perfect example of what mysteries are all about—deft plotting, believable characters, well-written dialogue, and a satisfying, logical ending. I loved it!" – *Suspense Magazine*

"I read an amazing book recently, y'all — *Scrapbook of Murder* by Lois Winston, #6 in the Anastasia Pollack Crafting Mysteries. All six novels and three novellas in the series are Five Star reads." – Jane Reads

"Well written, with interesting characters." – Laura's Interests

"...a quick read, with humour, a good mystery and very interesting characters!" – Verietats

Drop Dead Ornaments

"I always forget how much I love this series until I read the next one and I fall in love all over again..." – Dru's Book Musings

"*Drop Dead Ornaments* is a delightful addition to the Anastasia Pollack Crafting Mystery series. More, please!" – *Suspense Magazine*

"I love protagonist Anastasia Pollack. She's witty and funny, and she can be sarcastic at times...A great whodunit, with riotous twists and turns, *Drop Dead Ornaments* was a fast, exciting read that really kept me on my toes." – Lisa Ks Book reviews

"*Drop Dead Ornaments* is such a fantastic book...I adore

Anastasia! She's clever, likable, fun to read about, and easy to root for." – Jane Reads

"...readers will be laughing continually at the antics of Anastasia and clan in *Drop Dead Ornaments*." – The Avid Reader

"I love this series! Not only is Anastasia a 'crime magnet,' she is hilarious and snarky, a delight to read about and a dedicated friend." – Mallory Heart's Cozies

"It is always a nice surprise when something I am reading has a tie in to actual news or events that are happening in the present moment. I don't want to spoil a major plot secret, but the timing could not have been better...Be prepared for a dysfunctional cast of quirky characters." – Laura's Interests

"This is a Tour de Force of a Murder/Mystery." – A Wytch's Book Review

"A series worth checking out." – The Ninja Librarian

"I flew through this book. Winston knows how to make a reader turn the page. It's more than a puzzle to solve—I was rooting for people I cared about. Anastasia Pollack is easy to like, a good mother, a good friend, and in a healthy romantic relationship, the kind of person you'd want on your side in a difficult situation." – Indies Who Publish Everywhere

"Lois Winston's cozy craft mystery *Drop Dead Ornaments* is an enjoyable...roller-coaster ride, with secrets and clues tugging the reader this way and that, and gentle climbs and drops of suspense and revelation to keep them reading." – Here's How It Happened

"Anastasia is a take-charge woman with a heart for her family–even her ex-family members who don't (in my opinion) deserve her kindness... What I like best about Anastasia is how she balances her quest for justice with the needs and fears of her family… I can't wait to read more of her adventures and the progress of her relationship with her family and her boyfriend." – The Self-Rescue Princess

"…a light-hearted cozy mystery with lots of energy and definitely lots of action and interaction between characters." – Curling Up By the Fire

"I thought the plot was well thought out and the story flowed well. There were many twists and turns…and I enjoyed all the quirky characters. I was totally baffled as to who the killer was and was left guessing to the very end." – Melina's Book Blog

"(Anastasia's) wit and sarcasm lend a bit of humor to this cozy, and the story kept me intrigued right up to the end." – The Books the Thing

Handmade Ho-Ho Homicide

"Handmade Ho-Ho Homicide" is a laugh-out-loud, well plotted mystery, from a real pro! A ho-ho hoot!" – *Suspense Magazine*

"Merry *Crises*! Lois Winston has brought back Anastasia's delightful first-person narrative of family, friends, dysfunction, and murder, and made it again very entertaining! Anastasia's clever quips, fun stories, and well-deserved digs kept me smiling, and reading the many funny parts to my husband…does that count as two thumbs up in one? What a great journey!" – *Kings River Life Magazine*

"Once again, the author knows how to tell a story that immediately grabbed my attention and I couldn't put this book down until the last page was read…. This was one of the best books in this delightfully lovable series and I can't wait to see what exciting adventures await Anastasia and her friends." – Dru's Book Musings

"This was such a fun quick read. I can't wait to read more of this series." – A Chick Who Reads

"The story had me on the edge of my seat the entire time." – 5 Stars, Baroness Book Trove

"Christmas, cozy mystery, craft, how can I not love this book? Humor, twists and turns, adorable characters make this story truly engaging from the first to the last page." – LibriAmoriMiei

"Take a murder mystery, add some light-hearted humor and weird characters, sprinkle some snow and what you get is *Handmade Ho-Ho Homicide*—a perfect Christmas Cozy read." –5 stars, The Book Decoder

Books by Lois Winston

Anastasia Pollack Crafting Mystery series
Assault with a Deadly Glue Gun
Death by Killer Mop Doll
Revenge of the Crafty Corpse
Decoupage Can Be Deadly
A Stitch to Die For
Scrapbook of Murder
Drop Dead Ornaments
Handmade Ho-Ho Homicide
A Sew Deadly Cruise

Anastasia Pollack Crafting Mini-Mysteries
Crewel Intentions
Mosaic Mayhem
Patchwork Peril
Crafty Crimes (all 3 novellas in one volume)

Empty Nest Mystery Series
Definitely Dead
Literally Dead

Romantic Suspense
Love, Lies and a Double Shot of Deception
Lost in Manhattan (writing as Emma Carlyle)
Someone to Watch Over Me (writing as Emma Carlyle)

Romance and Chick Lit
Talk Gertie to Me
Four Uncles and a Wedding (writing as Emma Carlyle)
Hooking Mr. Right (writing as Emma Carlyle)
Finding Hope (Writing as Emma Carlyle)

Novellas and Novelettes
Elementary, My Dear Gertie

Once Upon a Romance
Finding Mr. Right

Children's Chapter Book
The Magic Paintbrush

Nonfiction
Top Ten Reasons Your Novel is Rejected
House Unauthorized
Bake, Love, Write
We'd Rather Be Writing

Decoupage
Can Be
Deadly

LOIS WINSTON

Decoupage Can Be Deadly copyright 2013 by Lois Winston. All rights reserved. No part of this book may be used or reproduced in any manner whatsoever without written permission except in the case of brief quotations embodied in critical articles and reviews.

This is a work of fiction. Names, characters, places, and incidents are either the product of the author's imagination or are used fictitiously, and any resemblance to actual persons, living or dead, locations, or events is coincidental or fictionalized.

Cover design by L. Winston

ISBN:978-1-940795-00-3

DEDICATION

For Jack, Zoe, and Chase
who have left permanent handprints on my heart.

ACKNOWLEDGMENTS

To my family: Rob, Chris, Scott, Jen, Megan, and the very special trio mentioned in the dedication.

To Irene Peterson and Donnell Bell for their second and third sets of eyes that caught what my own eyes missed.

To Sue Evens for her Malice Domestic donation which entitled her to be named as a character in this book.

To Sandy Sechrest for her Bouchercon donation which entitled her to be named as a character in this book.

For offering her expertise during the research phase of *Decoupage Can Be Deadly*, special thanks to attorney Barbara Doyle Frentz.

And finally, to Michael "The Gluologist" Assile of Beacon Adhesives for allowing me to use his experience with the consumer who broke a tooth.

ONE

"What happened?" I stopped short at the entrance to our exhibition booth. My fellow *American Woman* editors and I had spent all day yesterday at the Jacob Javits Convention Center, setting up for the *Celebrating Women* weekend consumer show. Now half our booth had been usurped, our carefully coordinated displays missing.

"Not what. Who," said food editor Cloris McWerther.

"Philomena." Travel editor Serena Brower practically spat out the name.

"Obnoxious people deserve a slow, painful death," said fashion editor Tessa Lisbon. She stood with hands on hips. Her perfectly painted, collagen-enhanced scarlet lips, deep in pout mode, matched the anger flaming on her cheeks.

Cloris turned to me and stage-whispered, "Not to spout clichés, but doesn't that fall under the heading of the pot calling the kettle black?"

Having an obnoxious personality was pretty much a prerequisite for the job of fashion editor at *American Woman*. However, Philomena Campanello, the target of everyone's ire belonged in the category of über-obnoxious.

"It's called *chutzpah*," said health editor Janice Kerr.

"Brass balls," added decorating editor Jeanie Sims.

"Same difference," said finance editor Sheila Conway.

I corrected them all. "No ladies, it's called sleeping with the CEO."

"Score one for our crafts editor," said Cloris.

I, Anastasia Pollack, being the crafts editor in question, executed a mock bow, then turned to Naomi Dreyfus, our editorial director. "So what do we do now?"

Naomi threw her hands up in the air. Little ever rattled the Grace Kelly perfection of our serene editorial director, but even she sported deep frown lines as we surveyed the devastation. "We make the best of a crappy situation for the next two days."

Trimedia, our parent company, was a major sponsor of the *Celebrating Women* show, with a display area that spanned both sides of the long center aisle at the convention center. *American Woman*, the monthly magazine responsible for our weekly paychecks, had been assigned four consecutive spaces, forty linear feet, on one side of the aisle. The remaining space was divided up between the rest of Trimedia's holdings that catered to women TV viewers, radio listeners, and magazine readers.

Each of our eight editors had received five feet of space. We'd spent the better part of the last two weeks coordinating our efforts to create a cohesive display where we'd each meet and greet attendees, hand out free copies of the magazine, do demos, and offer make-it/take-it projects. With schematics in hand, we'd spent most of yesterday setting up the booth.

Now, with the show opening to the public in a matter of minutes, we stood in the aisle, our mouths agape at the destruction of all our hard work. Overnight our forty feet had shrunk to twenty, half our booth appropriated by Philomena Campanello, the self-proclaimed Queen of Bling, otherwise known as Trimedia's newest star and CEO Alfred Gruenwald's newest arm candy.

When we'd finished setting up the *American Woman* booth late yesterday afternoon, Philomena hadn't even arrived. An army of minions must have worked late into the night to create the flashy extravaganza now occupying half our space plus her originally allocated forty feet.

Philomena had begun her career as Philly-Mean-A, a twenty-something white *gangsta*, often called the female Eminem. Whether through savvy business advisors, her own smarts, or sleeping with the right people, the potty-mouthed street rapper from Philadelphia had morphed into the first-name-only Philomena and parlayed herself into a business empire replete with her own line of perfume, fashions, and accessories, plus a multitude of endorsements.

Now, thanks to the help of one besotted CEO who'd convinced the Trimedia board to buy into her *Bling!* concept, the first issue of *Bling!* was on newsstands. A combination fashion, lifestyle, and entertainment monthly, the magazine featured ten percent fashion, ten percent lifestyle, and ten percent entertainment. The remaining seventy percent consisted mostly of ads for the various products Philomena hyped, thanks to her lucrative endorsement deals. But as anyone who has ever worked in the magazine business knows, advertising trumps content. Big time. Ads pay the bills and keep the company in the black.

Philomena's *Bling!* bling currently encroached over half our designated exhibit space.

"Where's our stuff?" asked Serena.

I stepped into the booth and ducked behind the eight-foot tall back panels, each covered with a larger-than-life blow-up of a page from the current issue of *American Woman*. Half were now missing, along with half our models and hand-outs. Just as I suspected, I found everything heaped on the floor in haphazard piles.

Retrieving the smashed remains of a Potichomanie decoupage bowl, I returned to the gaggle of editors and held up the shards of broken glass. "Five hours to create, five seconds to destroy."

"Good thing it was already photographed and appears in the current issue," said beauty editor Nicole Emmerling. "At least you don't have to pull an all-nighter to make another."

I'd been down that road before when a psychopath had fixated on my mop dolls and used them as props in an act of vandalism and a couple of murders. However, even though the bowl had already been featured in the magazine, I had planned to keep it. You never know when a Potichomanie decoupage bowl might come in handy as a prop. Or as a gift.

Given that our current issue featured decoupage crafts, I wondered if any of my other missing models had survived intact, but I didn't have time to dig through the mound of discarded items. Within minutes the doors would open, releasing a stampeding horde of women into the exhibition hall.

"Speaking of the *blinga donna*," said Cloris. She cocked her head, directing our attention down the aisle where a blinged-out Philomena strutted toward us as if she were on a Fashion Week catwalk.

Looped over one arm she held a behemoth of a chainmail-draped and gold sequin-studded red patent leather bag, a relatively tame statement compared to the rest of her streetwalker chic outfit of skin-tight turquoise leopard leggings, red-sequined bustier, and a pair of purple stiletto high top sneakers. Peacock feathers sprouted from her platinum pouf hairdo. A large script *P*, covered in diamonds, hung from her neck, the bottom of the letter disappearing into her massive cleavage.

A Marilyn Monroe impersonator stood beside Philomena. Her toned body wore an extremely short tiger print silk sheath like a second skin. She towered over the vertically challenged Philomena, who was barely five feet tall minus her stilettos, by at least a foot and a half. Something told me Marilyn was actually a guy. Even so, I'd kill for his hourglass figure.

Philomena's other arm looped through the arm of CEO Alfred Gruenwald who apparently had lost whatever common sense he once possessed as he approached his seventieth birthday. Behind them strutted Philomena's entourage and Gruenwald's combination driver/gopher boy. The guy's intimidating stature alone would keep the riffraff at bay.

"Are you going to say something to him?" I asked Naomi.

"Would it matter?"

"No, but we'd all feel better if you let him know how pissed we are," said Jeanie.

"Once more unto the breach," muttered Naomi, reminding me of Ralph, my Shakespeare quoting parrot. She stepped to the center of the aisle. The rest of us closed ranks on either side of her, blocking the conquering army's path to the *Bling!* display. With no easy way to maneuver around us, they were forced to stop.

"I'd like a word with the two of you," said Naomi.

Philomena set her mouth into a tight line and stared straight ahead, ignoring Naomi. I think. It was hard to tell. For all anyone knew, hidden behind her enormous rhinestone encrusted sunglasses, she may have been spearing Naomi with the Evil Eye.

Gruenwald offered Naomi one of those affable businessman smiles that really means he knows he's top dog, and you'd better not mess with him. Ever. "Certainly," he said. "What's on your mind?"

"After my editors spent all day yesterday setting up our booth, your girlfriend here pranced in last night and helped herself to half our space."

Gruenwald the Clueless turned to Philomena. "Really?"

"You said you wanted to make a statement," said the Blinged One. "How the hell do you expect me to make a statement with a measly forty feet of booth space?"

"Yes, but—"

I noticed that activity had halted in the surrounding booths. Various Trimedia staffers inched closer, some with smart phones in hand, already snapping photos and sending the latest Trimedia gossip out into the Twittersphere.

"No buts about it, sweetie. What's more important to Trimedia, a third-rate supermarket rag or *Bling!*?" She waved her arm toward her sixty feet of prime exhibit space. "Now *that's* a statement!" Then she turned to Marilyn. "Am I right, or am I right?"

"Right on!" shouted Marilyn, punctuating her agreement with a fist bump. The rest of Philomena's entourage echoed the sentiment.

"She made a statement, all right," said Serena.

"At our expense," added Cloris.

I studied the garish *Bling!* booth. A giant disco ball, centered over the display, hung from a steel girder. As it rotated, pulsating laser lights within the ball flashed the *Bling!* logo across the convention center. I'm sure the other exhibitors loved that. Was *gangsta* chic really the sort of statement Trimedia wanted to make?

"So cathouse couture is the next big trend?" asked Tessa. "I must have missed that memo."

Philomena got up too close and too personal with Tessa's nose, dragging Gruenwald along with her. "Are you calling me what I think you're calling me?"

Tessa didn't flinch. She held her ground and offered Philomena a smile that was anything but friendly. "If the Manolo fits..."

"Why you—! Alfred, you gonna allow her to diss your woman like that?"

Gruenwald finally extricated his arm from Philomena's and inserted himself between her and Tessa. "Now let's all calm down." He then addressed Naomi. "Your magazine has an established readership. We're trying to tap into a new demographic with *Bling!* To do so, we need to go big and splashy."

"That doesn't give her the right to trash our booth," I said. "If you wanted to give her more display space than us, we should have been told about it weeks ago, not ambushed this morning."

Gruenwald glanced over at our reduced space, then down the aisle to Philomena's enlarged area. "Well, what's done is done. You'll have to make do with the space you currently have. The show is about to open, and there's nothing I can do at this point."

With that, Philomena did exactly what I'd expect a spoiled brat celebrity to do: she flipped us the bird. Then she looped her arm back through Gruenwald's and they, along with the entourage and Gopher Boy, proceeded down the aisle to the *Bling!* display.

"There's no fool like an old fool," muttered Naomi.

The rest of us cast sideways glances at each other. Naomi's longtime significant other had made a similar spectacle of himself not that long ago with our magazine's former fashion editor. Marlys Vandenburg now resides six feet under, thanks to my not-so-dearly departed husband's loan shark.

In Naomi's case, Hugo Reynolds-Alsopp, the former publisher of *American Woman*, had come to his senses, and the two had gotten back together. I wondered if Mrs. Gruenwald would be as forgiving of her husband's lapse of sanity.

"What do you think he sees in her?" asked Sheila. "She's so crass and low-class."

"Beats me," I said. "Maybe she's stroking his ego. After all, he's old enough to be her grandfather."

"Oh, she's stroking something all right," said Tessa, "but I guarantee it's not his ego."

"Thank you very much," said Janice. She screwed up her face and shuddered. "That's one image I really didn't want imprinted into my cerebral cortex."

"So the old geezer's a horn dog," said Nicole. "What the hell does she see in him?"

"Can't be his money," said Serena. "She's worth millions on her own."

"Well, it's certainly not his looks," said Tessa.

"That's for sure," said Sheila. "The guy resembles Ernest Borgnine. On a bad day."

"Who's Ernest Borgnine?" asked Tessa.

"*Marty*? *From Here to Eternity*?"

"Huh?"

"*McHale's Navy*?" I offered.

When Tessa remained clueless, Sheila rolled her eyes and shook her head. "Google him."

Further conversation concerning Philomena and Gruenwald halted with the onslaught of the first wave of show attendees making their way down the aisles.

Naomi clapped her hands together. "Show time, ladies."

Since our space had been chopped in half, we quickly revised our game plan for the day. Half the editors grabbed copies of *American Woman* and stepped toward the edge of the booth to hand them out as people passed by in the aisle, the job Naomi had originally assigned herself. The rest of us took up positions behind our remaining podiums where we proceeded to demonstrate various techniques or dispense information. We'd switch off hourly.

While I decoupaged, Cloris decorated cupcakes, Tessa demonstrated scarf tying techniques, and Janice handed out refrigerator magnets listing the various signs of heart attack in women under forty. Oddly enough, chest pain wasn't one of the symptoms. "Reading *American Woman* might save your life," she told the women reaching for the magnets.

~*~

By six o'clock when the show closed for the day, I remembered why I hated working trade and consumer shows. "My aches have aches," I said to no one in particular. My feet burned from standing for hours in heels, but I knew if I slipped my shoes off for some relief, I'd never get them back on.

I also knew from experience that we'd wait at least an hour in the cab or bus line to transport us to Penn Station. Hoofing it would get us on a train home much faster. If my feet survived the nearly mile-long walk. I meant to bring a pair of sneakers with me to switch into after the show, but I forgot to grab them as I rushed out the door that morning to catch the train into the city.

"Did you notice the only booth space where Trimedia coughed up the extra dough for thicker carpet and padding is *Bling!*'s?" asked Jeanie.

I hadn't, but sure enough, when I glanced down the row, the *Bling!* carpeting rose a good two inches above the carpeting under our feet—including the twenty feet that used to belong to us. "Must be nice to have that kind of pull," I said.

Philomena and her entourage had darted out the moment the show officially closed for the day. The *Bling!* booth had been jammed non-stop throughout the day. Even when I walked past during a break, I hadn't seen much of it, given the crowds of women gathered in and around the booth. Now that people were streaming out of the convention center, I wandered over to take a close-up. The others followed my lead.

The décor matched the tackiness of Philomena's outfit. "She makes Vittorio Versailles look sedate," said Nicole.

Vittorio Versailles was an over-the-top designer our former fashion editor had sliced and diced in an issue last winter. He'd threatened to sue Trimedia, but Ricardo the loan shark got to Vittorio before Vittorio's attorneys had a chance to draw up the papers.

"This booth seems more appropriate for one of those adult expos," said Jeanie.

"Oh?" asked Janice.

"Not that I have personal experience," Jeanie quickly added.

"You think *Bling!* will be successful?" I asked Naomi.

She shrugged. "Eventually people will wise up to the fact that the magazine is mostly ads. They'll stop buying copies. Once that happens, ad revenues will dip, and the magazine will fold. I give it a year tops."

"Even with most of the ads for products Philomena's endorsing?" asked Tessa.

"Advertisers are fickle," said Naomi. "As her contracts near expiration, the advertisers will be courting the next hot spokesperson. Philomena has no staying power."

"Yet she's raking in megabucks right now," said Serena.

"I'd kill for an endorsement deal," said Tessa. "I wouldn't care if it only lasted a year or two."

"One can only hope Naomi is right," said Sheila. She glanced around the garish exhibit. "I feel dirty just standing here."

"And yet her booth was mobbed all day," I said.

"For what? Lollipops?" She picked one up out of a large fishbowl on the back counter. "Omigod!"

"What?" We all turned to stare at her. Sheila's normally peach complexion was now as flaming red as her hair. "These aren't lollipops." She passed one to each of us.

"They certainly aren't," said Tessa. "I wonder if the Trimedia board knows she's passing out condoms with the *Bling!* logo emblazoned on them."

"Maybe you should put in a call to your Uncle Chessie," said Cloris.

Tessa's Uncle Chester Longstreth sat on the Trimedia board. The connection had scored her the fashion editor position but hadn't helped her when Trimedia forced us into what amounted to indentured servitude last spring.

Tessa grabbed a handful of rubber lollipops and slipped them into her purse. "I might just do that."

"So what's with the Marilyn Monroe impersonator?" I asked no one in particular.

Tessa's eyes grew wide. "You don't know who that was?"

"If I knew, would I be asking?"

"That's Norma Gene," said Tessa.

"You're kidding."

"You've never heard of Norma Gene?"

"I know Norma Jeane was Marilyn Monroe's real name, but she died decades before you were born."

"And she didn't stand nearly seven feet tall," said Sheila.

Tessa rolled her eyes. "Do you people live under a rock?"

"Hey, you didn't know Ernest Borgnine," said Cloris, sticking up for Sheila and me.

Tessa turned to her. "Has Ernest Borgnine been on the cover of *Us* and *People* lately? Is he mentioned on *Page Six*? Or on *TMZ*?"

"Doubtful, considering he's dead."

"Well, Norma Gene has. Several times over the last few months."

"So, are you going to tell us who she is or not," asked Janice.

Good to know I'm not the only clueless editor on the *American Woman* staff when it comes to Norma Gene.

Tessa heaved a huge sigh before answering. "Norma Gene is Gail to Philomena's Oprah. They're BFF's."

"Is she a he?" I asked, curiosity winning out over political correctness.

"Norma Gene is in the process of gender reassignment. Everyone knows that. You should really keep abreast of current events, Anastasia."

"I'll add it to my to-do list." I picked up a copy of *Bling!* and started leafing through the pages. Even though I'd been aware of Trimedia's newest baby, I hadn't paid much attention to the birth. The *Bling!* staff occupied offices on another floor of our building, and this was the first time I'd had a chance for an up-close-and-personal with the newest corporate rugrat.

A quick scan of the Table of Contents piqued my curiosity. "What in the world is Vajazzling?" I asked as I flipped pages to find the article.

"They've got an article about Vajazzling?" asked Nicole. "Are they including pictures?"

"Oh yeah!" I stared at the eight-by-ten glossy depiction of a certain normally covered-up section of Philomena's anatomy. "This makes rubber lollipops tame, ladies."

"Let me see." Serena grabbed the magazine out of my hands. Everyone else clamored around her to ogle.

"Why would anyone want to do that to themselves?" asked Sheila.

"I wonder if it's painful," said Cloris.

"Not the Vajazzling," said Tessa, "but the full Brazilian you get beforehand hurts like hell."

We all turned to stare at her. "You know this from personal experience?" I asked.

She executed another eye roll directed toward me. "How can you work at a women's magazine and not know about the latest trends in beauty and fashion?" She glanced up and down the aisle to make sure no one else was around. Then she unzipped the fly front of her designer trousers and pulled down a scrap of pink silk fabric to show off her own Vajazzling, a series of crystals decorating the upper area of her hairless nether region.

"That's sick," said Jeanie.

The rest of us concurred except for Nicole who seemed more than a little interested. "How long does it last?"

"About five days," said Tessa as she zipped up her pants. "Then they start falling off."

"And you paid how much for this?" asked Sheila.

"Nothing. Many spas are giving them away free with a Brazilian, but it depends where you go. I've heard of places charging up to a hundred dollars."

"What a waste of money!" proclaimed our finance editor.

Cloris elbowed me in the ribs. "So when are we going to see a column on the hot new craft trend of vagina bedazzling?"

Naomi answered for me. "When hell freezes over."

~*~

My mother ambushed me the moment I arrived home. "Anastasia, we need to talk."

TWO

I dropped my purse and keys onto the hall table and kicked off my heels. Catherine the Great, Mama's enormous Persian cat, leaped from Mama's arms, gave a disdainful sniff to my shoes, then headed for her favorite perch on the back of my living room sofa.

"Mama, it's after seven. I've been on my feet all day and haven't eaten anything besides a cupcake (or three or four) since breakfast. Can't it wait?"

"No, it can't. Lawrence is picking me up shortly. This has gone on for too long. I can barely look him in the eye."

I sighed. My mother had a way of carrying on a conversation that made sense only to her. "What's gone on for too long?"

"Your appalling lack of manners. I brought you up better than that."

"You've lost me, Mama. How about starting at the beginning, but before you do, where is everyone else? Did the boys and Lucille have dinner?"

"Alex and Nick are off with friends, and I have no idea where the commie pinko is. She's been gone all day, probably out rabble-rousing with her commie pinko cohorts. If we're lucky, she'll get herself into so much trouble, the police will lock her up for good this time."

"Don't start, Mama." There was no love lost between my mother, a life-long member and past social secretary of the Daughters of the American Revolution, and my mother-in-law, the president of the Daughters of the October Revolution. Mama insisted Lucille and her octogenarian followers, all twelve of them, were plotting to overthrow the government.

Unfortunately, circumstances beyond my control have forced me to share my home with both Mama and Lucille and forced them to share a bedroom. That goes a long way toward explaining the *fun* part of my dysfunctional family dynamic. I have the man I now not so fondly refer to as Dead Louse of a Spouse to thank for saddling me with his mother and so much more.

"What about Mephisto?" Mephisto, whose real name is Manifesto (only my mother-in-law would name a dog after a communist treatise) was Lucille's runt of a French bulldog. The Devil Dog and I had belonged to a mutual animosity society up until one dreadful day this past summer when he'd proven his worth. I now owe my life to Mephisto. Literally. Needless to say, we'd bonded. And that really doesn't sit well with my mother-in-law.

"What about him?"

"Has anyone walked him?"

"How should I know? She took the mongrel with her."

One less chore for me. I headed to the kitchen and opened the refrigerator in search of something to eat. The nearly empty interior reminded me I needed to squeeze in a trip to the supermarket tonight. I grabbed the last two eggs and the dregs from the vegetable crisper—half a tomato and a two-inch chunk of slightly wrinkled zucchini. A search of the deli drawer uncovered a lone slice of cheddar cheese.

If I only had a bottle of wine to go with my omelet.... But wine was a luxury I could no longer afford. Yet something else to blame on the man who'd dropped dead at a roulette table in Las Vegas, leaving me with debt the size of the gross national product of some third world nations.

I set a frying pan on the stove to heat up, cracked the eggs into a bowl, added some milk, and began whisking the mixture together.

"Anastasia, are you listening to me?"

Actually, I had tuned her out, a skill I'd adopted as a teenager. I loved my mother, but I loved her best in small doses. Luckily, she was planning a sixth trip down the aisle. I hoped her marriage to Lawrence Tuttnauer lasted longer than her last four attempts at happily-ever-after. Mama's husbands had a habit of dying on her shortly after the *I do's*. Her last fiancé didn't even make it to the altar, thanks to a crazy woman who stabbed him in the heart with one of my knitting needles.

"Sorry, Mama. What did you want to discuss?"

"When are you going to invite Ira and his family for dinner? It's been over two months since their barbecue, and you've yet to reciprocate. It's embarrassing."

Ira was Ira Pollack, my dead husband's half-brother. No one knew of his existence until twelve weeks ago when he showed up on my doorstep. Ira was searching for his deceased father's long-lost love, my curmudgeon of a mother-in-law. He'd since wheedled his way into our lives, playing cupid to Mama and his father-in-law. I was happy Mama had once again found a soul mate, but Ira's arrival seriously complicated my already complicated life.

I poured the egg mixture into the frying pan, adjusted the flame, and began cutting up the zucchini and tomato. As I chopped, I glanced out my kitchen window at the darkened apartment above my garage. Zachary Barnes, my tenant turned boyfriend, had once again jetted off to some remote corner of the globe on another photo-journalism assignment. Or possibly some covert government activity he swore he didn't do. I had my doubts. Don't all government operatives swear they aren't government operatives?

I sighed. *Saturday night and I ain't got nobody*. Except Mama driving me nuts.

"Exactly when have I had time to entertain lately? In case you've forgotten, I worked a second job all summer." Although grateful for the extra paycheck I'd earned working weekends as the arts and crafts instructor at the Sunnyside of Westfield Assisted Living and Rehabilitation Center, the stint had taken both an emotional and physical toll on me. And almost gotten me killed.

A brief getaway with Zack to Barcelona had proved no respite, either. Sometimes I think that along with leaving me with debt up the wazoo, Karl also tattooed a target on my back. Ever since he died, people keep trying to kill me. Even in Barcelona.

"People do entertain during the week, dear," said Mama.

"Yes, people who arrive home from work at a reasonable hour and don't have a houseful of responsibilities to contend with once they do get home." Not to mention no husband and both a mother and mother-in-law genetically incapable of helping around the house.

"You can invite them for next weekend."

"First of all, I doubt Cynthia would lower herself to step foot in my home."

Cynthia was Ira's wife, or maybe his trophy wife. I still wasn't clear about their relationship. She had treated us as if we were society's castoffs, not fit to enter her Hunterdon County McMansion. During one of the hottest evenings of the summer, we were kept on the patio instead of being entertained in the comfort of that air-conditioned McMansion. When my sons got fed up with the heat and jumped into her pool, she acted like they'd contaminated the water.

"Besides," I reminded her, "she nearly stroked out when you and Lawrence announced your engagement."

"True, but that doesn't mean Ira and his kids won't come. Alex and Nick need to get to know their cousins better."

After their first and only encounter with their half-cousins this past summer, my sons had no desire to bond further with what they described as three extremely spoiled brats.

"There's also the problem of Lucille," I said. So far I'd been successful at keeping Lucille from meeting Ira, a dead ringer for his deceased half-brother.

"Why is that a problem?"

"She'd probably have another stroke if she saw Ira."

"So?"

"Mama, have a little compassion!"

At that moment Ralph swooped into the kitchen and settled on top of the refrigerator. "*And sir, it is no little thing to make Mine eyes to sweat compassion,*" he squawked. "*Coriolanus.* Act Five, Scene Three."

It never ceased to amaze me how the parrot I inherited from

my Great-aunt Penelope Periwinkle can not only quote Shakespeare, but always manages to come up with a situation-appropriate line from the Bard.

Mama was less than impressed by Ralph. She hated the African Grey. After shooting him a look of disdain, she continued, "Like that woman has ever had any compassion toward you? She'd throw you under a bus if it suited her communist agenda."

"That may be so, but she's lived a delusion for most of her life. I'm not going to be responsible for confronting her with the truth."

"I'd be happy to—"

"And neither will you!"

"Suit yourself, dear, but the truth will come out at some point."

I'd since learned that Lucille and her beloved Isidore had never married. She'd taken his name after he left her. Or she'd kicked him out. No one knows exactly what happened or whether Isidore knew Lucille was pregnant at the time. Lucille has always claimed Isidore was abducted by the government, never to be seen again. Mama and I now know Isidore was very much alive up until a few months ago.

Mama persisted. "You at least need to extend an invitation."

"I'll think about it."

She didn't seem all that pleased with my response, but at that moment the doorbell rang. Lawrence to the rescue. Mama would leave for the evening, and I'd get to eat my omelet in peace.

~*~

Nine-thirty the following morning found me and my protesting feet back at the Javits Center. "Who invented the high heeled shoe?" I asked Tessa. "He must have been a misogynist."

"High heels have been around since ancient times. Both men

and women wore them."

"Masochistic men and women, no doubt."

"Hardly. Heels served a practical purpose."

"Practical?"

"Sure. They kept your shoes out of all sorts of yucky street gunk and helped horseback riders keep their feet in their stirrups."

"Well, we don't have to worry about either anymore," said Cloris. "We have indoor plumbing, paved streets, and motorized means of transportation. Yet we're still forced to shove our tootsies into these torture devices. The guys wised up ages ago. Why haven't we?"

Tessa executed another one of her classic eye rolls, but this time she directed it toward Cloris. "Because high heels are extremely sexy."

"I could do with a little less sexy and a lot more comfort. We've got five and a half hours on our feet ahead of us. Minus the perk of plush pile and extra padding."

That said, I ducked behind the display panels to haul out a carton of magazines. Farther down the narrow alley created by our booth and the ones backing up to us, I spied Philomena. With her back toward me, she wasn't aware of my presence as she spoke into her cell phone. I wasn't about to clue her in. Instead, I ducked behind a stack of cartons and settled in to eavesdrop. Why pass up such a perfect opportunity?

"What are you saying? After all I've done for you?...How dare you!...Don't even think of it, you hear me?...Try it, and you're dead. No one messes with me."

A woman I recognized as part of Philomena's goon squad poked her head behind the section of booth dividing *American Woman* from *Bling!* "Philomena?"

"What!"

"Sorry to interrupt but the hair and makeup stylists are ready for you."

"They'll have to wait."

"Uhm...the crew said they really need to tape before the show opens to the public."

"I said they'll have to wait! What part of that don't you understand?"

The woman mumbled something under her breath before disappearing back into the booth.

Philomena returned to her caller. "You listen to me, and you listen good because I'm only saying this once. I'm gonna pretend this call never happened, but don't you *ever* try to pull a stunt like this again. You hear what I'm saying?"

With that she ended the call and stormed back into her booth. I counted to fifty before slipping from my hiding place. Grabbing a carton of magazines, I returned to the booth and communicated what I'd heard to my fellow editors.

"You think someone is trying to blackmail her?" asked Cloris.

"I'm not sure what else it could mean, but what about her threat to the caller?"

"Ask me if I care," said Tessa.

"Weren't there rumors of her being mixed up with some gang back during her rapper days?" asked Serena.

Tessa yawned. "Again, do I care?"

I glanced in the direction of the Blinged One, now seated in a director's chair while a makeup artist and hairdresser performed touch-up on her. Our besotted CEO sat in a matching chair beside her while an *E! Network* camera crew congregated in the aisle in front of the *Bling!* booth.

Once the makeup and hair stylists had completed their tasks, a reporter settled into the vacant chair alongside Philomena and proceeded to interview her, totally ignoring our CEO. If I had any spare change, I'd bet the cameraman framed the shot to exclude any hint of Gruenwald.

My fellow editors and I, along with other Trimedia personnel from surrounding booths, were barred from getting too close by a phalanx of convention center security guards. Aside from an occasional loud exclamation or burst of laughter from the Blinged One, we were too far away to hear any of the Q and A.

The interview was still in progress when the show opened to the public for the day. Within minutes we were smack in the middle of a logjam with no one able to pass in front of the *Bling!* booth. From either end, consumers strained to squeeze as close as possible to see what was going on, but the guards held everyone back.

Until one very determined woman broke through the pack.

"Here comes trouble," said Naomi.

I craned my neck to catch a glimpse of a Park Avenue sophisticate as she darted around one of the security guards and stepped between Philomena and the camera. The woman wore a Hermes scarf stylishly draped around her neck and secured with a large sapphire brooch that mirrored the midnight blue anger in her eyes. "Isn't that—?"

"Oh yeah," said Janice. "It most definitely is."

"Cut!" yelled the *E!* producer. "What the hell do you think you're doing, grandma? We're taping an interview here."

Grandma? I pegged her at late-forties, early-fifties at the most, but I suppose to a twenty-something, that's ancient.

"Nice suit," said Tessa. "Classic Armani. Who is she?"

"Sylvia Gruenwald," several of us said in unison.

"Hell hath no fury like a trophy wife scorned," said Naomi.

I couldn't help but notice the hint of a smile on her face.

Sylvia turned to the producer. In a voice loud enough for all to hear, she said. "I'm not your grandmother, but don't let me stop you, young man. Keep the camera rolling. I promise, you won't regret it." She then turned to Philomena. "Philomena Campanello?"

Norma Gene stepped in front of Philomena and glared with contempt at Sylvia. "Who wants to know?"

Instead of answering, Sylvia darted around Norma Gene and dropped an envelope into Philomena's lap. "You've been served." She then turned to her husband and dropped a second envelope onto his lap. "You, too, you randy old coot."

Sylvia then spun around on her red-soled Christian Louboutins. With her ash blonde not-a-hair-out-of-place head held high, she marched back in the direction she'd come, the mass of onlookers parting to make way for her.

"You're suing me?" shouted Philomena to Sylvia's departing back. She then let loose with a string of expletives that made Eddie Murphy's character in *Beverly Hills Cop* sound like an altar boy. After pausing for a breath, she finished with, "You won't get away with this! Who the hell do you think you are?" Then she turned and pounced on Gruenwald. "Don't just sit there, Alfred. Do something!"

But our CEO wasn't paying attention to his demanding mistress. All color had drained from his face as he stared at his own set of papers.

Meanwhile, the camera had captured every juicy moment, including Philomena ripping the document into confetti and tossing it into the aisle.

I couldn't help but chuckle. "I suppose Sylvia's mantra is *don't get mad; get even.*"

"Always the best revenge," said Tessa.

I wondered if that was also from personal experience. "Assuming Sylvia served Gruenwald with divorce papers, what could she be suing Philomena for?"

"Probably alienation of affection," suggested Cloris.

"Not possible," said Nicole. "Not in either New Jersey or New York."

"How do you know that?" I asked. To my knowledge Nicole had never been married.

"Pressure from the 'rents. They expected me to go into the family business—divorce law. But I hated law school. I did pay attention in class, though. There are only seven states that still have alienation of affection laws on the books."

"Is Hawaii one of them?" asked Naomi.

"Yes, but Gruenwald isn't commuting from Hawaii to New Jersey every day."

"He and Sylvia have a home on Oahu," said Naomi. "They may list it as their permanent residence."

"Could they legally do that?" asked Janice. "Even if they live here most of the year?"

"And could Sylvia have a complaint against Philomena drawn up in Hawaii?" asked Sheila.

Naomi shrugged. "Beats me. I'm no lawyer." She turned to Nicole. "Anything more to offer?"

"Sorry. Those sorts of intricacies were probably covered in an advanced class. I never made it past the intro courses."

~*~

In-between product demos, handing out issues of *American Woman*, and chatting with show attendees, my fellow editors and I kept a watch on the occupants of the *Bling!* booth, as much as we could through the crowds that filled the booth. The tone had changed dramatically since Sylvia's departure, from that of a party atmosphere to a wake.

"Lots of forced smiles over there," said Cloris.

"They're probably worried whether they'll have jobs once that video goes viral," said Nicole.

"Why?" asked Tessa. "Look at all the free publicity the magazine will get."

"Not all publicity is good publicity," I said. "Most likely Philomena has morality clauses written into all those endorsement contracts. If she's dropped as a spokesperson, there goes all that advertising revenue for the magazine."

"And there goes the magazine," added Nicole.

"Not to mention a huge chunk of her personal income," said Cloris. "Miss Potty Mouth just killed the goose that was mass-producing all those golden eggs for her."

"Such a pity," said Tessa.

"Spoken with all the sarcasm you can muster?" I asked.

Tessa offered me a catbird smile. "What do you think?"

"Anyone notice how Philomena keeps ducking behind the booth?" asked Cloris. "Sometimes she sneaks back there with Norma Gene; other times she drags Gruenwald with her."

"I doubt it's for a little nookie," said Jeanie. "That man is one seriously unhappy dude right now."

"His days as CEO are numbered," I said. "The board will force him out over this."

"Now that would be a shame," said Naomi, joining us.

Cloris and I exchanged knowing glances. Alfred Gruenwald had led Trimedia's hostile takeover of the Reynolds-Alsopp Publishing Company.

"Spoken with all the sarcasm she can muster," whispered Cloris as she headed back to her demo table to decorate more cupcakes.

I continued to pass out copies of *American Woman* to the women strolling up and down the aisle. When I ran out, I once again stepped behind the booth for another carton. Just as I was about to leave, I heard Philomena say, "If you don't take care of this, I will."

"You can't be serious!"

"I'm dead serious, Alfred. I have connections."

"You don't mean—"

"That's exactly what I mean. I'm talking about people who will make this problem disappear permanently. Do you understand me?"

"All...all right. Promise me you won't do anything. I'll deal with the uhm...situation."

"You better. That's all I'm saying."

"Everything will work out, Sugar."

"It damn well better if you ever want any more sugar, *Sugar*."

Gruenwald muttered something under his breath.

"You think what was a bad idea, Alfred? You and me? You know something? Maybe you're right about that."

"I didn't mean—"

I ducked out from behind the back of the booth in time to see Philomena grab Norma Gene and storm off down the aisle, headed for the exit. Within seconds, a very worried-looking Alfred Gruenwald followed, and the head of every *Bling!* staff member turned to watch all three of them.

THREE

As soon as the show officially closed Sunday afternoon, my fellow editors and I headed for the ladies' room to change into jeans and sneakers. When we arrived back at the *American Woman* booth, we began breaking down and packing the booth for transport to our New Jersey offices.

While we wrapped models in bubble wrap, we discovered more damage. Much of what Philomena's minions had tossed behind the booth Friday night either needed repair, cleaning, or both. The remainder, like my Potichomanie decoupaged bowl, were unsalvageable. I tossed the broken models on the pile of discarded cartons that had held issues of our magazine.

"Would it have killed them to take the time to place items in a box?" I asked no one in particular.

"Chalk it up to the *Me* generation," said Cloris, frowning at some dented bake ware that looked like someone had stepped on it. "They don't care about anything but themselves."

"If you ask me," said Jeanie, "this looks like deliberate

destruction."

"But why?" I asked. "Our magazine is no competition to *Bling!* We target a completely different demographic."

"Maybe someone doesn't see it that way."

Next door, the *Bling!* booth stood empty of employees. Neither Philomena nor Gruenwald ever returned that afternoon, and the others darted for the exit the moment the show closed. The booth remained empty while we all worked, and it continued to stand empty after we'd packed up everything except for the back panels and counters Philomena and her entourage had appropriated from us.

"Maybe they think the convention center fairies appear at night to break down the booths," suggested Janice.

"The same ones that set up their booth for them?" asked Jeanie.

I turned to Naomi. "Now what? I'm not breaking down their booth."

"Me, neither," said Cloris. The others echoed our sentiments.

"I wouldn't think of asking you," said Naomi. "Just pack up what remains of our booth."

"What about the stuff they have displayed on our panels and counters?" asked Serena.

"We should treat all of it with the same care they treated our stuff," said Tessa.

"I didn't hear that," said Naomi. She stepped out of the booth and headed toward the ladies' room.

Cloris turned to me and whispered, "Plausible deniability, Sherlock?"

"Indubitably, Watson."

Naomi returned as we were attaching the address labels to our shipping containers. "Drinks are on me, ladies."

Naomi suggested a tapas bar on Ninth Ave. The nine of us hiked the distance, a more comfortable trek than the previous night, thanks to my Nikes. Drinks segued into dinner, and by the time I arrived home, night had descended on Westfield. Which is probably why I didn't notice Ira's gray minivan parked in front of my house when I turned into the driveway.

The moment I stepped into my kitchen, I realized the confrontation I'd hoped to avoid for the next millennium, or at least the remainder of Lucille's life, was in full swing in my living room. I stood out of sight and listened.

"I don't know what kind of con you're running, young man, but I'll have you arrested! How dare you barge in here spouting such lies? My Isidore was certainly not your father! I should know."

"The only lies are the ones you've been spewing for decades, you Bolshevik cow." This from Mama. "*Your* Isidore wasn't kidnapped by the government; he ran out on you."

"You don't know any such thing!" yelled Lucille. "I'll bet you hired this imposter to confront me. Admit it."

"You're crazy," said Mama. "Look at him. He's the spitting image of Karl."

"All part of his scheme, no doubt," said Lucille. "How much did the plastic surgery cost you? What do you expect to get out of this scam? Money?"

"You don't have any money," I said, stepping into the living room. "And Ira isn't running a scam, Lucille."

She clutched Mephisto to her chest and glared at me over his squirming body. "I suppose I shouldn't be surprised you know this imposter."

"Yes, I know Ira, and I also know he's Karl's half-brother."

"Lies! All lies!" As she pounded her fist on the arm of the sofa, Mephisto wriggled free of her grasp and lumbered off her lap. "You're in on it, too!"

Ralph chose that moment to fly across the room and squawk his two cents. "*Gods, what lies I have heard!*" *Cymbeline*. Act Four, Scene Two."

"To what end?" I asked my mother-in-law. "What possible motive would I have for lying to you?"

Lucille jutted out her chin. "I know I'm not wanted here. You're all trying to drive me crazy and force me back into that horrendous nursing home. You'd stoop to anything to get rid of me."

Yes, including replicating Karl's DNA, apparently.

Lucille leveraged her cane to force herself off the sofa. She still wasn't all that steady on her feet after her stroke and brain surgery, but she refused to use her walker. For a moment I feared she'd topple forward onto the floor. I lunged to steady her, but she slapped my hand away. "Don't touch me!"

She raised her cane and pointed at Ira. "I'm not listening to any more of these blatant lies. If you show up here again, expect to be arrested for fraud and false impersonation. Come, Manifesto." She then turned her back on all of us and shuffled off to her bedroom, expecting her dog to follow. Devil Dog had other ideas, though, and instead headed for the kitchen.

"Well, that went as well as expected," said Mama.

"Was this your doing?" I asked her.

"Really, Anastasia! It was only a matter of time before she found out. I told you that."

I ignored her to confront the real culprit. "Why are you here,

Ira?"

Before he could answer, Nick and Alex burst through the front door. "Hey, Mom! Did you hear?" asked Alex. He threw his arms around me and crushed me in an exuberant bear hug. "Isn't it the coolest birthday present ever?"

"Whose birthday?"

"Mine."

"Your birthday was three months ago. Trust me, I was there the day you were born. It's not a date I'm likely to forget."

Alex laughed. "I know, but Uncle Ira didn't know me back then. It's a belated birthday present."

I extricated myself from Alex's lanky arms and turned to the giver of the as yet undisclosed gift. Ira's neediness rankled me from the moment I first met him back in early July. He'd been worming his way into our lives ever since. This wasn't the first time he'd tried to buy my kids' affection. The man had more money than common sense. "What did you give him, Ira?"

He opened his mouth to speak, but Alex beat him to it. "A Jeep! He gave me a Wrangler, Mom! Look!"

Alex grabbed my hand, pulled me into the foyer, and swung open the front door. A Jeep sat parked at the curb in front of Ira's minivan.

"It's pre-owned," said Ira, coming up behind us. "But it's certified. And extremely safe."

"I'm sure it is," I said, a fact that was so beside the point at the moment, that it didn't even belong in the same galaxy with the conversation I needed to have with him. "Ira, you and I need to talk. In private."

"Mom, you're not—"

"Please go to your room, Alex, and take your brother with

you."

"But—"

"Now." I hated playing the villain, but if I didn't set firm boundaries now, I'd have an even bigger problem on my hands in the future.

Alex stood his ground. "You're not going to let me keep the car, are you?"

Instead of answering, I pointed in the direction of his bedroom. He nodded toward his brother, and the two of them reluctantly dragged themselves down the hall.

"Ira," I said after the boys were out of earshot, "I know you mean well, but you can't give my son a car."

"Why not?" asked Mama.

"Because it's inappropriate."

"We're family," said Ira. "How is it inappropriate?"

Did I really need to explain? "You didn't give Alex a video game, Ira. You gave him a gift that costs tens of thousands of dollars."

"I picked it up wholesale," he said. "It wasn't all that expensive."

Ira owned a string of car dealerships in Mercer and Hunterdon Counties, but the cost of the vehicle was totally beside the point. I stared at the hurt look on his face. "You really don't get it, do you? Ira, you can't buy your way into our lives."

Mama placed her hand on my arm. "He's just being generous, dear."

"Look," said Ira. "I have a lot of money. More than I know what to do with. What's the point of being rich if I can't derive pleasure from spending my money on people I care about? You have financial problems, thanks to my half-brother. Why shouldn't I help?"

"A half-brother you never knew," I reminded him. "And my financial problems are not your problems."

Mama threw her arms up in the air. "For goodness sake, Anastasia. Stop being so stubborn. Family helps family. That's why you opened your home to that pinko commie, isn't it? Alex needs a car. For that matter, so do you."

She turned to Ira. "Have you seen that rattletrap she's driving?"

"Mama!"

"Don't *Mama* me. Stop being a martyr for once and accept Ira's help. Lawrence and I have."

"What's that supposed to mean?"

"Ira bought us a condo in Scotch Plains. Now Lawrence and I can get married."

"How does Cynthia feel about that?" I asked Ira.

"She left me."

FOUR

"I'm sorry," I said, even though I wasn't sure I meant it. My one and only encounter with Cynthia Pollack had me convinced she married Ira for his money.

"It wasn't working out," he said.

"What about the kids?"

"She didn't want to have anything to do with them. I never should have married her, but I was terribly lonely after Kristin died."

"Kristin?"

"My first wife. I lost her to cancer two years ago."

I had suspected Cynthia was a trophy wife. Now I knew she was actually a gold-digger. I suppose that also explained Ira's spoiled brat kids. I'd never met them, but from what Alex and Nick told me, I wasn't looking forward to the prospect.

Learning about Ira's past went a long way to explaining his neediness and why he wanted to be a part of our lives. I felt sorry for him, but that didn't mean I wanted him as any more of a fixture in my life. I dreaded the inevitable *quid pro quo*. If I accepted a car today, I'd probably get stuck babysitting three spoiled brats every weekend while their father dove back into the dating pool.

"About Alex's car?" asked Ira.

"Please, Mom!"

I turned to find my son eavesdropping from the hallway. So much for my private conversation with Ira.

"You have enough money for the insurance?" I asked. Alex had worked all summer at Starbucks and continued working a few hours a week since the start of school.

"I think so."

"And paying for driver's ed lessons?"

"I'll teach him," offered Ira.

"He still needs to take driver's ed for the lower insurance rate."

"I can work a few extra hours a week," said Alex.

"Along with the driver's ed, your sports, and homework. I don't see how you'll have the time—"

"I'll make the time, Mom."

"Without your grades suffering? You need to keep your GPA up to qualify for scholarships."

"I'll keep my grades up. I promise. Please!"

A second car would certainly make my life easier, but I couldn't shake the feeling I was about to enter into a Faustian bargain. "I'll sleep on it," I finally said.

"Thank you, thank you, thank you!" Alex lifted me into the air and swung me around.

"I didn't say yes," I reminded him.

"But she will," said Mama. She winked at Alex before he raced down the hall to tell his brother the news I hadn't as yet agreed to.

"I should be going," said Ira.

"How did you get both your car and the Jeep here," I asked as I walked him to the door.

"Two of my guys helped me. That's why I got here so late tonight. I had to wait for both of them to be available this weekend."

"One more thing," I said as he stepped outside. "No more surprises. Next time you consult with me before you do anything for or give anything to my sons."

"So Alex can keep the car?"

"I haven't made up my mind yet."

"I'd be happy to find one for you, too, Anastasia."

"I have a car."

"No, you have a rattletrap."

"But it's *my* rattletrap. Goodnight, Ira."

"Goodnight, Anastasia." He bent down and kissed my cheek, which creeped me out a bit, given his strong resemblance to Dead Louse of a Spouse.

"We need to find a nice girl for Ira," said Mama after I closed the front door. "What about some of the women you work with, dear? Are any of them single?"

"Forget it, Yente."

"Really, Anastasia!"

"Don't *really* me, Mama. How long have you known about the car for Alex?"

"A few weeks. Ever since Ira started shopping around for one."

"And it never occurred to you to mention anything about it to me?"

"And spoil the surprise?"

I channeled Tessa and did a fair representation of one of her

39

eye rolls. "How does Lawrence feel about his daughter walking out on Ira?"

"He's not exactly certain Cynthia walked out."

"What do you mean?"

"Lawrence suspects Ira actually threw Cynthia out, even though Ira claims Cynthia left him."

"Why?"

"She insisted he send his kids off to boarding school. They were having some huge fights about it."

"And Lawrence still lives with Ira?"

"He's on Ira's side."

"But he's her father!"

"It's called tough love, dear. Cynthia needs to grow up. She's a spoiled brat. Whether she left Ira or Ira sent her packing, doesn't really matter."

"What do you mean? She'll probably walk away with a huge settlement, given Ira's apparent bottomless pot of gold."

"Not according to their pre-nup."

I raised an eyebrow. "A pre-nup?"

"Ira insisted on one," said Mama. "He might come across as a milquetoast, but according to Lawrence, he's a barracuda when it comes to his money."

"That Jeep parked out front claims otherwise."

"A generous barracuda, but a barracuda nonetheless. He and Cynthia weren't married long enough for her to benefit financially in a divorce. Ira made sure of that."

~*~

Morning arrived, finding me no closer to a decision regarding Alex's car. Instead of sleeping, I'd spent most of the night debating with myself. Did I have the right to deny my son the gift based solely on my uneasiness regarding Ira's generosity? Would I feel the same if Mama had gifted him with the Jeep? Probably not. Had Karl not left me doggy paddling in an ocean of red ink, I would have bought Alex a car for his birthday. I'd planned to. *We'd* planned to. Back in those bygone days of our comfortably middleclass American Dream life, now a distant memory.

I had promised my son an answer this morning, and in the end, I found no logical reason to justify making him hand back the keys. Before he left for school, I reluctantly allowed Alex to keep his birthday present from Ira.

After one of Trimedia's less-than-stable employees had tried to kill me a few months ago, Naomi used the opportunity to leverage some much-needed benefits for her staff by leading the board into believing I intended to sue Trimedia. Along with receiving a cash settlement that allowed me to pay off a huge chunk of my Karl-induced debt, I and my fellow editors were now entitled to comp time.

Even though our planning meetings for the issue six months out normally fell on the last Monday of the month, Naomi had bumped the meeting back a week due to the consumer show. So I took Monday off and caught up on all the errands, laundry, and cleaning that had piled up over the weekend.

~*~

The next morning, as I drove to work in my rust bucket Hyundai, holding my breath through the constant creaks, rattles, and squeaks, I thought about compromising my principles even further. Car years, I decided, were equivalent to dog years, which made my Hyundai fifty-six years old. Not ancient but the car already suffered from an acute case of car-thritis. Any day now I expected something major to fail.

I managed throughout the summer without air-conditioning. I could manage without heat. I couldn't manage without an alternator or a carburetor, even if I had no idea what either did. However, although tempting, I also couldn't cross the line that would allow me to let Ira purchase a car for me. Such generosity suggested a level of intimacy I refused to encourage with my newly acquired half-brother-in-law.

Yet I wondered if I'd stick to my high principles if it were Zack offering to buy me a car.

I also wondered if it made sense to start playing the lottery. If anyone ever needed an extra million or two or ten, I was that someone. Hell, I'd settle for winning a few hundred thousand. Too bad I couldn't bring myself to part with even a dollar of my hard-earned money while red ink ruled my life.

The first thing I did after arriving at work was hit the break room for a cup of coffee and something chocolate. I found a freshly brewed pot of coffee but not even a leftover crumb of a chocolate anything.

On my way to my cubicle, I popped my head into Cloris's cubicle. "No goodies this morning?" I could count on few things in this life, but one of them was that Cloris kept the break room supplied with goodies from her test kitchen and samples sent by vendors who wanted her to feature their products in her food articles.

"Going through withdrawal?"

"Hand over whatever chocolate you're hoarding, or I won't be responsible for what happens."

"That bad, huh?" She pulled a plastic container from her tote and popped the lid.

A decadent fudgy aroma wafted toward me. I grabbed a cookie

and took a bite. Around a mouthful of pure Heaven I said, "You've performed a miracle. I'm calling the pope to nominate you for sainthood."

"Good thing I'm Catholic. What's up with you?"

"I'll tell you all about it while we unpack the show models and equipment, assuming the shipment arrived yesterday."

"It did. I noticed them off-loading the cases when I left work last night."

I grabbed three more cookies before we headed to the models' room to retrieve the hand truck. As we waited for the elevator to take us down to the ground level, I devoured my entire horde.

"Binging on chocolate. Zack out of town?" asked Cloris.

I nodded. "And so much more."

"Lucille?"

"And Mama and Ira. If I'd known what was waiting to ambush me Sunday night, I never would have gone home." I gave Cloris the abridged version of events, finishing as we arrived at the entrance to the building's physical plant. Dozens of cases holding the booths and models for all the magazines that had taken part in the show sat in the middle of the large concrete block room.

The two of us stood in the doorway. "This place always freaks me out," said Cloris. "I can never shake the feeling someone's hiding in a dark corner, waiting to pounce."

"Ditto." With its huge hissing furnace, clanking overhead pipes, wall of electrical panels, and one flickering low-watt bare bulb hanging from a fixture in the middle of the room, the place reminded me of too many suspense novels I've read. "The serial killer always sets up shop in places like this."

Cloris punched me in the arm. "You had to mention that, didn't you?"

"Let's grab our stuff and get out of here before something crawls up our legs. You know how I hate spiders."

An odor of decay hit us as we approached the five large cases that housed our booth and models. I pinched my nostrils closed. "I think something hitched a ride back from the convention center in one of our cases." I backed away. "Do you think it's still alive? I don't want to open the lid and have a rat jump out at us."

"I don't think there's any chance of that, not with such an overpowering stench."

"What if more than one rat climbed in and some are still alive?"

"We'd hear them scratching around, wouldn't we? It's probably just one small mouse."

"Smells way too much for one small mouse," I said.

Cloris shook her head. "You'd be surprised how much one tiny dead mouse can stink. I found one in my basement last winter. I thought the sewer system had backed up, the place reeked so much."

I walked up to the case we needed to empty. "Let's get this over with. If we're lucky, Mickey kicked the bucket in one of the booth cases, not the models' case."

We unfastened the strapping on either side of the case holding the models and flipped the lid's metal latches. Cloris lifted the lid, and I proceeded to toss my cookies—literally—all over what was definitely not a dead mouse.

FIVE

Cloris grabbed my arm, and we both raced from the room, slamming the steel door behind us. I ran to the outer wall and pushed the button to raise the overhead door of the loading bay. We collapsed against the outer wall and sucked in fresh air.

"Was that—?" asked Cloris, her body still shaking several minutes later.

"I think so." But neither of us had hung around long enough to get up-close-and-personal with the corpse. Given the way the body was shoved face down in the case, all we saw was the back of a blonde head, no face. "Either Philomena or one of her entourage."

I whipped out my phone and scrolled through the address book, searching for Detective Winifred Batswin's direct line.

"Mrs. Pollack," she said, answering on the second ring, "I hope you haven't stumbled across any new dead bodies."

Detective Batswin, along with her partner Detective Robbins (someone in the Morris County police department had a wicked sense of humor pairing up those two,) were the lead investigators last February when I discovered the murdered body of our former fashion editor in my cubicle. They were also involved in the aftermath of the Morning Makeovers fiasco when producer Sheri Rabbstein and her lover pulled a Thelma and Louise.

I'm hoping Batswin never finds out about the murders that occurred while I moonlighted this summer at the Westfield Assisted Living and Rehabilitation Center. Since Westfield is in a different county, my fingers are crossed. Along with my toes, eyes, and all extremities. Batswin is already convinced I'm a twenty-first century Jessica Fletcher: Wherever I go, murder follows.

"I'm afraid so," I said.

Batswin moaned. "Where are you?"

I gave her a quick rundown of the last few minutes, minus the cookie tossing.

"Stay put, and don't touch anything. I'm on my way."

"Don't worry," said Cloris when I relayed Batswin's orders. "I'm sure you're not the first person to lose it over a dead body, and you won't be the last."

"We should alert Naomi," I said.

"What about Gruenwald?"

"Probably not a good idea. Let the police deal with him."

"You don't think he did it, do you?"

"No, but I think the police will want to question him as a person of interest. More often than not, the spouse or significant other of the murder victim winds up being the killer."

"Look at Sherlock Pollack spouting police-speak!"

I've learned quite a bit over the last few months from my reluctant involvement in murder investigations. Emphasis on *reluctant*.

Within minutes Trimedia segued from magazine publishing to crime scene investigation. Work came to an abrupt halt as the Morris County police herded every employee in the building, from the bean counters to the janitor, into various conference rooms on each floor, the better to keep an eye on us, I supposed, while they did their CSI thing.

"How long do we have to stay here?" asked Janice. "I'm beginning to understand what sardines go through."

The conference rooms we were in normally held no more than a dozen people seated around a long table. Besides the lucky dozen who had secured chairs, I counted nearly fifty people lining the walls and squatting on the floor of our holding pen.

"Anyone know how many people work in the building?" asked Serena.

"Approximately two hundred," said Naomi.

"And those two detectives are interviewing each one of us?" asked Tessa. We'll be here for days."

"Let's hope they called in reinforcements," I said.

Batswin and Robbins appropriated the *American Woman* conference room for their interviews. Having called in the grim discovery, I received the honor of first in line for a police brow beating, even though Cloris and I were questioned in the loading bay as soon as Batswin and Robbins arrived.

A uniformed officer escorted me to the conference room where I settled into a seat opposite the two detectives. Batswin, Robbins, and I had danced this dance before, back when they suspected me of killing Marlys Vandenburg. After I helped them catch the real killer, I'd earned a modicum of grudging respect from them. It didn't hurt that I knew they'd illegally borrowed a stash of counterfeit bills from the police evidence locker during an unsuccessful sting operation, thus giving me my very own Get Out of Jail Free card.

"Mrs. Pollack," said Batswin. She expelled a deep sigh and shook her head in a gesture that suggested she was disappointed in me, I suppose for contaminating her crime scene. Or maybe for complicating her day with another dead body.

Even sitting down, Batswin exuded a commanding presence. A big-boned woman, nearly six feet tall, she was dressed in her standard outfit: a no-nonsense conservatively cut gray suit with a tailored white shirt. She wore her silver streaked sable hair tied back in a low ponytail, her face devoid of makeup other than a swipe of lip gloss. The only hint of personality came from her earrings, always Native American. Today purple feathered dream catchers swayed from her lobes.

"I had no idea magazine publishing was such a deadly occupation," she said.

"You may find this hard to believe, Detective, but before we moved into the middle of this Morris County corn field, we had a spotless record. Not a single murder in all our years in Manhattan."

Detective Robbins spoke for the first time. "Yet now you're racking up an impressive body count. What is it at this point? Seven? And all somehow connected to you, Mrs. Pollack."

Nine. But who's counting? The other two murders occurred in Union County. I fought back the urge to release my inner bitch and simply looked Robbins in the eye. A compact, beefy man of all muscle and no hair, he played Mutt to Batswin's Jeff, coming in a head shorter than his partner. He, too, dressed in conservative suits but had a penchant for cartoon crime fighter ties. Today he sported one featuring the Gotham City duo. *Holy irony, Batman.*

"That's not fair," I said. "I don't even know who the victim is. I didn't see a face."

"We haven't made a positive ID yet," said Batswin. "Any ideas?"

I shrugged. "From the blonde hair and clothing, possibly Philomena Campanello or one of her entourage." But if Philomena's the victim, wouldn't the police have recognized her? "Is it Philomena?" I asked.

"We're not sure," said Batswin. "The body sustained quite a bit of trauma. We'll probably need dental records for a conclusive ID."

I assumed that meant someone had beaten the crap out of her, although neither elaborated. "You should see if our CEO can make a positive identification," I said. I looked at Batswin, then Robbins. Neither seemed to understand. "I guess you're not up on the latest celebrity gossip."

They both raised their eyebrows. "What gossip?" asked Batswin.

"Alfred Gruenwald and Philomena Campanello. She's his mistress."

"Isn't he old enough to be her grandfather?" asked Robbins.

"I suppose that didn't matter to either of them," I said.

Batswin muttered something under her breath that sounded like, "That's sick."

"What else can you tell us?" asked Robbins. "How long have you known Philomena Campanello?"

"We've never formally met."

"But you work together."

"On different magazines on separate floors of the building. I don't even know how often, if ever, she actually shows (or was it now *showed*?) up at Trimedia."

"So she's more like a figurehead?" asked Robbins.

I shrugged. "I can't say for sure. Her name and photos fill the pages of the magazine, but most likely others do the bulk of the work. I saw her for the first time this weekend during a consumer show at the Javits Center."

I proceeded to tell Batswin and Robbins what I could about the show, including the telephone call and conversation I'd overheard. I certainly had no motive to kill Philomena or one of her minions. Offering as much as I knew might help the detectives in their investigation, thus allowing all of us to get back to work as soon as possible. We had production deadlines to meet.

~*~

After being questioned, I was allowed to return to my cubicle. Since I was too stressed to do anything important, I decided to tackle some of the reader mail, something Daphne normally handled for me. These days most readers contact me through email, but I do still receive a dozen or so snail mailed letters each month.

Reader mail generally falls into four categories. There are the readers who saved a picture but misplaced the directions, often for an issue from several years ago. Luckily, all back issues are archived. We either email or print out and snail mail the missing pages to them.

Then there are the readers who proudly send me photos of their original designs, hoping I'll feature them in a future issue. I never do. Most have only made minor changes to an original design from a competing magazine or even an old issue of *American Woman*. Rather than explain copyright infringement to them, I send a standard thank-you-for-thinking-of-us form rejection letter.

Some readers take extreme pleasure in telling me I screwed up. Although I have been known to make the occasional mistake, enough people pour over every word of each issue that errors are quite rare. If a reader does find a mistake, a correction is printed in the next issue, and the reader receives a nice thank-you note. Often their motives are more avaricious than altruistic. Some write back demanding a free subscription for their efforts.

I had dispatched half a dozen replies when I came across a snail mail letter from the last category of reader mail, the would-be blackmailer:

Dear Anastasia Pollack,

Yesterday I decided to decorate a pair of sneakers according to the directions in your June issue. I wasn't going to be using them for a wedding, though. I've been happily married to the same man for forty-two wonderful years.

The cap on my fabric glue was stuck on the bottle, and when I tried to pry it off with my teeth, a large chunk of what my dentist said was my #13 premolar came with it.

This is a direct result of your crafts project, and I expect to be compensated for the expense. I've enclosed a copy of my dental bill.

If I don't receive a check from you in a timely manner, I'll be forced to turn this matter over to my attorney, who I am sure will suggest I also sue you for pain and suffering and that my husband sue you for deprivation of spousal affection. Obviously, because of the pain, I couldn't give him any affection from the time the tooth broke until after my dental appointment.

Sincerely,
Mrs. Henry (Josephine) Holmes

The glue manufacturer probably received a similar letter. Josephine Holmes, like so many before her, thought she could make money from her own stupidity. I placed the letter and dental bill back in the envelope and walked it upstairs. Josephine would be hearing from one of our sharks. Trimedia didn't take attempted shakedowns lightly.

~*~

At the end of the day, Cloris and I headed for the parking lot together. "I should've stayed in bed all day. At least I could've caught up on some sleep," said Cloris.

"You and me both. All I did was answer reader mail. I didn't check off a single item on my to-do list today."

"Not even *Find a Dead Body*?"

"That was on tomorrow's list."

"Then you're ahead of schedule."

"We shouldn't be joking. Poor Philomena. Or whomever. No one deserves what happened to her."

"What did happen?"

I shrugged. "Beats me. Batswin and Robbins remained tight-lipped, other than they hadn't yet made a positive ID. Could be Philomena. Or not. Information only flows one way with those two, and it's not from them to me."

"At this point they probably don't even know where she was killed."

"Where is irrelevant," I said. "With the body dumped in our models' case, either she was killed at the Javits Center and dumped into the case after we packed up, which seems highly unlikely, or she was killed somewhere else, then brought here sometime last night after the cases were delivered. Either way, the killer is somehow connected to Trimedia."

"Wouldn't be the first time we discovered a killer in our midst," said Cloris.

I sighed. "You had to say that? People are looking at me like I'm some homicidal version of Typhoid Mary."

"There's another possibility. If the murder occurred at the Javits Center, the killer may have used our models' case simply because it was the most convenient place to dump a body."

"A Dumpster or the Hudson River would have been more convenient. The case was packed. He had to unload at least half the contents first in order to stuff her into it. That takes time."

"Right. I didn't think of that. He'd risk someone seeing him."

"Exactly. Which is why it's highly unlikely the murder occurred at the Javits Center. Think about all the workmen busy breaking down one show to get ready for the next. That place is a beehive of activity in-between exhibitions. Batswin inferred the woman was beaten beyond recognition. Even with all the noise of forklifts moving up and down the aisles, hammering and banging, someone would have heard her screaming. Someone would have seen the killer dragging off a dead body."

"Besides," said Cloris. "I'm sure the Javits Center has security cameras monitoring every nook and cranny. Even if no one saw the killer, he'd show up on the security tapes."

I stopped abruptly. "Security cameras!"

"What about them?"

I grabbed Cloris's hand and race-walked us toward the loading dock. The area had been cordoned off while the crime scene investigators continued processing the scene. News vans circled the perimeter. Camera crews and reporters had set up shop, hoping for something to broadcast in time for the six o'clock news.

Trimedia had installed security cameras at each entrance to the building after Marlys Vandenburg's murder. "If the killer brought the body here," I said, "he was recorded."

We inched our way as close as possible on the opposite side of the crime scene tape. I shaded my eyes against the late afternoon sun that was beginning to dip behind the building and craned my neck. "What happened to the cameras?" Empty brackets stood several feet above either side of the overhead loading bay door. Brackets that used to hold security cameras.

"I think we're dealing with one very smart killer," said Cloris. "How did he remove the cameras without being captured by them?"

"By rappelling down from the roof?"

"That would indicate a very methodical killer prepared for all contingencies."

"True but beating someone to a pulp is more a crime of passion, and those occur on the spur of the moment rather than by detailed planning."

Cloris gaped at me. "And you know this how?"

"Excellent question, Mrs. McWerther."

We both spun around to find Detective Batswin standing behind us. I swear that woman is part cat the way she creeps up without warning. "Well, Mrs. Pollack?"

"I've been reading up on murder lately."

"And why is that? Planning one?"

I have to admit, the thought had crossed my mind over the last several months, but Dead Louse of a Spouse was already dead. Unless he showed up on my doorstep as a zombie, I'd have no need to kill him. And although a certain mother-in-law has provoked me countless times, I'd never consider acting on my fantasies.

I offered Batswin a smile. "Because as you recently pointed out to me, Detective, I keep getting plunked down in the middle of murders. Knowledge is power."

"And a little knowledge is a dangerous thing. I'm sure I don't have to warn you to keep your nose out of this investigation."

"Of course not, Detective. My nose, along with the rest of me, is heading home right now."

Cloris and I walked back toward our cars. I settled in behind the wheel of my mud brown Hyundai rattletrap and turned the key. *Click.* I tried again. *Click.* Nothing but click.

SIX

I exited the car and lifted up the hood. Don't ask me why. At *Casa Pollack* anything to do with cars fell under Karl's realm of responsibilities, a perk of being married to an auto parts salesman. Now I wished I'd paid more attention when he waxed poetic over spark plugs and distributor caps.

Cloris pulled up behind me. "Trouble?"

"The engine won't turn over."

She parked her car and walked over to where I stood making faces and cursing at my engine. At least I knew which piece of equipment was the engine. That was the extent of my car knowledge. This was New Jersey. We don't even pump our own gas in this state.

Like a good friend, Cloris made faces and cursed along with me. Then she said, "You probably need to call a tow truck."

"You have any idea what a tow truck from Morris County to Westfield will cost?"

We went back to making faces. I reprimanded the Hyundai,

hoping to shame the car into starting. At one point I resorted to physical force and kicked the front bumper. The car still didn't start, but I'd succeeded in inflicting a grapefruit-sized dent in the chrome.

A black Lincoln pulled up behind my car. The driver side window lowered. Alfred Gruenwald's chauffeur stuck his head out and asked, "You ladies need help?"

"Love some!" I said.

He parked his car and joined us, poking his head under the hood. "Try turning it over when I tell you."

I climbed in behind the wheel and waited.

"Now," he said.

I turned the key. *Click.* Whatever was wrong hadn't magically healed through his fiddling. Nor had my dirty looks, cursing, and kicking had any effect on the situation.

Gruenwald's driver approached my door. "It's definitely electrical. Could be the battery. Could be the alternator. Could be the whole electrical system."

"That sounds expensive."

"More like terminal if it's system-wide. Batteries aren't that expensive. Alternators are a different story. They'll set you back a few hundred dollars."

On top of the cost of the tow truck. How I wish I still owned my dependable Camry! Unfortunately, that car became one of the first casualties of my plummet from middleclass comfort. Once I'd learned the extent of the debt Karl stuck me with, I could no longer afford the car payments.

"I can give you a jump," he offered, "but there's no guarantee it will hold until you get home."

With my luck? Especially today? I'd have better odds of

winning both MegaMillions and Powerball. In the same week. "I don't relish the idea of finding myself stranded on Rt. 287, tying up traffic during the height of rush hour." I held out my hand. "Thanks anyway, Mr.—"

"Martinelli. Martino Martinelli but you can call me Tino. Everyone does."

"Thank you, Tino."

"Wish I could've been more help."

"That makes two of us."

He nodded in the direction of the police activity. "What's going on down there? Accident?"

"We found a dead body this morning," said Cloris.

"No! In the parking lot? Must've happened after I dropped Mr. G off. Someone have a heart attack or something?"

"You haven't been here all day?" I asked.

"Not since eight. Mr. G. had me running errands for him and his lady friend."

Cloris and I exchanged a quick glance. "You saw Philomena?" she asked.

"Nah, I just had a long list of stuff to take care of for her."

"When was the last time you saw her?" I asked.

"Why? What's that got to do with anything?"

"The body we found was murdered, and the police think it might be Philomena," I said.

The color drained from Tino Martinelli's ruddy complexion. "Does Mr. G. know?"

"Of course, he knows," I said. "The police spent the day questioning all of us, but they haven't made a positive ID yet. The victim could be someone else."

"Huh?"

"You should probably go talk to them."

"The police? Why?"

"To help in the investigation," said Cloris.

"If it is Philomena," I added, "you may have been one of the last people to see her alive yesterday."

Tino drew his brows together and leaned forward in a menacing Cro-Magnon manner. "What are you saying? You think *I* had something to do with it?"

I inched backwards until my rear made contact with my Hyundai. "No, of course not."

"But you might have seen or heard something that could help the police catch the killer," said Cloris. "Until they do, no one is safe."

Tino took a step back and scanned the parking lot. "You mean there could be a serial killer on the loose?"

"No one is even sure who the victim is yet," I said. "Let alone why she was murdered. Until the police have answers, anything is possible."

Tino stepped backward and relaxed his body, his brows separating until the Cro-Magnon Tino morphed back into Homo Sapiens Tino. He rubbed his broad jaw. "Yeah, I see what you mean. Sorry I jumped all over you. I'll go talk to them. Anything to help."

He climbed back into the Lincoln. "Sorry I couldn't fix your car," he said before heading toward the crime scene.

"Me, too," I mumbled.

"Are you going to call a tow truck, or do you want a ride home?" asked Cloris.

I lowered the Hyundai's hood. "A ride home if you don't mind."

"Always put off today what you can do tomorrow?"

"More like put off till tomorrow what you can't pay for today."

"How will you get to work without a car?"

As much as I still bristled over Ira giving Alex that Jeep, the timing worked in my favor. Alex couldn't drive the car until he took driver's ed and passed his tests. A perfectly good vehicle sat parked in front of my house. I'd worry about the Hyundai later.

~*~

Cloris pulled into my driveway behind Zack's silver Porsche Boxster. "At least you'll have a way of relieving some stress tonight."

"You're forgetting about Mama, Lucille, and the boys."

"I'm sure three of the four will be happy to accommodate you, and the fourth can't climb the apartment stairs. Go for it."

I so needed some mind-numbing sex right now, but nothing kills the mood like murder.

Hi, honey, how was your day?

Oh, the usual. Stumbled across another dead body.

Any chance I could postpone the catching up until after the sex? Doubtful. I hopped out of Cloris's car. "Thanks for the ride. See you tomorrow."

I found everyone minus Lucille congregated in my kitchen. For all the chaos my duplicitous husband had caused me, the gods must have thought I needed something—or someone—to keep me sane. That someone arrived in the guise of Zachary Barnes, the photo-journalist who had rented the apartment above my garage shortly after Karl's death.

Why a to-die-for stud who looks like Pierce Brosnan, George Clooney, Patrick Dempsey, and Antonio Bandares all contributed to his gene pool would be interested in a pear-shaped, cellulite-riddled, slightly overweight, more than slightly in debt, middle-aged widow like me is beyond my comprehension, but I'm not complaining. I simply tell myself the universe works in mysterious ways.

At first, propriety kept my hormones in check. Recently widowed moms of teenage sons shouldn't jump in bed with near-strangers. However, as Zack insinuated himself more and more into my life (Did I mention he loves to cook? In my kitchen?), propriety began sounding downright Victorian—especially since Mama and the boys set about working in cahoots to get Zack and me together.

This past summer, after I decided I'd mourned Karl long enough, propriety went the way of the dodo bird. The result? One massive conflagration of Vesuvian proportions that showed no signs of waning.

"You're back," I said, stating the obvious.

Zack stepped away from whatever epicurean delight he was concocting on my stove to wrap me in his arms and plant a toe-curling kiss on my lips. I never knew what I was missing until I'd experienced one of Zack's kisses. When Alex and Nick started hooting and applauding, I stepped back, breaking the kiss.

"Don't stop on our account," said Nick.

I shot him a Mom Look that yielded little effect, given that my cheeks flamed.

"Have a successful trip?" I asked Zack.

"Definitely."

"Overthrow any dictators? Rescue any hostages? Save the world from imminent destruction?" No matter how often Zack protested to the contrary, I suspected he used the photo-journalism gig as a cover for his real work—that of a spy for one of the alphabet agencies.

His numerous, award-winning photographs notwithstanding, given the places Zack traveled, often at a moment's notice, I thought my suspicions justified. After all, some men must be capable of multitasking.

He thought I was nuts.

"Do I look like a spy?" he asked.

Ralph squawked from his perch atop the refrigerator. "*You spy! What do you spy?*" *Troilus and Cressida.* Act Three, Scene One."

"I spy a filthy bird," said Mama who sat at the kitchen table with Catherine the Great curled up in her lap. "Really, Anastasia, must you allow that winged rat in the kitchen?"

"Mama, Ralph is as clean as or cleaner than your cat."

Mama stroked Catherine the Great's fur and planted a kiss on the top of the cat's head. "I sincerely doubt that. Catherine the Great is meticulous in her grooming habits."

Alex came to our African Grey's defense. "Yeah, but Ralph doesn't lick his privates, Grandma."

Score one for my eldest son. "He's got you there, Flora," said Zack.

Mama had no rebuttal, so she changed the subject. "Come to think of it, you do look like a spy, Zack. At least the kind in movies. You'd make a far better James Bond than that Daniel Craig fellow. Have you ever done any acting, dear?"

"Not since I played a stalk of celery in fifth grade."

"I'm sure you were a very convincing stalk of celery," said Mama. "You should consider going into acting."

"When he gives up spying?" asked Nick.

Zack threw his hands up in the air. "I am not a spy!"

"If you say so," I said.

Mephisto lumbered into the kitchen and stood by the back door. "Where's Lucille?" I asked.

"Sulking," said Mama.

Mephisto was Lucille's responsibility. Not only was he her dog, she needed the exercise of walking him several times a day, even though one of us had to retrace her footsteps afterwards to pick up the dog's poop. If Lucille bent down, she might not get back up. "Alex, take Devil Dog out for a walk," I said. "Nick, set the table."

Alex returned five minutes later. "Hey, Mom, where's your car?"

"At the office."

"How'd you get home?" asked Nick.

"I flew." When no one accepted that explanation, I said, "My car died." Along with someone else but I wasn't about to bring that subject up just yet. "Cloris drove me home."

"We'll drive up after dinner," said Zack. "It's probably the battery. I'll give it a charge and follow you home."

"What if it won't hold a charge?"

"We come up with Plan B."

~*~

"It's definitely not the battery," said Zack after repeatedly trying the jumper cables.

Why did that not surprise me. "So what's Plan B?"

"Ira?"

"Why do you know more about my life than I do?"

"Flora said he offered you a car."

"Ira is trying to buy his way into our lives. Did she also tell you he and Cynthia are kaput?"

"That came as no surprise."

"No wonder Cynthia made a play for you during the barbecue.

64

She was already trolling for her next meal ticket."

"This is going to sound cynical," said Zack, "but maybe you should accept a car from Ira. He's lonely and insecure. Not to mention having all sorts of unfounded issues of guilt over what the brother he never met did to you and your kids. If giving you a car makes him feel better about himself, why not let him?"

"Because I don't want to owe him anything."

"Then offer to pay him."

"Sure, I'll pick a few hundred Franklins off the money tree in the backyard." I smacked my forehead with my palm. "Silly me! Why didn't I think of that earlier?"

"Pay him what you can when you can."

"I'd be paying him back into my nineties."

"You're either going to have to accept Ira's generosity or buy a car from a stranger."

"You don't think this is fixable?"

"Maybe."

"I see a *but* coming."

"The car is old, sweetheart. Once stuff starts going wrong, it doesn't stop. How much money are you willing to spend on repairs to postpone the inevitable? Ira will give you a safe, reliable car, unlike the crook who sold you this rusted out piece of crap."

I sighed. "I'll call Ira."

After we got back into Zack's car, he placed his hands of the steering wheel but didn't start the engine. "Something wrong?" I asked.

"I was just wondering when we were going to discuss the elephant in the parking lot. Or were you hoping I wouldn't notice the crime scene tape swaying in the breeze?"

"That was the plan." I had hoped it would be dark enough by

the time we arrived back at Trimedia that Zack wouldn't notice the aftermath of the police investigation, but between daylight savings time and the parking lot flood lights, the yellow and black tape was quite clearly visible.

"What happened?"

"I found a dead body."

Zack shook his head. "Why does that not surprise me anymore?"

After I recapped the events of the day, he said. "Were you planning on telling me about the murder, or am I only learning about it because I'm here?"

"I was going to tell you."

"When?"

"I was hoping to wait until after you jumped my bones."

Before Zack could answer—or act on my suggestion (which would have been more than a little awkward in his Boxster)—my cell phone rang.

"Did you hear the news?" asked Cloris when I answered.

"What news?"

"The medical examiner ID'd the body. It's Philomena."

SEVEN

Zack definitely lived up to my expectations later that night, almost making me forget about the dead Hyundai and the dead rap star-turned-entrepreneur. Reality set back in the next morning as I drove to work in Alex's Jeep. At least reality came accompanied by air-conditioning, something I'd suffered without all summer while driving the Hyundai.

Although the calendar claimed autumn began last week, the scorching temperatures we'd sustained throughout the summer never received the memo. For the first time in nearly five months, I drove to work in comfort, not needing a shower and a change of clothes once I arrived.

Given that we'd all left work yesterday still unaware of the identity of the murder victim, I expected to find a gaggle of gossiping coworkers congregated in the break room. Instead, I discovered the break room empty except for a freshly brewed pot of coffee and half a cinnamon streusel coffee cake. I poured myself a cup, cut a slice of cake, and headed for my cubicle.

I'd taken all of one bite and two sips when my office phone rang. "Anastasia Pollack."

"Mrs. Pollack, this is Marie Luscy, Mr. Gruenwald's secretary."

"Yes?"

"Mr. Gruenwald would like to see you."

"Now?"

"Right now."

"I'm on my way." I placed the handset back in its holder and stared at the phone. Why was Gruenwald even here today? Shouldn't he be home mourning his mistress's death? Making funeral arrangements? Who shows up at work the day after his girlfriend is brutally murdered?

"Good morning," said Cloris, poking her head into my cubicle. "I see you snagged some coffee cake before the vultures consumed the last crumb."

"Huh?"

"Hey, you okay? You look dazed."

I realized I still clutched the phone. I released my death grip and withdrew my hand. "Why on earth would Gruenwald want to see me?"

"Gruenwald? *Our* Gruenwald?"

I nodded. "Since when does the corporate CEO call meetings with staff members?"

"Since never. He won't even make time for our editorial director. I once overhead Naomi complain that she had to set up an appointment with him three weeks in advance. And then he stood her up."

"His secretary just called. He wants to see me. Immediately." A boulder the size of Seattle settled in my stomach. "What if I'm being laid off? I'm barely making ends meet now."

Cloris placed her hand on my shoulder. "If you were getting laid off, you'd be summoned to Human Resources, not the CEO's office."

"I suppose. What do you think he wants?"

"Only one way to find out."

I forced myself out of my chair and willed my feet to carry me toward the elevator. Cloris followed along for moral support. "Whatever he wants, I doubt it's good news," I said.

"You don't know that it's bad news." She pressed the elevator button. When the doors opened, my feet remained planted until she pushed me inside.

"You're not coming with me?"

"He didn't send for me; he sent for you."

With that the doors whooshed closed, and I was on my own. The last time I'd ventured onto the marble-tiled, mahogany-walled fourth floor, two crazed women were speeding down the Interstate, bent on killing me. The time before that, I'd sneaked into Hugo's office to figure out if he'd killed Marlys Vandenberg, only to bump into the real killer a few minutes later. Needless to say, I wasn't keen on making another trip to the fourth floor.

Before the birth of *Bling!*, I don't think Alfred Gruenwald ever set foot in his office here in our little neck of the Morris County cornfields. We housed corporate headquarters only for the magazines, a small part of the Trimedia stable.

Up until recently, Gruenwald oversaw his fiefdom from the luxury of the Trimedia Building, a thirty-five-story high-rise on Lexington Avenue in Midtown Manhattan. That changed once he offered Philomena her own magazine. Not that I ever bumped into him, but rumors circulated among the staff each time he deigned to grace our steel and concrete abode.

The elevator came to a stop, and the doors slid open. After taking a deep breath, I swiped my sweaty palms down either side of my khaki pencil skirt, stepped out of the elevator, and headed for the double glass doors that separated Gruenwald's real estate from the rest of the fourth-floor suits.

An enormous Carrara marble-topped reception desk sat opposite the glass doors. A plaque on the desk told me the woman seated in the leather chair behind the desk was Marie Luscy, Gruenwald's secretary.

She offered me a friendly smile. "Mrs. Pollack?"

I nodded.

"Please have a seat." She indicated an area off to the right where a deep umber leather couch and two matching club chairs flanked a free-form Carrara marble coffee table.

I crossed the room and perched nervously on the edge of one of the club chairs while she picked up the phone. "Mrs. Pollack is here, sir." When she hung up, she turned to me. "He'll be with you shortly."

Shortly being a relative term. The minutes ticked away, and with each passing one, I grew more nervous. After ten minutes my nervousness segued to annoyance. For someone who wanted to see me *immediately*, Gruenwald was certainly taking his sweet time. Was this some sort of power play? If so, I failed to see the point.

After fifteen minutes I stood and walked back over to the secretary's desk. "If he's tied up, I can come back later."

"No need," she said, again smiling sweetly. "I'm sure he'll be out momentarily." Then she dismissed me by turning her attention to the computer monitor on her desk.

I refused to take the hint. "Do you know what this is about?"

"Sorry," she said, keeping her attention focused on the monitor while her fingers raced around her keyboard. "You'll have to wait to speak with Mr. Gruenwald."

A minute later her phone rang. She picked it up on the first ring and said, "Yes, sir? Very well, sir." She hung up the phone and turned to me. "He'll see you now, Mrs. Pollack. Just go in. No need to knock."

I opened the massive mahogany door and stepped onto snow white carpet so plush, I nearly lost my balance. I thought about removing my shoes, fearful that I'd deposit a trail of debris in my wake, and stole a quick glance at Gruenwald's feet. Since he wore his shoes, I abandoned the idea and kept my toes curled in mine.

Gruenwald ushered me to one of two black suede upholstered accent chairs positioned in front of an ebony cabinet that held a massive flat screen television. Matching bookcases on either side of the cabinet contained a collection of leather-bound books and various service awards, the kind designed by Tiffany, Waterford, and Baccarat.

After I sat, he took the seat opposite me. "Thank you for coming, Mrs. Pollack."

An odd comment, given I hardly had a choice in the matter. When the CEO summons, the peons appear for an audience.

I debated bringing up Philomena's death. I suppose common courtesy dictated I say something, but I worried over choosing the proper wording. Finally, I settled on, "I'm sorry for your loss, sir."

"Yes, a terrible tragedy." He lowered his head and shook it side to side, taking a deep breath as he did. When he exhaled, he raised his head and faced me. "Which is the reason I wanted to see you."

"Sir?"

"I'd like your help, Mrs. Pollack."

"In what way?"

"From the tone of the questioning, I suspect the police believe I had something to do with Philomena's death. They may also suspect my wife. They questioned her quite extensively as well. I need you to find the real killer."

"Me? Sir, I'm no detective."

"Don't be so modest, Mrs. Pollack. Over the past year you've discovered both Marlys Vandenburg's killer and Lou Beaumont's killer."

"That's not exactly what happened. The killers discovered me. And both times nearly made me their next victim."

"I'll supply you with adequate protection while you investigate."

"Protection?"

"My driver, Tino Martinelli, will accompany you throughout your investigation. He's a former Marine." Gruenwald stood, strode over to his desk, and returned with a business card that he handed to me. "This is his cell number. He knows to expect your calls and that you're now his top priority."

I stood to leave, holding the card out to him, but he kept his hands at his sides. "I'm honored that you think so highly of my investigational skills, Mr. Gruenwald, but you've tremendously inflated my abilities. You need to hire a professional." And an attorney, but I kept that thought to myself.

"A detective nosing around would raise suspicions. You'd blend in better. You work here."

"You think someone from Trimedia is responsible for Philomena's death?"

"I do."

Given Philomena's connections to the rap world, I thought it far more likely her questionable past had finally caught up with her, but I opted for discretion, adding that thought to the others I didn't voice. Instead, I asked, "Why would you think that?"

"I know many people here were jealous of Philomena."

Jealous, maybe. But jealous enough to kill? I didn't think so. "That's not a very persuasive argument for convincing me to stick my nose into a murder investigation."

"I have other arguments. Five thousand to be exact." He slipped his hand into his suit jacket, removed a rectangular piece of paper, and handed it to me.

My jaw dropped. I sat back down and stared at a check for five thousand dollars, made out to me, from Gruenwald's personal account.

"I know you can use the money," he said.

"What if I'm not successful?"

"You will be."

"How can you be so certain?"

"You have incentive."

"So I only get to cash the check if I catch Philomena's killer?"

"No, the money is yours. I have faith that you're an honorable woman and will work hard to accomplish the task for which I'm paying you."

"I could still fail."

"I'm confident you won't."

I decided Alfred Gruenwald was certifiable. However, if he was willing to pay me five thousand dollars for a wild goose chase, who was I to complain? I folded the check in half. "Before I agree, you'll need to clarify a few things for me. Full disclosure. No holding back."

"Such as?"

"What were you and Philomena arguing about behind the

booth Sunday afternoon?"

Now it was his turn to drop his jaw. The color leached out of his face. "How do you know about that?"

"I overheard you."

Gruenwald's demeanor quickly segued from overconfident to mightily pissed. "So you're the one who told the police. That's why I'm their prime suspect." He pointed a finger at me. "This is all your fault. I should fire you right now."

Great. Me and my big mouth. "You'll also have to fire the entire *Bling!* staff."

"Why would I do that?"

"Because every single one of them in that booth also heard you and Philomena. She's not exactly quiet and reserved, and your voice carries even when you're not shouting."

Gruenwald dropped his bluster. "They all heard?"

I nodded. "Everyone watched the two of you and Norma Gene leave the Javits Center. They stood around whispering about it afterwards."

He waved his hand in the air as if trying to swat away my words. "The argument was nothing important."

Bull. "Sounded much more than nothing to me. Philomena made threats. You both second-guessed your relationship with each other. Then she stormed out, grabbing Norma Gene on her way. You followed, looking less than happy. As far as I know, that could be the last time anyone saw Philomena alive."

"Damn. No wonder the police suspect me. You all fingered me."

"I'm sure the police would have suspected you whether they heard about the fight or not."

"Why is that?"

"The spouse or boyfriend more often than not turns out to be the killer."

He began pacing, repeatedly covering the short distance between where I sat and the matching chair before turning and retracing his steps. After four laps he sat back down and shoved his hands into his pockets. Staring at his feet, he said, "Sylvia—my wife—served me with divorce papers Sunday."

"Wouldn't that make Philomena happy?"

"It would have if Sylvia wasn't also suing Philomena for alienation of affection."

"Which isn't legal in New Jersey."

Gruenwald's head shot up. "How do you know that?"

I shrugged. "Doesn't matter."

"No, I suppose not now. The papers were drawn up in Hawaii where we have a vacation home. For various reasons, we list it as our permanent residence."

Score one for Naomi. Maybe Gruenwald should ask her to investigate the murder. "Philomena made threats against your wife, didn't she?"

He nodded.

"Forgive me for saying this, Mr. Gruenwald, but given Philomena's associations with a certain seamier element of society, isn't it more likely that someone from her past killed her? Maybe he had a score to settle." Which made far more sense than someone at Trimedia knocking off the Queen of Bling.

"She cut all ties with those people except for Norma Gene when she went mainstream. She'd cleaned up her act. They both had."

"Yet, she was willing to contact someone concerning your wife. It sounds to me like she hadn't severed *all* ties with her past."

Again, he swatted away my words. "Idle threats to get me to convince Sylvia to drop the lawsuit."

"You seemed more than concerned about those threats on Sunday."

He had no answer for that. I continued. "People hold grudges. They fester and grow. At some point they seek revenge. If Philomena reached out to some of her old associates—"

Gruenwald jumped up and began pacing once again. With his back to me, he said, "No. You're wrong. Someone connected with Trimedia killed Philomena."

"How can you be so sure?"

He spun around and pierced me with a determined look. "I just know. I feel it in my gut."

Gruenwald the Clairvoyant? What wasn't he telling me? "When was the last time you saw Philomena?"

"Monday. Late afternoon. We had another fight over Sylvia. Philomena left for a Zumba class but never came home that night. I figured she was still fuming and spent the night either at her apartment or with Norma Gene."

"Have you spoken with Norma Gene?"

He nodded. "She didn't spend the night with her."

"You do know that Norma Gene is a guy, right?"

"I wasn't born yesterday, Mrs. Pollack. I'm well aware of Norma Gene's situation. If you're inferring what I think you're inferring, you're way off base. Philomena and Norman never had that kind of relationship."

"Norman?"

"Norman Eugene Mortenson, his birth name."

Weird. If I remembered correctly, Mortenson was Marilyn Monroe's real last name. Norma Jeane Mortenson. Norman

Eugene Mortenson. I half expected to hear the theme music from *The Twilight Zone* playing in the background.

I pushed the coincidence from my mind and asked, "Did this happen often, that you'd fight over something, and Philomena would leave for the night?"

"Sometimes. Philomena was a very passionate woman."

I resisted the urge to squirm. I so didn't want this conversation veering into TMI territory.

"Passionate people often have control issues," he added.

I raised my eyebrows.

"My therapist explained that to me."

His therapist? I didn't want to go there, either. "Your driver mentioned a list of errands Philomena left him yesterday."

That caught Gruenwald by surprise. "When did you speak with Tino?"

"My car died. He stopped to help me yesterday afternoon and asked about the police activity in the parking lot."

"How did the list come up in conversation?"

"It's not important. What matters is how he got the list and when."

"She left it for him Monday afternoon."

"You're sure of that?"

"Positive. I handed it to him myself yesterday when he picked me up."

"I can understand why the police consider you a suspect, Mr. Gruenwald, but why do you think they're also looking at Mrs. Gruenwald?"

"Because I left her for Philomena."

Through the Trimedia grapevine I knew Gruenwald had walked out on his first wife of nearly twenty years for the much younger Sylvia two decades earlier. Did philanderers come in different varieties with cycles similar to cicadas?

"Sylvia was suing Philomena. Why kill her when she'd gone to the trouble of filing a lawsuit?"

"That's the obvious question, isn't it? Maybe the police think Sylvia used the lawsuit to deflect suspicion away from herself."

"I saw your wife, sir. She's hardly capable of beating another woman to death. Even though Philomena was short, she was much younger and quite fit."

"The police must think Sylvia hired the killer."

"Is that what you think?"

"I told you, Sylvia had nothing to do with this. I know my wife."

"If that's the case, the police won't find any evidence linking her to the crime."

Gruenwald checked his watch. "I have a budget meeting, Mrs. Pollack. We may have to make some cuts in the magazine group. Will you be accepting my offer or not?"

Budget cuts? Was that a veiled threat? Was Gruenwald blackmailing me into investigating for him? I glanced down at the check, still in my hand. Five thousand dollars. Mine. And all I had to do to earn it was snoop around Trimedia in search of a killer that was anywhere but at Trimedia. I was certain no one here had any motive for killing Philomena, even if none of us particularly liked her.

"You still want me to investigate?" Didn't he just threaten to fire me?

"From what you've told me, you're not the only one who told the police about that argument. As much as I wish otherwise, I can't expect anyone to withhold evidence during a murder investigation, and as you pointed out, the police would suspect me anyway."

I guess that meant I wasn't fired. I slipped the check into my skirt pocket and stuck out my hand. "Then you have a deal, Mr. Gruenwald."

"One other thing," he said, gripping my hand so hard I winced. "Yes?"

"No one can know about our agreement."

"And if someone happens to figure things out?"

"Make certain they don't."

EIGHT

"Why all the cloak and dagger, Mr. Gruenwald?"

"I have my reasons."

"None of which you've shared with me. How can I investigate for you if I don't have all the facts? I requested full disclosure, remember?"

"You have all the facts you need." He strode across the room and opened his door. "Now if you'll excuse me, Mrs. Pollack, I'm late for that budget meeting."

In other words, shut up and do the job I've asked you to do, or find yourself on the unemployment line.

And what if that veiled threat encompassed not only my job but all the *American Woman* employees? Laying off a crafts editor wouldn't solve any budget problems, but folding an entire magazine might. If I refused Gruenwald's offer, would I take the fall for all my friends and co-workers losing their jobs?

I headed for the elevator, my mind made up. Gruenwald had me over the proverbial barrel. I slipped my hand into my skirt pocket and fingered the check. Could be worse. At least he was paying me.

"So what did he want?" asked Cloris when I returned to our floor.

We stood in the corridor between our cubicles. "Not here," I mumbled, afraid someone might overhear. If Gruenwald had paid me to investigate, he may have paid someone else to make sure I kept to the terms of that agreement—even though I hadn't actually agreed not to tell anyone about working undercover for him.

Cloris's brows knit together. "Where?" she whispered.

Before I could answer, Naomi rounded the corner and headed toward us. "Anastasia, I've had the oddest request. You're on temporary assignment to *Bling!*"

I quickly turned to Cloris and mouthed, "Shh," then responded to Naomi, "Me?"

Obviously Gruenwald's doing. Actually, having a reason to nose around the *Bling!* staff would make ferreting out Philomena's killer far easier—if I believed I'd find Philomena's killer among the *Bling!* staff. "I don't know the first thing about twenty-something fashions, lifestyles, and entertainment," I reminded Naomi.

"That's exactly what I told Gruenwald's secretary. I thought maybe someone had confused you with Tessa."

Cloris laughed. "Probably the only time that will ever happen."

"Still, it's damned odd," said Naomi.

"What am I supposed to do down there?" I asked.

Naomi shrugged. "Beats me. I guess you'll find out once you arrive."

"And what about my work here?"

"Daphne will fill in for you as best she can. How caught up are you?"

Daphne Jervis, the one assistant shared by the four bottom feeder editors, already juggled far too much. "Right now, I'm ahead of schedule, but how long do they want me downstairs? Daphne can handle editorial copy but not the actual craft projects or writing the directions."

"Gruenwald's secretary didn't say."

But I already knew the answer to my question. I was exiled to *Bling!* for as long as it took me to discover Philomena's killer.

~*~

Stepping into the *Bling!* editorial department, was the equivalent of tumbling down Alice's rabbit hole. Rap music blared from ceiling speakers, the thump-thump-thump of the bass rattling through my entire body. The staff all dressed in outfits that paid homage to Philomena's unique sense of style. In my khaki pencil skirt and pinstripe oxford shirt, I stood out like a nun at a rave.

But I wasn't the only one. Standing off in a corner, I noticed Tino Martinelli, looking every bit the part of a Secret Service agent. Or perhaps an extra in the next *Men In Black* movie.

Except for a twelve hundred dollar pair of Bulgari shades (which I only recognized because Tessa had recently showed off the pair she bought for her boyfriend's birthday,) Tino's obviously custom made black suit, conservative tie, white shirt, and buzz cut certainly didn't fit in at *Bling!* any more than I did. He nodded in recognition but remained at his corner observation post.

I marched up to him. "Gruenwald give you orders to keep an eye on me?"

"Yes, ma'am."

"You know why?"

"I do."

"You okay with that?"

"I get paid to do what Mr. Gruenwald requests."

And obviously paid very well, judging from his attire. Maybe I should quit my job and become a chauffeur to a corporate CEO.

The *Bling!* editorial department had moved into the space vacated by the now defunct *Bear Essentials*, a magazine dedicated to the collection of teddy bears. However, the space was the only thing *Bling!* had inherited. An open concept floor plan now took the place of the former rabbit warren of cubicles. All the tables, desks, and chairs looked brand new and expensive, unlike the battered furniture that moved with us from our old headquarters in Manhattan to our current cornfield location.

"Who are you, and what are you doing here?"

I spun around to find Norma Gene towering over me, her hands on her hips, a glare on her face that didn't mask her red-rimmed puffy eyes or mascara streaked cheeks.

Funny how she didn't recognize me. Or maybe not. I thought about Cloris's comment regarding the *Me* generation. Norma Gene often stood feet from me all last weekend but never once bothered to make eye contact. I wasn't even worthy of an occasional glance, let alone acknowledgment of my existence.

"I'm Anastasia Pollack, an *American Woman* editor, and I've been assigned here temporarily."

"What's *American Woman*?"

Really? I tamped down the urge to keep from spouting the comment itching to break free of my mouth. "One of the other Trimedia magazines. We were in the booth next to you at the consumer show."

She shrugged. "If you say so. You need to talk to Sue."

"Where do I find her?"

Norma Gene pointed to a woman bending over a light table, then shouted, "Hey, Sue!" When the woman looked in our direction, Norma Gene waved her over. "She says she's assigned here."

"Who assigned you?" asked Sue. "And why?"

"Corporate assigned me. I haven't a clue why."

"We don't need you. We're quite capable of running *Bling!* on our own."

Good. Because I wouldn't know how to help them. They certainly didn't need my input on fashion, lifestyle, or entertainment. I had none to offer. Or at least none of the kind they'd accept.

"Look, I don't want to be here anymore than you want me here. So how about if I simply wander around, pretending to give you advice? We act friendly, make small talk from time to time, and I let you do whatever it is that you all do. Hopefully, this won't last long. I'd like nothing better than to return upstairs to my own magazine."

She thought about that for a moment, her arms folded across her chartreuse leopard print spandex-covered chest. She glanced at Norma Gene. "You okay with that?"

"You won't start ordering us around?" asked Norma Gene.

"Wouldn't dream of it."

"Okay by me," said Norma Gene.

Sue nodded and offered her hand. "I'm Sue Evens. The *Bling!* editorial director. What did you say your name was again? Annabelle?"

"Anastasia."

"Whatever."

As Sue introduced me to the other staff members, Tino followed us around but kept out of the way. Sue didn't seem to notice him. I wondered if Tino had performed a similar task for Gruenwald before Philomena's death, keeping an eye on her.

"Just ignore Annabelle here," Sue told the staff. "Gruenwald thinks we can't function without Philomena. We know better." She turned to me. "Philomena really didn't do anything on *Bling!* We did all the work."

"I suspected as much," I said.

"She got all the credit, though."

And how did that make you feel, Sue Evens? "Isn't that always the way with celebrities?"

"You got that right, girlfriend."

Hmm...was Sue jealous enough of Philomena that she killed her? Maybe Gruenwald wasn't as offbase as I thought.

~*~

After observing the inner workings of *Bling!* for a couple of hours, I came to the conclusion that the staff definitely knew what they were doing. Except for Norma Gene. Unless her job assignment was to mope around all day doing nothing except cry every twenty minutes or so. When that happened the nearest *Bling!* staff member would console her until the last of her sniffles subsided.

"You've all worked at magazines before, haven't you?" I asked Sue at one point.

"Of course. Except for Norma Gene. I have no idea where she'll go or what she'll do without Philomena. Those two were as tight as two peas in a Spanx pod."

Sue eyed me for a moment. "You thought we were all just Philomena groupies, didn't you?"

"I never had an opinion one way or the other. Even though I

work a floor above you, I didn't know much about *Bling!* or even Philomena before this past weekend."

"Hard to believe, given Philomena's popularity."

"I've been living under a rock for nearly a year."

"Apparently." She sighed. "It won't last. Now that Philomena's gone, the magazine will die. Just like *George*."

"Who's George?"

"Not a who. A what. The magazine JFK, Jr. ran?"

Sue hardly looked old enough to remember that. She also didn't fit the image of a typical *George* reader, but maybe she'd been forced to adopt a certain persona in order to work on Philomena's baby. Magazine jobs were hard to come by in today's economy, and image was everything for Philomena and *Bling!*

"We're putting together a memorial edition," she said. "I expect it will be our last. You know if there are openings at any of the other Trimedia magazines?"

Scratch Sue Evens as a suspect.

I excused myself and headed for the ladies' room. A howl of despair greeted me as I pushed open the door and stepped into the room. The sequin decorated turquoise patent leather stilettos I spied under one of the stalls confirmed the howler's identity. "Norma Gene? It's Anastasia. Is there anything I can do for you?"

She blew her nose, then wailed, "It's all my fault."

"What is?"

"I let Mommy down. I promised her I'd always look out for Philomena." A fresh onslaught of sobbing followed.

"Philomena was your sister?"

After a few minutes, the crying jag subsided. She blew her nose again, then hiccupped back one last sob before opening the stall and stepping out into the room.

"Not by blood. We grew up in the same foster home. Mommy was worried about the rap crowd. Drugs and guns, that's all they cared about. She didn't want Philomena mixed up with them.

"I promised I'd always take care of Philomena, and I did. I even convinced her to give up that life. Mommy was so happy and so proud of me. Now Philomena's dead, and it's all my fault. I should've protected her better."

Fresh tears streamed down her mascara-streaked face. I reached out to touch her arm, and she collapsed against me, nearly bowling me onto the tile floor. I patted her back until she collected herself again.

"Do you have any idea who might have killed her?" I asked once this latest bout of tears subsided.

Norma Gene slumped down on one of the vanity chairs and stared at her reflection in the mirror. A steely determination settled over her face. "No, but when I find out, he's gonna wish he never crossed paths with Norma Gene Mortenson."

~*~

Shortly before the end of the workday, I left the *Bling!* offices and headed back upstairs to find Cloris. Tino followed. "I'm only heading upstairs to *American Woman*," I said. "No need to follow me."

"Sorry, but I have my orders."

"How am I supposed to explain your presence to my co-workers when I'm not supposed to tell anyone what I'm doing for Mr. Gruenwald?"

Tino shrugged. "You'll think of something."

"Feel free to offer suggestions."

I wondered if he planned to follow me home and camp outside my front door all night. The one place he wouldn't dare follow me, though, was into the ladies' room. I texted Cloris to meet me there.

"What in the world is going on?" she asked once she arrived.

"How do you feel about ditching family responsibility for the evening and going out to dinner with me?"

"I'm in."

"Good." We made arrangements to meet at an Italian bistro at the Short Hills Mall. I grabbed my purse from my locked desk drawer and headed back downstairs. Tino followed me to the Jeep, but once I pulled out of my parking spot, he waved and headed back into the building.

I called home while stopped at the first red light. Mama picked up on the third ring. "What do you mean you're going to be late?" she asked. "How late?"

"Late enough that you, the boys, and Lucille should eat without me. There's a frozen lasagna defrosting in the refrigerator and plenty of salad fixings."

"You won't be home for dinner?"

"Not tonight."

"You have to!"

"Why? What's going on, Mama?"

She hesitated, then sighed heavily into the phone. "I invited Ira and his family for dinner tonight."

"And when exactly were you planning to tell me this? When I walked into the house this evening?"

"You were never going to get around to inviting them, so I did it for you."

"Great. And what did you plan to serve them?" The lasagna certainly wouldn't stretch far enough to include Ira, his three kids, and his father-in-law. I figured Cynthia for a no-show, given recent events.

"I knew you wouldn't have time to cook. So I phoned in an order to that catering place in downtown Westfield."

The one that charged twenty-five dollars per person? "Your treat, Mama?"

"Don't be silly, dear. Not at their prices. I'm sure Ira will cover the cost."

"You assume quite a bit sometimes, Mama." Especially when it comes to other people's money.

"Anyway, that's why you need to come home in time for dinner tonight."

"Not going to happen."

"But, Anastasia, you're the hostess!"

"No, Mama. You are." With that I disconnected the call.

~*~

Forty minutes later, as Cloris and I sat sipping frozen Bellinis, awaiting our dinners, I told her about Mama's latest attempt at bonding between our family and Ira's family.

"What do you suppose will happen when the food delivery arrives and Flora has no money to pay the driver?"

"She'd better hope Ira shows up before the food. I can't believe my mother pulled a stunt like that."

"Really?"

Who was I kidding? "You're right. On second thought, I'm not at all surprised." In her own way Mama was quite the manipulator. She'd proven so on more than one occasion.

"When is she moving into her new apartment with her current fiancé?"

"Not soon enough." When Cloris raised her eyebrows, I added, "Don't get me wrong; I love my mother."

"I know."

"I'd simply like a bit less chaos in my life."

"Which brings us to why we're here. Why *are* we here? What the hell did Gruenwald want?"

"First, you have to swear you won't breathe a word of what I'm about to tell you to anyone."

"This sounds ominous."

"Swear?"

Cloris shrugged. "Why not? Cross my heart."

"Gruenwald has it in his head that Philomena's killer is one of us."

"Us? As in *American Woman* us? That's crazy." Cloris slammed her glass onto the table hard enough that some of the yellow slush spilled over the rim and onto her hand. "Why would any of us kill that self-centered bitch?" She paused for a moment to reach for her napkin, then added, "Besides Tessa. I could definitely see her knocking off Philomena. I swear that girl turned fifty shades of green with envy."

"Tessa didn't kill Philomena. She's not smart enough to plan a murder and get away with it."

"True. Besides, she might break a nail. She does have the money to hire someone to do her dirty work, though."

"Green with envy isn't enough motive for murder. Killing Philomena wouldn't give Tessa her own magazine, and that's what she wants."

"I don't know. She's delusional enough to believe it might happen. After all, she does have her Uncle Chessie."

"Who hung her out to dry when we all got roped into those unpaid gigs at *Morning Makeovers*." I shook my head. "No, I think Gruenwald meant someone at Trimedia in general. Specifically, someone working at *Bling!*"

"So that's why he transferred you?"

"I'm supposed to prove his theory for him by figuring out who killed Philomena. Right now, he's convinced he's the prime suspect."

"He's probably right. I'm assuming you told Batswin and Robbins about those conversations you overheard?"

"Of course. Gruenwald's also convinced the police won't bother to investigate much further if they find enough evidence to indict him for her murder."

"Why you? Why doesn't he hire a private detective?"

"I asked him that. He wants someone who will blend in and not raise suspicions."

Cloris laughed. "I hate to tell you this, but you don't exactly blend in with the *Bling!* crowd, either."

"Tell me about it."

"And what do you get out of all this snooping around? Did Gruenwald blackmail you or something?"

"In not so many words." I told her about his veiled threat, which I interpreted as all the *American Woman* employees risked losing their jobs.

"You should go to the police. Not to mention Human Resources. Look at all the money Trimedia will save by not paying his exorbitant salary. Better yet, you should sue the creep for harassment."

I reached into my skirt pocket and withdrew Gruenwald's check. Handing it across the table to Cloris, I said, "He also gave me this."

Cloris frowned at the check for a moment before passing it back to me. "What if the police are right? What if Gruenwald is the killer, and he's using you in the hope of diverting attention away from himself?"

"That crossed my mind, especially after what I observed on Sunday. I don't think he and Philomena had the smoothest of relationships."

"No kidding."

"But how would asking me to investigate have any impact on the police investigation?"

"Unless you discovered someone else killed Philomena."

"Except Gruenwald does have motive. Philomena flipped out big time over that lawsuit Sylvia Gruenwald filed. I questioned him about the argument I overheard, and he filled in the blanks. As I suspected, Philomena's threats involved contacting some of her old cronies from the 'hood to have Sylvia permanently dispatched if Gruenwald didn't handle the problem himself."

"Are you suggesting Philomena wanted Gruenwald to kill his wife?"

"Sounds like it."

"And Gruenwald flipped out over Philomena's threat against Sylvia?"

"Exactly. He may have walked out on her for Philomena, but divorce is one thing, murder quite another."

"Yet you're suggesting he killed Philomena because she wanted him or someone else to kill Sylvia. It's okay for him to kill, but it's not okay for someone else to kill?"

"In his mind. I suppose if he's charged, he'll claim he was protecting his wife from a killer."

"If he's the killer."

"If. There's always the possibility that he's innocent, and someone else killed Philomena for a completely different reason."

Our dinners arrived, and we ate in silence for a few minutes until Cloris finally asked, "If not Gruenwald, though, then who? Someone from her entourage? Norma Gene?"

"Norma Gene, being a guy, certainly has the strength, but she's wandering around like a teary-eyed lost puppy without Philomena."

I told Cloris about my conversation with Norma Gene. "I swear she's on the verge of a nervous breakdown. She blames herself for letting her foster mother down and not preventing Philomena's death."

"What about someone on the *Bling!* staff?"

"Definitely not the *Bling!* staff unless someone acted without thinking. They're all reluctantly polishing up their resumes. *Bling!* can't survive without Philomena, and they know it. Even though they did all the work, she provided the big draw."

"Rumor has it Trimedia poured a boatload of money into the launch of *Bling!*"

"And with only one issue in print so far, they'll lose a bundle on their investment."

"Hence Gruenwald's budget meeting?"

"Probably. I'd say his job is on the line."

"Finding the killer isn't going to save his job."

"No, but if the police charge him with murder, as he's worried might happen, Trimedia executes the morals clause in his contract and won't have to pay to get rid of him. If I can determine that someone else killed Philomena, Gruenwald still loses his job, but he walks away with an extremely large platinum parachute."

"And he's paying you a measly five grand? You should hold out for ten times that. After all, he's asking you to put yourself in possible danger."

"Except I don't think anyone at Trimedia killed Philomena,

and he never asked me to look elsewhere, even though he did say Tino Martinelli was at my disposal."

"For what?"

"Protection."

"He has the brawn, but even if you wanted to, how would you insinuate yourself into Philomena's inner circle? You're certainly not insane enough to drive down to Philadelphia to question her gangbanger friends, are you?"

"Definitely not."

"Looks like Gruenwald just bought you a new car."

A new *used* car but who's quibbling? "The universe works in mysterious ways," I said around a mouthful of vodka penne.

NINE

Cloris and I left the restaurant shortly after eight o'clock, and even though I first stopped at the bank to deposit Gruenwald's check, I still arrived home to find Ira's van parked at my curb. As I pulled into the driveway, I glanced up at Zack's apartment and contemplated slipping upstairs to avoid Ira and his kids. The last thing in the world I wanted to do right now was deal with dinner guests I hadn't invited.

However, knowing Mama, she was monitoring the driveway every few minutes, awaiting my arrival. I parked the Jeep and reluctantly headed up the path to my back door. Taking a deep breath, I forced a smile onto my face before stepping into the house.

My kitchen looked like the Tasmanian Devil had taken up residence. Dirty dishes covered nearly every square inch of the table and counters. Mephisto sniffed around the garbage that overflowed from the trash can onto the linoleum. Ralph pecked at a glop of something sticking to the seat of one of the kitchen chairs. How could Mama make such a mess when she'd ordered in a catered meal?

From the dining room, over a series of bleeps, dings, and swooshing noises, I overheard Alex, Nick, and Ira discussing the Mets' slim chances of clinching the National League pennant. Either everyone else listened in rapt silence, was bored to death, or was too busy stuffing their faces with the pricey meal I hoped Mama hadn't charged to the one credit card I'd nearly paid off from moonlighting at Sunnyside over the summer.

I scooped up Ralph and deposited him in his cage in the den. Then I returned to the kitchen, hoisted Mephisto into my arms and shut him in the den with Ralph. After taking another deep breath but not bothering with pasting on a smile this time, I marched into the dining room.

Seated around the table, I found Alex, Nick, and Ira continuing to discuss batting averages and pitching stats. Mama and Lawrence gazed starry-eyed at each other while sharing a slice of cherry pie a la mode. Lucille, head down, rapidly shoveled enormous forkfuls of the dessert into her mouth. A set of twin girls sat texting while a younger boy played a handheld video game. A half-empty container of Turkey Hill vanilla ice cream sat melting in the middle of the table.

No one seemed to notice me. I cleared my throat. "Good evening."

"Nice to see you finally made it home," said Mama, tearing her gaze from Lawrence. "These are Ira's children, dear." She waved in the direction of the boy and girls as she rattled off their names, "Melody, Harmony, and Isaac. Children, this is your Aunt Anastasia."

I didn't receive so much as a nod of recognition from any of them. Their attention continued fixated on their mini-screens while their fingers flew across keyboards and controls, each stroke punctuated by those bleeps, dings, and swooshes.

"Children, say hello to your aunt," said Mama.

I glanced at my sons. Alex mouthed, "I told you so," while Nick rolled his eyes. They previously had the misfortune of spending a day with Ira's kids, and that in itself had been reason enough for me to keep postponing this get-together.

Taking matters into my own hands, I walked up behind Ira's three kids and whipped the phones and video game out of their hands before they realized what was happening.

"Hey!" yelled the girls in unison.

"Give that back," shouted the boy.

"Phones and video games are not allowed at the dinner table," I said.

"Dad! Make her give my phone back," demanded one of the girls.

"She has no right," said the other.

The boy jumped out of his chair, knocking it over behind him, as he grabbed for his Game Boy. "Give it back, bitch!"

Mama gasped.

"Isaac, apologize at once!" said Lawrence.

"You're not my real grandfather. I don't have to do what you tell me."

Lucille stopped shoveling food into her mouth and speared Ira with a narrow-eyed glare. "My Isidore would never have such insolent grandchildren. You can't possibly be his son."

Ira glanced first at his kids, then at the rest of us, seemingly unable to speak. He looked like he wanted to crawl under the table. Granted, the man was overwhelmed raising three young kids, but he desperately needed to grow a backbone.

Silence descended on the room. "Jump in any time, Ira." I finally said.

He cleared his throat. "Anastasia is right. You shouldn't be texting or playing games during dinner," he told his children.

"Since when?" asked one of the girls, Harmony or Melody. I didn't have a clue which was which.

"We do it at home," said the other.

"She's not my mother," said the boy. "I don't have to listen to her."

"My house, my rules," I said.

"Screw you!" He made one more futile attempt at grabbing his Game Boy from my hands. When that failed, he ran from the dining room, through the living room, and out the front door, slamming it so hard the dishes on the table rattled. A moment later, his sisters followed him out in the same manner, but both first tossed me a third finger salute.

"Ira, you've got to do something about those children," said Lawrence. "They're totally out of control."

"They're only acting out because they've lost their mother," said Ira.

"Two years ago. Stop using that as an excuse. You've got to set rules and make them abide by them. Trust me, you'll regret it later if you don't do something now."

I wondered if Lawrence spoke from personal experience, given the way Cynthia turned out.

"Well, that went well," said Mama. "Don't you think you were a bit harsh, dear?"

This was my fault? "I'm just getting started, Mama. Since you went behind my back and organized this dinner party, you can clean up. I'm leaving. When I return, I expect to find my kitchen in the state I left it this morning." With that, I headed back through the kitchen, out the back door, and up the garage steps.

Zack opened the door before I knocked. "I've had a really bad day," I said, collapsing into his arms. "How about you?"

He drew me into the apartment and closed the door. "Want to talk about it?"

All of it? Did I? I knew what Zack would say about my newest side job. He'd lecture me and try to talk me out of investigating Philomena's death. I sighed. "Not all of it, but you'll probably wheedle it out of me anyway, so we might as well get it over with now."

"I don't like the sound of that."

"Trust me. You'll like it even less once you know more about it."

He grabbed a bottle of Sauvignon Blanc from the refrigerator and poured two glasses, carrying them to the sofa. "Out with it," he said.

I placed the Game Boy and the phones on the coffee table. Zack raised both eyebrows in question. "Hardly worth the effort of an explanation," I said.

I curled up into a corner of the sofa, and accepted one of the glasses of wine. After a sip, I decided to take the coward's way out and work backwards. "I'm surprised Mama didn't invite you to her little shindig this evening."

Zack sat down next to me. "She did. I told her I had work to do."

"Smart man." I took another sip, then gave him the thirty second recap of the state of my kitchen and Ira's obnoxious kids. "Maybe I shouldn't have acted the way I did, but after the day I've had—"

"Which you haven't gotten to yet."

"I'm working up to it. Drink your wine."

Zack drained his glass. "No more excuses. Out with it."

"Promise you won't yell at me?"

"No."

"No?"

"No. I'm not promising anything until I know what's going on."

"Have another glass of wine first."

"That won't change anything. Out with it."

So I told him.

He jumped up from the sofa and lit into me. "Are you out of your mind?"

"Probably, but what choice do I have?"

"You could have said no."

"And risk being responsible for the entire staff of *American Woman* losing their jobs?"

"He was bluffing."

"I don't think so."

Zack strode over to the kitchen, retrieved the bottle of Sauvignon Blanc and refilled our glasses. "You can't keep sticking your nose into murder investigations. Three times now you've nearly gotten yourself killed."

I didn't need him to remind me of that. I'd made the same argument to Gruenwald. "But I'm certain no one at Trimedia killed Philomena. So I'm not placing myself in jeopardy."

"Really? No one at Trimedia is a suspect?"

"What would be the motive? More likely someone from her *gangsta* past is involved."

"Then explain to me, Sherlock, how her body wound up in the Trimedia boiler room?"

"Oh." A lead balloon settled into the pit of my stomach. Why hadn't I realized that? Obviously, Gruenwald had. "What a clueless idiot I am!"

Before Zack could respond, someone knocked at his door. "Who is it?" he yelled.

"Ira. Is Anastasia with you?"

I shook my head, not wanting to deal with Ira at the moment. Zack ignored me and opened the door.

Ira stepped inside and turned to me. "I wanted to apologize for what my kids said to you."

"Your kids should be the ones doing the apologizing," I said. "Lawrence is right. They walk all over you, Ira."

"I know." He sat down without being invited. "You have to understand, though. They've had to deal with so much the last few years. First Kristin's illness. Then her death. Then bringing Cynthia into their lives, which in hindsight was probably the biggest mistake of my life."

I thought about mentioning that my kids also lost a parent and much more recently, but they hadn't turned into juvenile delinquents as a result. However, given Ira's hangdog appearance at the moment, that seemed too much like kicking a puppy.

"I also didn't know Flora hadn't cleared tonight's dinner with you," he continued.

"Speaking of manipulators. Did she also stick you with the dinner bill?"

Ira shrugged. "I don't care about the money."

"But I do. Mama is using you to get what she wants, just like your kids use you."

"Flora doesn't want anything from me."

"Didn't you just buy her and Lawrence an apartment?"

"Yes, but they needed a place to live."

"My point." Mama always knows when to bring out her inner Blanche DuBois and take advantage of the generosity of men. Too bad I didn't inherit that trait from her instead of her stubby legs. "She's even manipulating you in ways you aren't aware of," I said.

"What do you mean?"

"She loves having you in my home because she knows how much your presence annoys Lucille."

"But I want to get to know Lucille better."

"Trust me, Ira. She doesn't want to get to know you better. You're a reminder of everything she sacrificed to her unyielding political agenda. Not to mention the lie she talked herself into believing for half a century."

"Does this mean you don't want me in your lives?"

"Of course not, but I need you to understand that this friendship you're trying to cultivate with Lucille isn't going to happen."

"Maybe in time."

"I doubt it." Was he really that dense? Forget about Lucille. No woman would want a constant reminder of her lover's child by another woman.

Ira heaved a huge sigh, then stood. "I should go. My kids are waiting in the van. I also came to retrieve their phones and the Game Boy."

"Which they shouldn't get back until they apologize to Anastasia," said Zack, joining the conversation for the first time.

Ira's shoulders slumped. He looked down at his shoes. "I know," he mumbled. And yet he scooped the phones and Game

Boy off the coffee table.

"Ira, before you go—"

He raised his head; his face lit up. "Yes?"

"I need a favor." Now who was doing the manipulating, but what choice did I have? Ira wouldn't take advantage of my lack of car knowledge the way the Hyundai dealer had.

"Anything," he said.

"My car died at the office yesterday. I need to know what it will cost to repair, assuming it's worth repairing."

"Which it probably isn't," said Zack.

"In that case, I have ten thousand dollars for a replacement. Not a penny more." Actually, I had five thousand dollars, the same five thousand Gruenwald gave me, but I knew I'd never find reliable transportation for such a small sum.

Had I paid off enough of Karl's debt that Ira would be able to finagle me a car loan for the balance? He must have some pull with the banks, given the number of dealerships he owned, but what would I do if every bank turned me down? I decided to pull a Scarlet O'Hara and not think about it for now, hoping the Hyundai only required a relatively minor repair.

"I'll send my guys over to your office tomorrow to pick the car up."

"Thanks, Ira. You'll find a spare set of keys hanging on a hook in the mud room. I'll email you the office address later tonight."

"Anything for you, Anastasia." He gave me a sloppy peck on my cheek, then left.

"That's one seriously needy guy," said Zack after we heard Ira descend the steps. "I feel sorry for him."

"I do, too, but my life is too complicated to get dragged into the drama of his life." Yet by asking a favor of Ira, I'd opened myself up for all sorts of future Ira drama.

"Which is why you dodged Flora's dinner, too?"

"I had dinner with Cloris. I was hoping Ira and his kids would be gone by the time I got home. No such luck."

"Is Ira at all like Karl?"

I laughed. "Had Karl been anything like Ira, he never would have bamboozled me into poverty. Ira is as transparent as Karl was deceptive."

"Speaking of deceptive, that brings us back to an earlier topic. What are your plans, and how do you intend to keep yourself out of a killer's crosshairs?"

Damned if I knew.

TEN

The next day Tino was waiting for me when I pulled into the parking lot. Before last night, I would have told him he needn't take his responsibility toward me so literally. This morning I was glad to see his protective ex-Marine bulk surveying the parking lot as I stepped from the Jeep.

I'd slept little last night, tossing and turning as I worried about once again placing myself in harm's way. I had no training as a sleuth and none of the tools available to the county detectives. All I could do was hope Batswin and Robbins made a swift arrest in this case. I wanted nothing to do with the investigation into Philomena's murder. Yet here I was, blackmailed smack into the middle of it.

As we headed into the building, I said, "You spent a good deal of time chauffeuring Philomena around. Do you have any ideas who might have wanted her dead? Mr. Gruenwald thinks the police suspect him."

"Mr. G. didn't kill her."

"How do you know that?"

"I know Mr. G."

"He also thinks the police might suspect Mrs. Gruenwald."

Tino narrowed his eyes and stared at me for a full ten seconds before bursting out in raucous laughter.

"Not on her own, of course, but she may have hired someone."

"Makes no sense. Why would she kill Philomena when she was suing her?"

"To divert suspicion away from herself?"

"Is that what you think?"

"Not really. What about Norma Gene?"

Tino laughed even harder this time. "No way."

"Why not?"

"That big baby passes out from paper cuts."

Why didn't that surprise me?

"I heard Philomena was beaten to a pulp," Tino continued. "Norma Gene and all that blood? Never gonna happen. Besides, she worshipped Philomena. She'd sooner take a bullet for her than harm her."

"So who do you think killed Philomena?

"My money's on some of those shady dudes she hung out with in Philly."

"Why?"

"They wanted a cut of the action. Got it, too, for a few years from what I hear. But once she went mainstream, she turned her back on them."

"Bad for her new image?"

"Exactly."

The gravy train drying up certainly sounded like motive for murder to me. "But if that's the case, how did her body wind up here? Why not just make her disappear? Dump her in the Hudson or bury her up in the Catskills."

Tino shrugged his wide receiver shoulders. "To frame someone else?"

"Possibly. But how did the killer get into the building? There were no indications of forced entry, and whoever he is, he knew about the surveillance cameras by the loading dock."

Tino pondered that for a minute as we waited for the elevator. "Maybe some of her homies work at *Bling!*"

I hadn't thought of that. Sue insinuated all the *Bling!* staff had magazine experience. Where would *gangstas* get magazine experience? Only one way to find out. "Tino, can you get me the personnel files of all the *Bling!* staff?"

"Don't see why not. Mr. Gruenwald said to make sure you had whatever you need."

"Good." The elevator doors opened, and we stepped inside. Tino pushed the button for the second floor. "I need those files. Bring them to me at my *American Woman* office, please." I pushed the button for the third floor.

"You're not going up to *Bling!*?"

"Not yet." Not until I read through all those files and figured out who knew Philomena from her days in the 'hood.

When the elevator stopped at the second floor, Tino stayed inside. "You don't need to accompany me to the *American Woman* offices."

"I'll make sure you arrive safely, then head down to Human Resources for those files."

The doors closed, and the elevator proceeded to the third floor. I stepped into the hallway, and Tino headed back downstairs.

"I didn't expect to see you here today," said Cloris when I stopped into the break room for coffee. She held an open box of cupcakes and offered me one. "Pineapple mango. Compliments of a new vegan bakery in Hoboken."

I hesitated. "Vegan cupcakes?" I broke off a piece from one and popped it into my mouth. Beggars can't be choosers when breakfast had consisted of an overripe banana and half a glass of orange juice. "Carlo's doesn't have to worry about competition," I said after forcing myself to swallow. "I hope the vegans didn't sign a long lease."

"That bad?"

"Worse. Anyway, I thought I'd check in with Daphne first to see how she's handling the extra workload."

Cloris took another cupcake from the box and sampled a piece. "Ugh! You're right." She tossed the remainder, along with the ten still in the box, into the trash, then guzzled down half her coffee. "There should be a law against baking with soy and tofu instead of butter and eggs. "So what's it like downstairs? Are you making enemies?"

"Not at all. The editorial director and I came to a quick and amiable understanding. I don't tell her what to do, and she doesn't carve me up with her switchblade."

"What!"

"Only kidding. Everyone is totally sane and extremely professional. The blaring rap music might render me deaf, though."

"So no suspects?"

"Shh!" I ducked out into the hall to make sure no one had overhead her, then stepped back into the room and closed the door.

"Why so paranoid?"

"Gruenwald didn't want anyone to know the real reason for my transfer. For all I know, he's paid off some *American Woman* spies to keep tabs on me."

Cloris laughed as she poured two cups of coffee and handed me one. "You are paranoid!"

"Maybe." Or maybe not. I still couldn't shake the feeling that two plus two didn't add up to four in Gruenwald World. Maybe this entire exercise was an elaborate scheme to send me on a wild goose chase because he worried I'd figure out he'd killed Philomena. If so, the man had far more faith in my sleuthing expertise than my experience warranted.

However, if Gruenwald did kill Philomena, he should be worried about Batswin and Robbins, not me.

Then again, given his age, I couldn't see Gruenwald rappelling down the side of our building to steal the security cameras. Of course, he may have hired someone to do his dirty work for him, but that brought me back to the stupidity of dumping the body at Trimedia. If Gruenwald was behind Philomena's death, why bring her body back here?

"Anyway, no one downstairs stood out as a homicidal maniac." I lobbed my cupcake into the trash after the others. Beggars might not be choosers, but even I had my limits.

"I wonder if the crime scene unit uncovered any forensic evidence," she said.

"Even if they did, Batswin and Robbins wouldn't divulge anything about an ongoing investigation to me."

"So what does Gruenwald expect you to do? Confront every staff member, asking if they killed Philomena?"

"That's one plan, I suppose."

"I wouldn't advise implementing it."

"No kidding, Watson."

"Got a better idea?"

I told her about my latest theory concerning the *Bling!* staff. "Tino headed down to Human Resources to collect employment records for me."

"Speaking of Tino, how does it feel to have your own personal hunk of a Secret Service detail?"

"Weird. And I haven't figured out how to explain his presence if I'm asked why he's following me around."

"You'll think of something. He's certainly nice eye candy. If things don't work out between you and Zack, you could do worse."

"I don't think so. He can't be more than thirty, and I'm not into the cougar thing."

"Never say never."

"On that note, I'm off to find Daphne."

"Give my regards to tall, dark, and drool-worthy when you see him."

~*~

Tino arrived about twenty minutes later and dumped a stack of file folders on my desk. "All these people work downstairs at *Bling!*?"

"That's all of them."

I quickly thumbed through the stack, counting. "Forty-two? No way are there forty-two people working downstairs." We didn't have anywhere near forty-two staff members at *American Woman*. "This must be a mistake."

"The secretary may have pulled files from other employees," he said.

"Only one way to find out." I divided the stack in half and handed one pile to Tino. "Start reading."

"What am I looking for again?"

"Anyone with a Philadelphia connection who now works for *Bling!*"

Tino wedged his bulk into the one spare chair in my cubicle and opened the first file. I settled into my desk chair and began reading from my stack.

First up on my pile was Sue Evens, *Bling!*'s editorial director. Sue listed *Philadelphia Magazine* as her former employer.

"Got one," Tino said. "Anthony Marzano. His employment application lists his last address as West Diamond Street, Philadelphia."

"What about former employers?"

"None listed. Looks like this is his first job."

"And his position at *Bling!*?"

"Copywriter."

First job and he scores a gig as a magazine copywriter when so many experienced copywriters are collecting unemployment? Unless Marzano accepted the job for peanuts, this sounded suspicious. "What's his annual salary?"

"Fifty big ones."

Definitely suspicious. "Did he gain experience while serving in the military?"

"He doesn't list military service."

I held out my hand for the file. "May I?"

When Tino passed me the file, I skimmed the employment application. "He didn't even go to college. Human resources signed off on hiring someone right out of high school as a magazine copywriter?"

"Looks like it."

"He lists his current address as a post office box in Morristown."

"He may not have found a permanent place to live yet when he filled out the paperwork and never bothered to update the information."

Possibly. I placed the file on my counter. "Suspect Number One? I'd certainly like to take a look at the copy this kid is writing. If he's even writing any copy."

If I weren't so hard up for cash, I'd bet my next paycheck that Anthony Marzano had scored himself a cushy no-show job, compliments of Philomena Campanello. But if that were the case, why kill the goose serving him twenty-four karat golden eggs?

"Found another," said Tino. "Pedro Alvarez. Last address Cecil B. Moore Avenue, Philadelphia. He's working as a layout artist for *Bling!*"

"Past experience?"

"None listed. And no college or military. Plus, he also lists a Morristown post office box for his current address. The same box as Marzano."

I pointed to the Marzano folder. "Add it to the pile." I then added Sue's folder. Three files so far. Three Philadelphia connections. At least Sue had prior magazine experience and didn't list a post office box for her current residence. However, if Marzano and Alvarez actually worked downstairs, she'd lied to me about the rest of the staff having experience.

As we continued reading through the folders, our pile of suspects with Philadelphia connections grew. Of the forty-two employees, nearly all came from Philadelphia. Two-thirds had no prior magazine experience and listed the same post office box for their current address. "I think it's time to head downstairs to have a talk with some of these people."

"How do you plan to do that without raising suspicion?" asked Tino.

"Good question." One I pondered for a moment. "I suppose I'll just say that as part of my assignment, I was asked to review the personnel files."

Tino shrugged. "Works for me."

We headed downstairs. I found Sue Evens doing paperwork in her corner office, an area separated from the rest of the room by only a two-sided four-foot high smoky gray glass pony wall. A break on one side of the wall allowed for entry.

"I need to speak with you," I said, half shouting over the thumping boom-boom-boom of the rap blaring from the overhead speakers. How did anyone think straight, let alone carry on business discussions, in such an atmosphere?

She motioned me into her alcove. Tino stood guard at the entrance. With no door to close to drown out some of the noise, I settled into one of the two chairs on the opposite side of Sue's desk and realized I'd have to shout to be heard.

"I see you inherited the puppy dog," she said.

"Excuse me?" I could barely hear her.

"Tino," she said a bit louder. "He used to dog Philomena. Now he's dogging you."

Tino was more pit bull than puppy dog. Gruenwald probably had him keeping an eye on Philomena to protect her from the Trimedia rabble. No one would dare get too close to the Queen of Bling with the hulking Tino Martinelli watching from the sidelines. "He's my assistant," I shouted. Not exactly a lie. Tino *was* assisting me.

She raised an eyebrow. "Funny. I thought he was the CEO's driver. Gruenwald sure works fast."

"What's that supposed to mean?"

"Just that poor Philomena isn't even six feet under yet, and Gruenwald has already moved on to his next bimbo. Although I must say, you certainly don't fit the bimbo mold."

"That's because I'm not. There's nothing going on between me and Gruenwald."

She shrugged. "If you say so. What did you want to talk about?"

I glared at her for a moment before opening the first folder. "Let's start with Anthony Marzano."

"Who?"

"Any chance you can turn the music down, so we don't have to shout at each other?"

Sue swiveled in her chair and pressed a button on the console behind her desk. "Better?"

"Slightly."

"Hey," shouted someone, "who's messing with the volume?"

"Annabelle can't hear me," yelled Sue. "I'll turn it back up as soon as she leaves." Then she turned back to me. "You were saying?"

"Anthony Marzano. Your copywriter?"

"Never heard of him. Who says he's one of my copywriters?"

"Human Resources."

"News to me."

"What about Pedro Alvarez?"

"Is he also supposed to be a copywriter?"

"No, a layout artist."

"Not here."

"You're sure?"

"Of course, I'm sure. I know my own staff."

"How many people work at *Bling!*?"

"What's this all about?"

"I'm not sure, but I'm beginning to have an idea. A number, please?"

She thought for a moment. "Around fifteen, I think. If you need an exact number, I'll have to look it up."

"Before you go to that trouble, tell me if any of these other people work here." One by one I opened folders and rattled off the names of the people without prior experience. After each name Sue shook her head.

"You're positive you don't know any of these people?" I asked after coming to the last name.

"Absolutely. Are they all listed on the *Bling!* payroll?"

I nodded. "To the tune of one point four million dollars annually. Each one of these supposed employees is collecting fifty thousand dollars in salary." Given that *Bling!* had commenced operations six months ago, that added up to nearly three-quarters of a million dollars so far. I asked her one last time, "You're sure none of these people works here?"

"I know my staff, Annabelle. I've never heard of any of those people."

"Anastasia."

"What?"

"My name is Anastasia, not Annabelle."

She waved her hand in the air. "Whatever. So you're telling me Philomena padded the payroll with no-shows?"

"Looks that way."

"Sonofabitch. Someone had to be in on this."

And that someone was probably Philomena's killer.

ELEVEN

"I need to find out if Human Resources and Accounting have any new staff members," I told Tino after filling him in on my conversation with Sue.

"Snooping around in either department isn't the best idea. You'd raise suspicions."

"Who else would know?"

"Probably Ms. Luscy."

"Mr. Gruenwald's secretary?"

"She knows just about everything that goes on here."

"And what she doesn't know, she can probably find out without alerting the killer we're on to him." Or her.

We headed up to the fourth floor. Along the way we passed Tessa in the hall. I think she tried to raise an eyebrow, seeing me with Tino, but given her love affair with Botox, I may have been mistaken. Either way, I needed a credible reason for Tino's sudden appearance in my working life, and I needed one soon.

We found Marie Luscy sitting behind her desk, her eyes glued to her computer screen. With one hand she held her phone to her ear while the other typed away at her keyboard. When she noticed us hovering at her desk, she placed her keyboard hand over the mouthpiece and said, "Mr. Gruenwald's at a meeting in the city."

"I don't want to speak with him," I said. "I'm here to see you."

"Me? What on earth for?"

"I need your help with something."

She held up a finger before going back to multitasking between the phone and computer. Tino and I sat down in the reception area to wait.

While killing time, I eavesdropped on Marie's end of the conversation, which seemed to deal with the Trimedia budget. The person on the other end of the line apparently kept asking for figures that Marie would hunt down on her computer and supply to him. I couldn't tell if the figures represented the current budget or the projected budget, but I suspected they were budget-related. I also thought it odd that Gruenwald's secretary would be supplying the caller with these figures rather than someone in accounting, but according to Tino, Marie Luscy was much more than just a secretary.

An unsettling thought struck me. How far did Marie's relationship with Gruenwald go? Was she a mistress cast aside for the high-profile Philomena? Had she killed Philomena to rid herself of the competition?

I studied Marie as she continued to supply figures to the caller. Although close to my age, she looked in far better shape, at least from what showed above her desk. No discernable arm flab jiggled as she moved.

Rappelling down the side of a building took far more skill than a lack of flabby upper arms, though, and Marie Luscy didn't strike me as the athletic type. Her upper body was all curves in all the right places, especially the area that spilled over the top of her neckline.

"How may I help you, Mrs. Pollack?" she asked, finally hanging up her phone and turning from her computer screen.

I stood and walked over to her desk. "Can I assume you're aware of what I'm doing for Mr. Gruenwald?" Although the CEO had attempted to swear me to secrecy, I suspected Tino was not the only member of his staff in the know.

Marie quickly scanned the room, searching for what, I had no idea. Heavy glass doors separated Gruenwald's fiefdom from the remainder of the fourth floor. Unless someone lurked in Gruenwald's office, Tino, Marie, and I were the only people within earshot.

She nodded. "Investigating Philomena's death."

Score one for the reluctant sleuth.

"What do you need?" she asked.

I filled her in on the no-show employees. Her eyes grew wide. She reached for her phone. "We need to tell Mr. Gruenwald and call the police at once."

"Not yet." I placed my hand over hers to prevent her from lifting the phone out of its dock.

"Why not?"

"If the police start questioning people about the no-show employees, the killer will be tipped off. We need more evidence before we contact the detectives. That way instead of just questioning people, they'll make an arrest."

"So what do we do?"

"Can you access employment records for Human Resources and Accounting?"

"I can access everything." She turned to her computer and began typing. "I doubt anyone in Accounting is involved, though. With Trimedia using a payroll firm, Accounting has no involvement in employee salaries. Human Resources sets up the accounts and sends the payroll information each week."

"Don't most employees either have their paychecks direct deposited into their bank accounts or handed to them at work?"

"Normally, yes, but there are some employees who prefer to have their checks mailed to their homes."

"But not to one address. No one at the payroll company thought it odd that each payday over two dozen checks are mailed to the same post office box?

She shook her head as she continued to type. "No one would notice. Trimedia employs thousands of people nationwide. The payroll is computerized."

"So the only person who'd know about the scam besides Philomena was the person who set up the accounts."

"Right."

I thought back to the phone conversation I'd overhead at the Javits Center. *Try it, and you're dead. No one messes with me.* Was the person on the other end of the phone Philomena's Human Resources co-conspirator? Was she shaking Philomena down for a larger cut? No one commits fraud for someone else without getting something in return.

"Trimedia employs four people in Human Resources at this location," said Marie, cutting into my thoughts. "No one relatively new. All have worked for Trimedia for years."

Yet one of them had to have a connection to Philomena. "Are any of them originally from Philadelphia?"

She turned the monitor to show me the four files she'd opened.

"Doesn't look that way. At least not from the information on their employment applications."

Then what was the connection? "Would you print out those files for me?" Maybe if I studied them more closely, I'd find a connection.

Marie printed off the pages, then slipped them into a manila envelope. "Good luck," she said. "Let me know if I can be of further assistance."

"You like working for Gruenwald?" I asked before leaving. How Marie answered might tell me a lot about her relationship with the CEO.

She shrugged. "It beats sitting in a cubicle."

Tino and I left Gruenwald's reception area and headed for the elevators. "I don't see the point of wasting my time on the second floor," I said. "I'm going back down to the *American Woman* offices."

"But Mr. Gruenwald said—"

"Mr. Gruenwald wants me to find Philomena's killer. Assigning me to *Bling!* was a cover to allow me to snoop around the *Bling!* staff. I've snooped. The investigation is moving in another direction, one that doesn't seem to involve the legitimate *Bling!* employees."

"So what are you going to do?"

I waved the envelope. "Figure out which one of these four people has some connection to Philomena. I'll be on the third floor until quitting time. You don't need to hang around."

"No can do. Mr. G. told me to keep you safe."

"I promise I won't go snooping around Human Resources. I'm going to my cubicle to read through these files and catch up on my own work."

"And I'll be right outside your cubicle, making sure no one disturbs you."

"You realize people will become suspicious and want to know what's going on."

"Not my problem. I'm just doing my job."

I craned my neck up at Tino. Definitely a pit bull of an ex-Marine. I was glad for his protection, but I certainly didn't need protecting from anyone on the *American Woman* staff. Besides, with Tino hanging around, I wouldn't be able to bounce ideas off Cloris.

"Fine. Anyone asks about you, you're Secret Service, assigned to protect me because I'm running for president."

"No one's gonna believe that. You need to come up with a better explanation."

"Not my job."

We stared each other down for a good minute. Finally, Tino said, "Some crazy person's sending you threatening letters. Trimedia hired me to protect you."

I wondered how many of my coworkers would believe our tightwad owners would spend a dime to protect any of us, but what did I care if they believed the excuse or not? It was an excuse I could use to explain Tino standing guard outside my cubicle.

I might be paranoid in believing Gruenwald had someone from *American Woman* spying on me, but Tino's first loyalty was to his boss. Logic told me the hulking chauffeur/bodyguard was under orders to report back to Gruenwald on my progress at the end of each day, not protect me from anyone. If he discovered I'd blabbed about my agreement with Gruenwald, I'm certain he'd rat me out. I shrugged. "Protect away, big guy."

~*~

After checking in once again with Daphne, who was more than relieved to see me back on our floor, I settled into my desk chair, pulled the Human Resources files from the envelope, and spread them out in front of me.

I knew all four women: Nita Holzer, Gwendolyn Keene, Catherine Chenko, and Sandy Sechrest. None stood out as the type to associate with Philomena. Just the opposite. These women, all ranging in age from mid-forties through early sixties, struck me as probably never having heard of Philomena before Trimedia handed her a magazine to run.

I pored over the files, reading every single line over and over, trying to figure out what connection one of these women had to Philomena. None had gone to school in Philadelphia, nor listed any previous places of employment within fifty miles of the City of Brotherly Love.

Could one of them be related to Philomena? I studied their ID photos, going so far as to enlarge their faces with a magnifying glass. No matter how much I scrutinized every feature on each face, I found no resemblance between Philomena and any of the women. Not scientific proof by any means but narrowing the suspect list down to someone with the same eyes or nose would have made my day.

I really needed to brainstorm with Cloris, but with Tino standing sentry outside my cubicle, he'd overhear every word, whether we talked in her cubicle or mine. The only place we were assured privacy was the ladies' room. I grabbed my phone and shot her a quick text: *U need 2 powder ur nose.*

"Just going to the ladies' room," I told Tino as I darted from my cubicle down the hall. Since he had a clear view down the corridor and would be able to watch me enter, he had no reason to follow. Which he didn't.

"Was the shine that bad?" asked Cloris when she entered the ladies' room a few seconds later, "Or are you dodging your Secret Service escort?"

"Tino means well, but I'm getting claustrophobic the way he shadows me like a puppy."

"He's keeping you safe."

"The question, though, is from whom?" I quickly caught her up on what I'd learned so far. "If we stay in here too long, Tino will get suspicious."

"What do you need me to do?"

"See what you can dig up on the four women who work in Human Resources. Ask Kim what she knows. She's always the best source for company gossip, given her daily forays into the corporate realm."

Naomi hated dealing with the suits upstairs. Whenever possible, she sent Kim to run interference, and Kim had become good friends with several of the secretaries on the fourth floor. If anyone knew anything about the four Human Resources women, Kim would scoop up all the dirt without drawing suspicion.

"I'll probably have to tell her why."

I shrugged. "I'm not worried about Kim. Gossip only travels one way with her—from corporate to us. She's totally loyal to Naomi and the rest of us."

"So you don't mind if I tell her what's going on?"

"Gruenwald demanded I swear not to tell anyone, but I never agreed." Even if he was under the impression that I had. "Besides," I continued, "he's only interested in one thing: making sure neither he nor Mrs. Gruenwald is implicated in Philomena's murder."

"We can probably rule out *Frau* Holzer," said Cloris.

"I'm inclined to agree with you." Nita Holzer, dubbed the Human Resources Attendance Nazi, sat in a first-floor office that gave her an unobstructed view of the building's entrance. Every morning she monitored the door, taking extreme pleasure in writing up employees who arrived so much as a minute late for work. I'd personally racked up enough demerits that my file bulged with little yellow slips of paper. Although, I suspected no one paid attention to those demerits besides the Attendance Nazi herself.

We also suspected Nita spent much of her day monitoring the Trimedia employee computers. Nothing would give her more pleasure than catching someone playing *Angry Birds*, watching YouTube videos, or shopping online on company time. Any personal activity on Trimedia computers was grounds for immediate dismissal.

"Then again," said Cloris, "isn't the person you least expect of doing something often the culprit?"

"True, but The Queen of Bling hooking up with the Queen of Mean to commit fraud?"

"It is hard to conceive of a connection between the two of them."

That's when something occurred to me. "Unless there is no connection. Not with Nita and Philomena and not with any of the other three women and Philomena."

"Then how—?"

"What if all those bogus employees are also bogus people? Maybe instead of padding the payroll with no-show jobs, the culprit stole the identities of dead people."

"So the entire scam was set up by someone without

Philomena's knowledge or participation?"

"It's possible."

"And gave them all a Philadelphia connection to throw suspicion on Philomena in case someone discovered what was going on."

"Exactly," I said. "The scam might be someone in Human Resources embezzling Trimedia funds, not Philomena padding the magazine's payroll to benefit her *gangsta* friends."

"And if Philomena somehow found out about the embezzling, that may have gotten her killed."

"Unless the two crimes have no connection."

We'd already stayed long enough in the ladies' room that Tino might push the door open at any moment to check on me. "Tomorrow is payday. We need to find a way to see who picks up those checks."

"How are we going to do that? You and I can't scope out the post office all day."

"We don't need to. If someone in Human Resources is stealing the money, she'll pick up the checks during her lunch break."

"What if she sees you?" asked Cloris. "She'll figure out you're on to her."

"I'll send Tino."

"He's not suppose to leave your side."

"I know, but I'm going to have to find some way to convince him to spend a few hours engaging in Human Resources surveillance, rather than shadowing me."

I waited more than an hour after returning from the ladies' room before I broached the subject with Tino. I didn't want him to suspect Cloris and me of plotting instead of peeing.

"Not going to happen," he said. "I'm supposed to keep an eye on you to keep you safe. What if you're wrong, and the killer strikes again while I'm gone?"

I played to his logical ex-Marine brain. "Since I have no idea who killed Philomena, the killer can't be worried that I'm getting close to fingering him. Besides, no one other than you, me, Marie, and Mr. Gruenwald even knows that I'm investigating Philomena's death."

Okay, so I lied, but I could trust the two other people who knew. Neither Cloris nor Zack killed Philomena. "I'm not in any danger," I continued, "especially if I stay at my desk. Besides, it's only a couple of hours, depending on when the thief takes her lunch break."

"What if I tail the wrong person?"

"You won't. Go to the post office before any of them leaves for lunch. See which one shows up to empty the box."

He mulled my plea over for a minute. "You promise you won't go anywhere?"

"Office, break room, and ladies' room. That's it. I won't even leave the floor."

Tino scowled. "Mr. G. will have my head if he finds out. I could lose my job."

"He won't find out." I held up two fingers. "Scout's honor."

Finally, he caved. "Okay, your theory makes sense, and someone needs to see who picks up those checks."

"So you'll do it?"

He heaved a huge sigh. "I'll do it, but you better not get yourself killed while I'm gone."

"Wouldn't dream of it."

TWELVE

The next morning I arrived at work to find my Hyundai gone and Tino once again waiting for me in the parking lot. I found Gruenwald's insistence of a bodyguard shadowing me only at work quite absurd. If someone wanted me dead, he could strike at any time—at my home, on my way to and from work, while I walked the supermarket aisles. Not to mention the killer would have to be dumb as dirt to strike again at the same place he dumped Philomena's body. All of this added to my conviction that Tino's main responsibility involved keeping tabs on me for Gruenwald, not protecting me from a killer.

~*~

Once Tino left for the post office later that morning, I called Kim. "Got anything?"

"Let's meet in the conference room," she said. "We'll have more privacy. Bring coffee."

Before heading for the break room to grab coffees for the two of us, I stuck my head into Cloris's cubicle. "Conference room.

BYOC."

Bakery box and coffee in hand, Cloris entered the conference room shortly after I arrived.

"Tell me those aren't vegan," I said, pointing to the bakery box.

"Not vegan." Cloris raised the flap to reveal half a dozen mini cupcakes. "These are adult-only cupcakes made with different flavors of liqueur." After she closed the door, the three of us settled into chairs around the table and each grabbed a couple of cupcakes.

"What did you find out?" asked Cloris.

"Quite a bit," said Kim. "Only I couldn't take notes because it would have looked odd."

Cloris raised an eyebrow. "You think?"

Kim laughed. "Anyway, bear with me while I try to remember everything."

She polished off a cupcake, took a swig of coffee, then said, "First, our favorite Human Resources employee, the Attendance Nazi. No one likes Nita, but I'm sure that's not news to either of you."

"Does she have motive to embezzle nearly three-quarters of a million dollars?" I asked.

"Three quarters of a million and counting," added Cloris. "The longer this scam plays out, the more money she collects."

"Except with Philomena dead, *Bling!*'s days are now numbered," I reminded her. "No *Bling!*, no payroll. No payroll, no payroll padding."

"Which makes you wonder why the embezzler would kill Philomena," said Kim. "She'd lose her ill-gotten revenue stream."

"Unless Philomena's death was an accident. What if the killer didn't mean to kill her?"

"The way she was beaten to a pulp?" asked Cloris. "You said so yourself: that's a crime of passion, not an accident."

"Perhaps Philomena's death was an accident, but the killer panicked and beat the body afterwards to make the death appear personal in nature."

"Thus, misdirecting the investigation," said Cloris.

"Anyway," said Kim, bringing the conversation back to Nita Holzer, "Turns out Nita and her husband bought themselves a McMansion at the height of the real estate boom."

"I'm guessing that her house is now worth a lot less than what she paid for it," I said.

"No need to guess," said Kim.

"Someone upstairs told you this?" I asked. "The Nita I know would never admit that to one of her co-workers."

"She didn't."

"Then how did you find out?" asked Cloris.

"She bragged about the house when they bought it, showing off pictures to anyone she could corner, not only at the time of the sale but for quite some time afterwards. Then the bragging suddenly stopped. I put two and two together and typed her address into Zillow."

"Sneaky," said Cloris. "You better hope she wasn't monitoring your computer."

Kim held up her iPhone. "I didn't take any chances."

"Is the bank foreclosing?" I asked. If Nita were at risk of losing her home, that would give her incentive to skim money from Trimedia.

"The house had been listed for sale but was taken off the market."

"When?" I asked.

"About six months ago, shortly after the inception of *Bling!*"

"Rather coincidental," said Cloris. "Sounds like she's our suspect, at least for the embezzlement if not the murder."

"Not necessarily," said Kim. "Wait until you hear what else I discovered."

"You found dirt on someone else?" I asked.

"I wouldn't call it dirt but definitely financial motive to pad the payroll."

"Who?" I asked.

"All three."

"Dish!" said Cloris.

Kim ate her remaining cupcake before she continued. "Wow, these are good! I thought the amaretto was fabulous, but this Mojito flavored cupcake is even better."

She washed down the cupcake with more coffee, then continued. "Two of the other women are dealing with major family medical issues. Catherine Chenko's husband suffers from Alzheimer's, and he's at the point where she needs to put him in a nursing home."

"That's rough," said Cloris. "And expensive."

"A husband with Alzheimer's doesn't excuse stealing," I said. "What about the others?"

"Gwendolyn Keene's son has cancer," said Kim.

As much as I felt sorry for both women, family health issues didn't give them a pass to commit fraud. "What about Sandy Sechrest?"

"Her husband lost his job over a year ago and hasn't found a new one yet. They've got a kid in college and one graduating high school next year."

"Any one of these women could have masterminded the

payroll plot," said Cloris.

"I just don't see any of them viscously beating Philomena and dumping her body in the models' case," I said.

"Unless one of them had help," said Kim. "Or maybe all four were in on it. They all need money. The four of them together could have killed Philomena and dumped her body."

"You're forgetting the missing security cameras," I said. "Do you honestly see any of these women rappelling off the roof and down the side of the building to disconnect and steal those cameras?"

"I can," said Kim. "Holzer has a photo on her desk of her and her husband mountain biking in the Rockies. Maybe she also rock climbs."

"She's brawny enough," said Cloris.

"What are you going to do now?" asked Kim.

"Wait to see who picks up the checks today," I said.

"And then?" asked Cloris.

"Place a call to Detective Batswin." I'd had my fill of tangling with killers.

~*~

Tino arrived back at my cubicle two hours later. "None of those women showed up at the post office," he said.

I glanced at my watch. "It's only two-thirty. Someone might take a late lunch. You should have stayed."

"No need. Some guy emptied the box a few minutes ago."

"An accomplice?" Perhaps Nita's husband? "Did he look familiar?"

"Not to me."

"I don't suppose you snapped a picture with your phone."

"I tried, but given where I parked, I couldn't get a clear shot."

"If you were in your car, how do you know he emptied the box?"

"High powered binoculars. When I arrived, I first checked the location of the box. I realized if I hung around in the post office lobby for too long, some employee would get suspicious. So I parked at an angle that gave me a sight line of the box just in case someone other than any of those women picked up the checks."

"Brilliant." Why didn't I think of that possibility? Maybe because I'm not an ex-Marine. "Did you get the guy's license plate?"

"MAN-TOY."

"You're kidding!"

"On a late model black Escalade. Shouldn't be hard for the cops to track down."

With all the money she'd embezzled, Nita could afford to pay off her mortgage *and* buy a luxury SUV. I picked up my phone. "I think it's time to give Detective Batswin a call."

She answered on the first ring. "Staying out of trouble, Mrs. Pollack?"

Damn, sometimes I really hated Caller ID. "Trying my best, detective."

"Why do I sense a *but* coming on?"

"I've uncovered information about Philomena's death."

"Didn't I tell you to leave the investigating to the professionals?"

"Have the professionals discovered embezzlement linked to the victim?"

"Embezzlement?"

"Nearly three-quarters of a million dollars so far and counting."

Batswin sputtered, letting loose a barrage of quite colorful expletives, then asked, "Where are you?"

"In my cubicle."

"Don't leave. I'm on my way."

~*~

Less than ten minutes later both Batswin and Robbins arrived, apparently breaking all local speed laws along the way. Neither showed any sign of surprise upon finding Tino filling up a good percentage of my cubicle floor space, but emotion rarely registered on the faces of those two. They definitely aced Blank Stare 101 at the police academy.

"Let's go somewhere private to talk." I grabbed the personnel files and led the way to the conference room.

"If you're heading for the conference room," said Cloris as we passed her in the hall, "it's occupied."

"That leaves the break room," I said, turning in the opposite direction.

Tino closed the door after the four of us entered. Batswin, Robbins, and I took seats around the table. Tino remained standing, his back to the door, posed in his usual don't-mess-with-me bodyguard stance.

As she helped herself to a cup of coffee, Batswin asked, "What's this about embezzlement?"

"When I came across something puzzling in the employment files of the *Bling!* staff, I—"

"What were you doing nosing around employment files?" asked Robbins, speaking for the first time since the dynamic duo's arrival. "Aren't you a crafts editor?"

"I was asked to check something, and in the course—"

"By whom?" asked Batswin.

"A superior."

"Which one?"

When I hesitated, Robbins stated matter-of-factly, "Withholding evidence in an ongoing investigation is a criminal act, Mrs. Pollack."

Subtle, isn't he? The Dick Tracy tie dangling from his neck did little to diffuse the implied threat. I took a deep breath and glanced at Tino as I slowly emptied the air from my lungs. Did he know Gruenwald had ordered me not to tell anyone about our arrangement? Would he rat me out to the CEO if I answered truthfully? I wasn't under oath; I hadn't sworn on a Bible. Still, I didn't think lying to the police worked to my benefit.

Thankfully, Tino let me off the hook by answering for me. "Mr. Gruenwald gave her the assignment."

Batswin raised an eyebrow ever so slightly. "Exactly what is your role in this?" she asked Tino.

"He's assigned to help me," I said.

Batswin studied Tino. "Aren't you Gruenwald's driver?"

"Among other things."

"Apparently so," she muttered, then turned her attention back to me. "Why did the CEO ask you to check personnel files? Isn't that something his secretary would do? Or someone in Human Resources?"

"Normally."

"But?"

"He asked me to help prove his innocence."

"I see. And exactly what did you find in those personnel files, Mrs. Pollack?"

Over the course of the next fifteen minutes, I told Batswin and Robbins everything I'd discovered. When I finished, Robbins asked Tino, "Did you get a good look at the driver?"

"I did."

"Enough to recognize him from a mug shot or pick him out in a line-up?"

"Maybe."

Batswin and Robbins exchanged looks, then both stood. "Let's go," said Batswin.

"Go where?" I asked.

"Not you, Mrs. Pollack." She nodded in Tino's direction. "Him."

"What for?" asked Tino.

"To sit down with a sketch artist," said Robbins.

"Can't," said Tino. "I'm needed here."

"That wasn't a request," said Batswin. She and Tino engaged in a stare-down, neither blinking. Finally, she said, "We can do this the hard way or the easy way." She removed a pair of handcuffs from her belt and jingled them in front of Tino's nose. "Your choice."

Tino grudgingly acquiesced, and the three of them headed for the elevators.

My phone rang as I left the break room to return to my cubicle. "Hello?"

"I've got good news and bad news," said Ira. "Which do you want first."

I groaned. "I'm assuming the Hyundai is beyond repair, so what's the good news?"

"I found you a sweetheart of a deal on a low mileage Jetta."

"How sweet?"

"Under five grand."

"Not in this century. What's the catch, Ira?"

"No catch. The car is ten years old—"

"Ten years? My Hyundai is only eight years old."

"As Indiana Jones said, 'It's not the years; it's the miles.'"

"He wasn't referring to cars."

Ira chuckled. "I know, but I love that line."

"Seriously?"

"Okay, in all seriousness, the Hyundai has nearly a hundred thousand miles on it. This Jetta has half the mileage and is in excellent condition."

Spoken like a true car salesman. Next he'd be telling me it was owned by a little old lady who only drove it on Sundays to and from church. "Then why is it so cheap?"

"I'm offering you the car for the exact amount I gave the former owner this morning on a trade-in."

"Meaning you could turn around and sell that Jetta for twice what it cost you."

"Anastasia, you're my brother's wife. I'm not going to make a profit off you."

So much for stereotypes about the honesty of car salesmen. Too bad Karl hadn't inherited some of the integrity swimming around Ira's gene pool. I sighed through the phone line. "I don't know what to say, Ira."

"Thank you will do."

"Thank you, Ira."

"You're welcome, Anastasia."

Back before my middleclass life imploded, Karl and I attended the theater at least once a month. As I hung up from Ira, a line from a song in *Wicked* popped into my head. Maybe—

"Earth to Anastasia. Hello? Anyone in there?"

"Huh?" I looked up to find Cloris waving a hand across my

face.

"What planet were you visiting?" she asked.

"I was just wondering, do you believe people come into our lives for a reason?"

"Why? Who are we talking about? Gruenwald's hunk? The dead Blinganista? Zack?"

"Karl's half-brother." I told her about the phone call. "If Ira hadn't been on a quest to connect with his father's first love, I'd now be stuck with a dead Hyundai and no way to get to work."

"So you think some celestial force or divine intervention sent Ira your way?"

"Possibly."

She shook her head. "I'm more a proponent of the random chaos theory of life."

"Personally, I could do with a little less chaos in my life, random or otherwise."

She shrugged. "Caca happens. The universe works in mysterious ways. Take your pick. Both mean the same in the end. And speaking of one or the other, where's your hunky shadow?"

I caught her up on events. "Tino's reluctantly sitting down with a sketch artist. Batswin and Robbins are probably investigating who owns the post office box and the Cadillac Escalade."

"Why reluctantly?"

I'd wondered the same thing. "Not sure. Except he's a guy trained to follow orders, and his orders are to keep me safe. He can't do that if he's discussing the width of a nose or the slant of someone's eyes down at police headquarters."

"Unless..."

"Unless what?"

"What if Tino is in on the embezzlement? Maybe he collected the checks from the post office box."

"No, Tino brought me the bogus employee files. Why would he do that if he was in on the scam?"

Cloris smacked her forehead. "This is why you're the sleuth, and I'm only the trusty sidekick."

"Reluctant sleuth," I reminded her.

THIRTEEN

Shortly before the end of the work week, we all received an inter-office email memo stating a private funeral service for Philomena would take place once the coroner released her body. A public memorial would be scheduled afterwards. Details of both to follow.

"Command performance?" asked Cloris, calling to me from across the hall.

"Most likely."

"Which means we can't use a comp day to get out of going. The only thing worse than attending a funeral, is attending one for someone you didn't like."

"Ditto." I'd attended far too many funerals and memorial services this year, and other than the one for my husband, most of them involved Trimedia employees.

A few minutes later Cloris stood at the entrance to my cubicle. "I'm cutting out. Are you ready to leave?"

Tino hadn't returned from the police station. After being

escorted to and from my car the last two days, it seemed strange to leave the building without his protection. Not that I expected a sniper perched on the roof. Why would anyone want to kill me? I'm no threat. Besides, if there were a sniper on the roof, unless he was a lousy shot and missed with the first bullet, what kind of protection would Tino provide me?

I shut down my computer, grabbed my purse, and joined Cloris for a TGIF exit of Trimedia. I looked forward to my first weekend off since the end of June and planned to celebrate by doing absolutely nothing. Or possibly a little bit more than nothing if Zack returned from wherever he had traipsed off to at the crack of dawn yesterday morning.

~*~

Unfortunately, Mama had other plans, and they involved me. I arrived home to find my living room and dining room set up to resemble an evacuation staging ground, minus the disaster victims, Red Cross volunteers, and medical supplies. Cartons and suitcases, some empty and some in the process of being filled, covered nearly every square inch of floor space except for a narrow path leading from the entry hallway to the kitchen. Every piece of furniture held haphazard piles of clothing, shoes, accessories, and the assorted trappings of Mama's life.

In-between husbands, Mama not only came to live with us, so did all her worldly possessions. Because she always lived above her means, whenever a husband died, she could no longer afford to keep her home. Mama habitually married men with champagne tastes, small bank accounts, and little life insurance. Thanks to five previous marriages, she owned an overabundance of worldly possessions, her own and those belonging to her *Dearly Departeds*.

She kept everything, storing some of her belongings in the

bedroom she shared with Lucille and some in my basement. The Dearly Departeds, all in bronze urns, lined a shelf in my dining room. The balance, including all her furniture, filled up most of my two-car garage, leaving just enough room for my lawn mower and snow thrower.

Mama lucked out when Ricardo trashed my house this past winter. With Seamus O'Keefe, her latest husband, so recently deceased, she hadn't yet transferred the contents of her apartment to my home. So when Ricardo mounted his search and destroy mission for the fifty thousand dollars he insisted I'd squirreled away, Mama's property had been spared the vandalism mine sustained.

Mama and Lawrence moving into their own condo meant I'd finally get my garage back and wouldn't have to scrape snow and ice off my car this winter. That thought alone nearly made me burst out in a Snoopy dance. Few tasks are worse than chipping away at inch-thick windshield ice in the pre-dawn hours of a snowy winter morning.

"Oh, there you are, dear!" Mama entered the living room and dumped a pile of sweaters into an open suitcase.

"Are you moving this weekend, Mama?"

"As long as everything is ready."

"What isn't ready?" And why did a sense of dread start to creep up my spine?

"The usual, of course. Cleaning. Painting. Now that you're home, you can help me narrow down color selection. I picked up paint chips the other day but haven't been able to decide. We can buy the paint this evening after dinner. That way we'll get an early start first thing tomorrow morning."

"We?"

"You are going to paint for me, aren't you? After all, you're the one with the art school degree."

Funny how I forgot to enroll in the House Painting 101 course while in college. "You expect me to paint your apartment this weekend?"

"Not alone. Lawrence and I will help. And I'm sure the boys will pitch in. Ira has to work Saturday, of course. Saturday is his busiest day of the week."

Of course. And if Lawrence were anywhere near as handy as Mama, I'd be better off tackling the job on my own. She conveniently forgot that between varsity football and Alex's part-time job at Starbucks, my sons had little free time most of Saturday and Sunday.

So much for my weekend of relaxation. "How come Ira Moneybags didn't hire a professional house painter along with the condo he purchased for you?"

"He offered, but I told him not to bother."

"And why is that?"

"Workmen are so unreliable these days. I'm much more comfortable with you doing the painting. I can trust you to do an impeccable job."

Should I strangle her now or wait until she finished packing?

I suppose I shouldn't complain. What was one more weekend of work when I'd finally have my garage back and one less person in the house? I loved Mama, but I loved her more when she and her corpulent kitty weren't instigating trouble with Lucille and Mephisto. I'd willingly trade one more weekend of my life for a little more peace and a lot less chaos under the *Casa Pollack* roof.

At that moment, the Queen of Chaos stormed into the house. Actually, she hobbled, but even using a cane, Lucille's entrance conveyed more storm than hobble, especially with the addition of the front door slamming against the foyer wall.

My mother-in-law stopped at the entrance to the living room and surveyed Mama's mess. "You'd better not be taking anything that belongs to me," she said.

"Is she kidding?" Mama asked me. Then she turned to Lucille. "What do you own that I would possibly want? Your orange paisley pantsuit? Your copy of *The Communist Manifesto*?" Mama waved her arm as if to swat a pesky gnat buzzing around her face. "Don't flatter yourself."

Lucille raised her cane and pointed it at Mama. "Every time you move out, something of mine is missing."

Good grief! Those two sounded more like squabbling adolescents than grown women. "Enough! Lucille, I'm sure Mephisto needs walking."

"Manifesto!" she screamed, pounding her cane. "How many times do I have to tell you his name is Manifesto?"

"She'll never get the joke," said Mama.

"Because it's not funny," said Lucille. "I'm not an idiot."

"Could've fooled me," said Mama.

"That's enough, Mama. Stop instigating."

"You're blaming me? What did I do? You're the one who calls the dog Mephisto."

Guilty as charged. And even though the devil dog and I had recently come to an understanding, he'd always remain Mephisto in my mind. And as a slip of my tongue.

Lucille muttered under her breath as she stomped her cane down the hall to the bedroom she shared with Mama. A few minutes later, she reappeared with Mephisto in tow and headed out the door.

I confronted Mama. "Have you taken anything of hers?"

"Really, Anastasia! Are you siding with that communist heathen over your own flesh and blood?"

"You didn't answer my question, Mama."

"And I don't plan to. It's downright insulting for you to even suggest such a thing." She turned her back on me and began to rearrange the flotsam and jetsam piled on my sofa.

I took her evasiveness as a yes. Mama wasn't above stooping to the level of a spiteful child. Lucille didn't own much, thanks to all her possessions going up in flames last year, and she didn't suffer from dementia now that a tumor no longer grew in her brain. She knew what she owned. One of them was either lying or deliberately pilfering in order to foment trouble. The question was, which one? Both were certainly capable of such tactics.

I left Mama in her snit and headed into the kitchen to start dinner. The boys would be home from football practice any minute. That's when I noticed the note on the kitchen table:

You. Me. Bottle of expensive bubbly. Romantic French restaurant. No kids or grandmothers allowed. I'll pick you up at 7. Zack.

P.S.: I ordered pizzas delivered for the starving masses.

My hero. A glance at the clock told me I even had time for a relaxing soak in the tub. Mama's paint chips and a trek to Home Depot would have to wait.

~*~

"You've officially fallen out of grace with Mama," I told Zack as we drove off in his silver Porsche Boxster shortly after seven o'clock.

"Me? What did I do?"

As much as Mama played Yenta the Matchmaker when it came to me and Zack, she wasn't above putting her need for wall color resolution ahead of my romantic dinner. I left her holding a handful of paint chips and pouting amid a sea of suitcases and packing cartons. "You gave me an excuse not to go to Home Depot this evening."

"And Flora is mad at me for that?"

"She expected me to help her decide on condo colors, then take her paint shopping. By the way, feel free to kidnap me for the entire weekend. I promise to be an extremely compliant kidnap victim."

"Your mother needs an entire weekend to buy a few cans of paint?"

"She needs an entire weekend for me to paint her apartment."

Zack slowed to a stop for a red light and turned toward me. "Your first weekend off in months and you plan to spend it painting walls?"

"Not my plan. Mama's. She sprang it on me the moment I walked in the house this evening."

"What about Lawrence? Isn't he capable of wielding a paint roller?"

"Apparently not."

"Dare I ask why?"

"He doesn't have an art degree."

"That makes no sense."

"It makes perfect sense in Floraworld."

"I see. And have you painted other apartments each time she reels in a new husband?"

"I'll admit I haven't put up much of a fuss in the past, but all those painting jobs occurred before Karl shafted me. I had plenty of time back then to help Mama."

"Not to mention an art degree."

"A housepainter requirement."

A few minutes later Zack turned into the parking lot of Chez Catherine. "Who did you kill to score a table here?" I asked. One of the state's finest restaurants, Chez Catherine normally required booking a reservation at least a month in advance. Usually longer.

He grinned. "You don't want to know."

"I'll take that as code for whatever alphabet agency employs you."

He parked the car, and we headed for the entrance. "Take it any way you want. If you're going to insist I'm really a spy, I might as well play along."

I stopped at the entrance and turned to him. "You're not packing heat, are you?"

Zack laughed. "Packing heat?"

"Isn't that what you spies call it?"

"Right. And here I thought you were way too busy to watch television. Have I ever mentioned how much I enjoy these inquisitions of yours?" He grabbed the lapels of his sports jacket and spread them wide. "Care to do a pat down? Or maybe you'd prefer a strip search?"

"In the middle of downtown Westfield? I'll save the strip search for later tonight."

He smiled. "I can't wait."

We entered the restaurant and were shown to our table. As we perused the menu, Zack casually asked, "Speaking of killers, did you unmask any today?"

"Maybe."

Both his eyebrows shot up over his menu, but before he could say anything, the sommelier appeared at our table. As soon as the sommelier left, the waiter appeared.

"Fun's over," said Zack after the waiter took our order and the sommelier had returned to pour glasses of champagne for us. The playful banter had disappeared, and his voice grew serious. "Define maybe."

I caught him up on everything I'd discovered yesterday and today. "If you hadn't been off saving the world, I would have told you last night."

He scowled his I-am-not-a-spy scowl.

"Anyway, all four women in Human Resources have financial problems. Any one of them could have doctored the payroll to embezzle that money. Once Batswin and Robbins track down the guy who picked up the checks, we'll know which one."

"I see one slight problem."

I sighed. "I know. The embezzlement might have no connection to the murder. As a matter of fact, the more I think about it, the more the two seem totally unrelated. In the unlikely chance that Philomena found out about the embezzlement, why would she care? She wasn't exactly a poster child for living a law-abiding life."

"Given her past, she'd more likely demand a cut of the action," said Zack.

"Which a savvy embezzler would have given her to keep her quiet and allow the scam to continue. After all, killing Philomena killed the magazine. No magazine, no payroll. No payroll, no money to embezzle."

"Perhaps a heated argument over the size of the cut got out of hand," he said. "We won't know if the two crimes are connected until the police figure out the embezzler's identity."

Come Monday morning would I arrive at work to find a vacancy in the Human Resources Department? At this very moment Batswin and Robbins might be at the Holzer McMansion, slapping handcuffs on Nita.

"You still uncovered a crime no one else other than the perpetrator knew about before yesterday," said Zack.

That put a smile on my face. "I did, didn't I? Maybe I'm not so bad at this sleuthing business after all."

"Don't get cocky. And don't quit your day job."

"Wouldn't dream of either. Anyway, if the two crimes are unrelated, I'm no closer to uncovering any credible suspects than I was before I discovered the embezzlement."

"For all you know, the police already have a prime suspect."

"They do. Gruenwald."

"Have you considered the possibility that Gruenwald paid you to keep you occupied on a wild goose chase?"

"Because he feared I'd figure out he killed Philomena? Yes. Especially since he's certain I solved the other Trimedia murders. And I'm still not convinced he didn't kill her, probably in a fit of uncontrollable rage. The last time I saw them together was during a heated argument. Philomena made some vicious threats. Gruenwald brushed it off as just a manifestation of her passionate personality, but something about his behavior doesn't add up."

"Like the killer bringing the body to Trimedia?"

"Exactly. Why not dump it in the Hudson? Or the Meadowlands swamps? I also don't see Gruenwald rappelling down the side of the building to steal the surveillance cameras."

"Because of his age?"

"The guy is pushing seventy." Zack whipped his iPhone out of his pocket. "What are you doing?"

"Googling Gruenwald." He spent a minute scrolling down his phone. "The man's built like a brick outhouse."

"Sheila said he reminds her of Ernest Borgnine back in his *McHale's Navy* days."

"I can see the resemblance. He's certainly far from handsome."

"That's another thing I don't understand. What did Philomena see in Gruenwald? She already had fame and plenty of her own money. All I can come up with is that she was so desperate to become a hip-hop Oprah, she prostituted herself to get that magazine."

"Women have prostituted themselves for far less," said Zack. "How much do you know about Gruenwald?"

"Other than him being the CEO of Trimedia?" I shrugged. "Nothing."

He passed his phone across the table to me. "Read."

I skimmed the bio Zack had pulled up from the Trimedia corporate website. My jaw dropped. "Oh. My. God." Albert Gruenwald listed his hobbies as participating in marathons and triathlons. He'd even placed in several recent races in his age division.

The waiter arrived with our appetizers, and I returned Zack's phone to him. As he slipped it into his pocket, he stated the obvious. "I'd say the man is quite capable of rappelling down the side of a four-story building."

"Can't argue with that. But assuming Gruenwald did kill Philomena, what would compel him to bring her body to Trimedia?" I wracked my brain as I nibbled on escargot. "I'm coming up blank. Nothing makes sense. Did he employ some twisted logic, thinking the cops wouldn't expect him to be that stupid, so they'd discount him as a suspect?"

"Possibly. You'd need a degree in criminal psychology to understand a killer's mind."

"Yeah, all I've got is an art degree, which apparently qualifies me to paint condo walls."

FOURTEEN

The next morning, I woke to banging on the door. I opened my eyes to find Zack stretched out beside me, one of his legs looped over mine. Sunlight poured through his bedroom window; the clock flashed eight. *Oops!*

I hadn't meant to spend the night. I always leave Zack's apartment and return to my own bed before anyone else in the house wakes up. Not that they don't know Zack and I have taken our relationship to the sex level. After all, Mama, Alex, and Nick practically pushed me into Zack's bed, and Lucille calls me a harlot at every opportunity. Still, I did try to play the role of responsible parent.

I inched out from under Zack's leg and searched the floor for my clothes. Once I tossed my dress over my head, foregoing bra and panties, I tiptoed barefoot from the room, closing the bedroom door behind me.

"Who is it?" I asked through the apartment door.

"It's your mother. Who do you think it is?"

Discounting Lucille because she'd never make it up the steep steps, there were two other possibilities, but I refrained from saying so. "What is it, Mama?"

"I'm ready to leave. You obviously aren't."

I swung open the door, and Mama pushed her way inside. "It's only eight o'clock."

"And we have a lot to do today. You still haven't even helped me decide on colors. Good morning, Zachary, dear."

I spun around to find Zack, dressed in a pair of boxers and a rumpled T-shirt, standing in the bedroom doorway. He scrubbed his jaw and yawned. "Morning, Flora. Would you like some help today?"

"I'm sure Anastasia can handle it. You might distract her too much."

I stared dumbfounded at my mother. "Carrying a bit of a grudge this morning, Mama?"

"I wasn't asking you," said Zack, coming up behind me and draping his arm across my shoulders. "I was asking your daughter."

Mama and Zack engaged in a stare-down for a few seconds. Finally, Mama broke eye contact and said, "Well, I suppose an extra pair of hands will make the job go quicker. Let's get going. We have lots to do today."

I saluted her retreating back as she descended the stairs.

"I'll have to figure out a way to get back in her good graces," said Zack after closing the door.

"She'll get over it. Just don't spill any paint on her carpets today."

"Maybe we'll get lucky, and the condo will have hardwoods and tile."

"Are you that sloppy a painter?"

He shrugged. "I have no idea. I've never painted a room before."

"Great. You'll be as big a help as Mama."

"I'm a much quicker study."

"Nice to know." I dashed into the bedroom to retrieve the remainder of my clothes. "Breakfast in twenty minutes," I said, heading out the door.

~*~

By the time I grabbed a quick shower, threw on a pair of old sweats, fed Ralph and changed his water, and set out fresh kibble and water for Mephisto, Zack was in the kitchen preparing a pot of coffee. I fired up my frying pan to scramble a dozen eggs.

Paint chips covered the kitchen table. As I cracked eggs, Mama cradled Catherine the Great in one arm while sticking one paint sample after another in front of my face. Ralph watched in rapt fascination from his perch atop the refrigerator.

"What do you think of this color? It's called Silver Cloud. Maybe for the living room? But Mother of Pearl is also nice." Mama shoved another chip so close to my nose that my eyes crossed. "That might work well in the powder room, though. And I thought an accent wall of Beaver Gray in the bedroom but can't decide which color to choose for the remaining three walls. Ash or Dove?" More paint chips crowded my vision. "What do you think, dear?"

"You're going to be the one living there. You should make the decision, not me." I'm not a huge fan of gray walls, no matter the hue, tone, or shade, but Mama had spent the last several weeks camped out in front of HGTV and pronounced gray the wall color *du jour* according to all the TV decorators.

"But you know color." She sounded like a whiney child in need of a nap.

"*Nay, pray you, seek no colour for your going,*" squawked Ralph. "*But bid farewell, and go. Antony and Cleopatra.* Act One, Scene Three."

Mama shot Ralph a vile look. "Filthy flying rat," she muttered under her breath.

At that moment, the remainder of the Pollack menagerie arrived. With Mephisto close on her heels, Lucille shuffled into the kitchen, plopped herself down in a chair, and waited silently for her breakfast. She offered not so much as a grunt in place of a *good morning*. Mephisto waddled over to his doggie bowl and attacked his kibble. No *good morning* from him, either. I live to serve.

Alex and Nick entered the kitchen a moment later. "Morning," they both mumbled, each planting a quick peck on my cheeks.

At least some members of my family have manners. "Good morning." I poured the egg batter into the frying pan. Zack had moved on to making toast. "One of you needs to set the table; the other can pour juice."

Nick glanced at the kitchen table. "I'll have eggs and toast, but hold the paint chips on mine, Mom."

"Very funny, Nick. If you become a stand-up comic you'll save me a bundle on college tuition. Mama, sweep up your chips, please."

"But we haven't decided on colors yet!"

I set down my spatula and turned to the table. One by one I pointed to random colors of gray. "Living room and dining room, kitchen, bedroom, bathroom, powder room. Done."

"What about the accent wall in the bedroom?"

I stabbed at a color three shades darker than the color I'd picked for the other bedroom walls. "This one."

Mama hesitated. "You're sure?"

"You asked for my help, didn't you?"

"I suppose, but I thought Silver Cloud would look nice."

"Then go with Silver Cloud."

"But you chose Stratus."

I sighed and moved back to the stove. "Nick needs to set the table, Mama."

"All right. I'll go with Stratus. After all, you're the one with the art degree."

I glanced at Zack. The poor man was trying desperately not to crack up laughing. If we made eye contact, he'd lose it. I turned back to Mama. "I think you'll be very happy with those colors."

"And if I'm not, that's the nice thing about paint, dear. You can always change the color for me."

~*~

Painting is mindless work, perfect for mulling over murder as I rolled color onto Mama's living room walls. Except Mama kept interrupting my thoughts with a steady stream of nattering. "Are you sure about the Stratus for this room, dear?"

"I'm sure, Mama."

"Well, if you're sure, I'll go check out Zack's progress painting the bathroom."

A moment later I heard Zack yell, "Flora, look out!"

A loud crash followed, then a shrieking howl, and finally a stream of language far more fit for a longshoreman than the former social secretary of the Daughters of the American Revolution.

I dropped my paint roller and ran to the bathroom. Mama

stood frozen in place in the middle of the room. A gallon of Mother of Pearl latex dripped from nearly every square inch of her body onto the tile floor. Rivers of paint flowed along the grout lines. A pattern of spatter covered the sink, toilet, and bathtub. Only the shower stall had been spared the latex baptism.

If my mother didn't look totally mortified and about to burst out in tears, I'd probably double over in laughter. The scene looked like something out of a slapstick comedy.

I glanced up to where Zack stood on the ladder, a paint brush still in his hand. "What happened?"

"Isn't it obvious?" she asked. "Look at me!" She shook her arms and sent paint sailing across the room to land in my hair and on my sweats.

"But how?"

"She banged the door into the ladder, knocking off the can of paint," said Zack.

"Don't just stand there," cried Mama. "Do something! I need help."

I surveyed the situation. "Any suggestions?" I asked Zack.

"We should stick Flora in the shower."

"Are you out of your mind?" asked Mama. I'm fully dressed."

"Your clothes are ruined. Zack's right. The first thing we need to do is get you into the shower.

"Like this?"

"How else?"

"But that's the one place without paint."

"We have no other choice."

Mama reluctantly stepped into the shower. I dodged paint puddles to make my way to the stall and adjust the water for her. "Stay there until the water runs clear. We'll start cleaning up this mess."

Zack descended the ladder. "How are we going to clean up the paint? We have exactly two rolls of paper towels, four rags and no towels."

"Let's start by sopping up the floor as best we can with the paper towels." I dug in my pocket for my phone. Lawrence hadn't arrived yet. I'd have him stop off at my house to pick up some clothes and towels for Mama and a pile of rags from the basement.

~*~

Thirty minutes later, Zack and I had mopped up the floor the best we could, using every single sheet of Bounty. So much paint had spilled on the white tile floor that the white grout was now Mother of Pearl. Much of the porous material had soaked up the latex from the initial spill, the rest as Zack and I attempted to wipe the tiles clean.

"Nothing we can do about that," said Zack, noticing me frowning at the darkened grout.

I shrugged. "At least it's a trendy color. According to the HGTV decorating mavens. Not to mention it will perfectly match the walls."

I heard the front door open and called to Lawrence, "We're in the bathroom."

He arrived empty-handed. "Where are the rags, towels, and clothes for Mama?"

"I tried," he said. "That mother-in-law of yours refused to let me in the house."

"Why?"

He shrugged. "I tried to explain what happened, but she wouldn't even open the door to me."

"Great."

"The commie pinko did that on purpose," shouted Mama from the shower stall. "I'm freezing in here. The hot water ran out. I'm going to catch pneumonia!"

I sighed. "I'll be back."

"I'll drive you," offered Zack.

"You can't leave," said Mama. What about painting the rest of the apartment?"

"No one's painting anymore today, Mama."

"Why not? It's early, not even lunchtime yet."

"Really? It feels like midnight to me."

"I don't know what you're so angry about, dear. I'm the one who was attacked by a can of paint."

"This is what I get for being nice," I complained to Zack as we left the apartment. "It's like that song from *Wicked* says, 'No good deed goes unpunished.' No more. If Mama wants her apartment painted, she and Lawrence can do it themselves. Or she can accept Ira's offer to hire someone."

"And you get your weekend back."

"Are you kidding? I'm about to kill Lucille. I'll be spending the rest of the weekend behind bars."

FIFTEEN

My impending night in lockup was postponed only because we arrived back at the house to find Lucille MIA.

"Looks like the old battle-axe lives to see another day," said Zack.

"She's probably off fomenting a government takeover. Now that she's mostly recovered from her stroke and surgery, she's back to her old tricks."

Lately, Lucille stayed home as little as possible. I suspected she and her comrades-in-arms, the twelve other members of the Daughters of the October Revolution, were up to something. I just didn't know what. However, as long as they didn't commandeer my living room and dining room, not to mention my office supplies, they could plot to their octogenarian hearts' content.

I began scurrying around the house, grabbing clothes and towels for Mama and an armload of rags from the basement. At the last minute I dashed into the bathroom for her hair dryer and a brush.

In less than twenty minutes we arrived back at the condo. Mama had stripped off her wet clothes and now wore a gray and navy Pollack Motors sweatshirt, the same one Lawrence arrived wearing. She'd wrapped her wet hair in what appeared to be Lawrence's white T-shirt.

Mama let loose a deep sigh when I handed her the bag containing her clothes. Her lower lip jutted out and trembled ever so slightly. Her voice quivered when she spoke. "I don't suppose I can change your mind about not continuing to paint. We won't be able to move tomorrow, otherwise."

Sarah Bernhardt lives! Mama made a valid point, though. I weighed spending the remainder of the day rolling shades of gray against another week of Mama versus Lucille warfare within the confines of *Casa Pollack*. Not to mention two less mouths to feed, one two-legged and one four-legged.

"We might as well finish," said Zack. "We're already here and covered in paint."

Mama brightened, rewarding him with a smile and a batting of her lashes. She placed her hand on his forearm. "Thank you, Zack dear." Zack had managed to find a quick way back into Mama good graces at my expense.

Mama turned her attention, along with pleading eyes, back to me. "Am I really asking that much, dear? Zack is willing to stay, and Lawrence and I will help."

I capitulated. "All right. As long as you stay at least five feet from any open can of paint."

"Really, Anastasia, you can't blame me for what happened in the bathroom. How was I to know Zackary had a gallon of paint precariously perched on a ladder behind the door?"

I bit my tongue. Hard. Zack appeared to be doing likewise. I mentally counted to twenty before speaking. "You and Lawrence need to pick up another gallon of Mother of Pearl for the bathroom after you change and dry your hair."

"Of course, dear. Did you bring my makeup?"

"Just a brush and hair dryer."

Mama turned to Lawrence. "We'll have to stop back at Anastasia's before heading to Home Depot. I'm not going to the store without makeup." Having dictated the agenda, she sashayed into the empty bedroom to dress.

After Mama and Lawrence left the condo, Zack asked, "That will keep them busy for a while. How much do you think we can accomplish before they return?"

"The way Mama primps? We should have the rest of the living room and the dining room painted before they return."

"At which point we can send them out to pick up lunch. If we keep them busy running errands all day, we should be able to avoid any further disasters."

I wrapped my arms around Zack's neck and kissed him. "I like the way you think." Bad move. A certain body part sprang to life between us. I quickly broke the kiss and stepped back. "Grab a roller."

"I'd rather grab you."

"After you help me finish painting."

"Killjoy."

"Me? I'm the one who wanted to walk out earlier, remember?" I picked up my roller, loaded some Stratus paint onto it, and returned to the wall I'd left half-painted after Mama's collision with a gallon of latex. "Start rolling. The sooner we finish, the sooner we can get out of here."

By five o'clock Zack and I had finished painting the entire condo. Lawrence offered to take us out to dinner, but all I wanted was a long soak in my bathtub. Every muscle in my body berated me for having overworked them.

"We'll bring something in," said Lawrence. "I'll see if Ira and the kids can join us."

I stifled a groan. Was it too late to change my mind and agree to dinner at a nice restaurant? But Lawrence had already whipped out his cell and placed a call to Ira. A moment later I learned I'd be having four additional guests at the dinner table.

~*~

Instead of a long soak, I had to settle for a short shower in order to make room in the house for dinner guests. Mama's cartons and suitcases still covered much of the living room and dining room, although by now most of them were packed. Since neither she nor Lawrence had helped paint, I gave them, along with Nick and Alex, the task of clearing space and setting the table while Zack and I showered and dressed. Separately, of course.

A short time later Ira and his brood arrived with two shopping bags filled with cartons of Chinese food. I eyed Ira's three kids. None of them looked happy to be back at *Casa Pollack*, but I noticed their hands were gadget free. Hopefully, we wouldn't have a repeat of our last encounter.

"Isaac and the twins have something to say to you, Anastasia," said Ira after giving me a wet peck on the cheek. I exerted extreme willpower to keep from wiping the slobber from my face.

I waited for the kids to say something.

"Children?" prompted their father.

The three of them mumbled something indiscernible. "I'm afraid I didn't hear you," I said. "Please speak up."

"We're sorry, Aunt Anastasia." The words came out in unison, sounding less than heartfelt and full of sing-song belligerence, but at least this time I heard them. I didn't push my luck by asking exactly what they were sorry for because I knew they weren't at all sorry. At least now, hopefully, I could expect not to have a repeat of our last encounter.

"Thank you for apologizing," I said.

"I'll help you with the food," said Ira. He carried the bags into the kitchen. I followed, wondering if Lawrence planned to reimburse his son-in-law for the dinner. Lawrence manipulated Ira more than Mama manipulated me.

Ira set the bags on the kitchen table. "Thanks for forcing me to wake up," he said. When I stared blankly at him, he continued. "About my children. Everything you said the other night?"

"I know it's hard to play the bad guy, Ira. Being a single parent isn't easy." I grabbed serving dishes and utensils.

"Understatement of the year."

"How are they adjusting to Cynthia's departure?"

Ira barked out a laugh. "They're thrilled to be rid of her. Frankly, so am I. I never should have married her, but then, Flora and Lawrence wouldn't have met. I guess everything happens for a reason."

"Have you spoken with Cynthia since she left?" I didn't let Ira know Lawrence suspected Ira had thrown Cynthia out on her Size Zero butt. That bit of gossip came from Mama, and years of experience had taught me to question everything my mother told me.

Ira opened a carton of fried rice and began spooning the contents into a bowl. "I tried calling her a few times. She's not answering her cell. Probably having too much fun with her new boy toy."

"She was having an affair?" Mama failed to mention that juicy tidbit of gossip. Either Lawrence didn't know or was too embarrassed by his daughter's behavior to discuss it.

Ira shrugged. "I've suspected for some time. The pool boy. How cliché is that?"

"When did Cynthia walk out on you?"

"A week ago. She didn't even bother leaving a note this time."

This time? "She's run off with someone before?"

"Twice. She'll come crawling back soon enough when she runs out of money. I cancelled her credit cards. Once the well dries up, the pool boy will dump her. This time I'm not taking her back."

"I'm sorry, Ira."

"Don't be. I've learned my lesson. I won't make the same mistake again."

"What will you do about childcare once Lawrence moves to the condo?" Ira's kids certainly weren't old enough to leave alone for hours at the McMansion.

"The kids leave for school before I have to leave for work in the morning. I'm hoping Lawrence and Flora will come to the house in the late afternoon and stay with them until I arrive home."

Red flags began waving in my mind. Ira's three kids were incorrigible. If they decided to stage a rebellion, I doubted Mama and Lawrence would survive the initial attack. "Have you spoken to them about this?"

"Not yet."

I was about to point out the downside of his plan, but Zack chose that moment to enter the house through the back door. Seeing me alone with Ira, his alpha male sprang into action and commenced territorial marking.

He crossed the room, wrapped his arm around my waist, and kissed me. Unlike Ira's wet pecks, Zack's kisses never made me think of a St. Bernard's slobber. Maybe I should suggest Zack give Ira kissing lessons. If Ira knew how to kiss, he might have better luck finding and keeping his next wife.

"Need any help?" asked Zack after finally separating his lips from mine.

"You're timing is excellent." I handed him two bowls of food to bring out to the dining room. "And have one of the boys tell Lucille dinner is ready."

Lucille and Mephisto had walked into the house shortly after Ira and his kids arrived. She took one look at the commotion in the living room, grunted, and headed for her bedroom.

I had glanced out the window in time to see Harriet Kleinhample, designated driver for the Daughters of the October Revolution, pulling her antiquated orange Volkswagen minibus off the curb and back onto the street. At least she'd missed the oak tree this time.

Ira's three kids wolfed down their plates of moo goo gai pan and chow mei fun before I had a chance to take more than three bites. "Can we be excused?" Melody asked Ira. Or was it Harmony? I needed a way to tell the difference between those two, especially now that Mama was marrying Lawrence. Something told me by default I'd drawn the short holiday hosting straw from now on.

"Me, too?" asked Isaac.

"Ask Aunt Anastasia," said Ira.

The three of them turned toward me, their silent expressions almost daring me to deny their request. If they were my kids, I'd make them stay at the table until everyone had finished eating. But they weren't my kids. For that I launched a silent prayer of gratitude heavenward. At least I'd won the genetic roll of the dice when it came to Pollack offspring. "You can watch television in the den, if you want, but leave Ralph alone."

"Who's Ralph?" asked Isaac.

"The parrot. Don't stick your fingers in his cage or open the door."

"Whatever."

The three of them raced from the room without so much as a thank you.

Less than a minute later they were back in the dining room, hands on hips, pouts on lips.

"You're TV's busted," said Isaac.

Great! Another expense I don't need. "Won't it turn on?"

"It turns on," said Harmony/Melody, "but it's only getting a couple of lame channels."

"Your cable is out," said Melody/Harmony.

"We don't get cable," said Nick. "Not anymore."

One of the major sore spots for my son when it came to accepting our new life of near-poverty—no ESPN. Cable hook-up, along with many other luxuries my family once took for granted, had gone the way of the dodo bird at the Pollack homestead.

Isaac's eyes grew wide. "How can you not have cable? That's like not having Internet."

"Jeez, you're practically pre-historic," said Melody/Harmony, rolling her eyes at me. She turned to her father. "There's nothing to do here, Dad. Why do you keep dragging us to visit these losers?"

"Melody, that's not a very nice thing to say," said Ira.

"Apologize to—"

"I want my phone!" demanded Harmony/Melody, planting herself next to her father's chair and sticking her hand out under his nose.

"Me, too," said Melody/Harmony, coming up alongside her sister and shoving another hand at Ira.

Ira caved immediately. So much for the lesson he claimed to have learned. He reached into his sports coat pocket and handed the girls their phones.

"What about me?" asked Isaac. "Where's my Game Boy?" Ira reached into his other pocket and produced Isaac's game. His son snatched it out of Ira's hand and started to head back to the den. Halfway into the living room he turned around and asked, "What are you, like poor or something?"

Ira turned to me and mumbled, "I'm sorry," as Isaac raced toward the den.

Right now, I felt sorrier for Ira than I did myself. It didn't take a clairvoyant to see into the future when it came to those kids of his. I glanced at both my sons. For all his wealth, I'd never trade places with Ira. I was far wealthier where it mattered most.

~*~

We were clearing the table when my doorbell rang. "That's for me," said Ira. He dropped an armload of dishes back on the table and headed for the front door.

The rest of us, minus Lucille, carried stacks of dirty dishes into the kitchen. A moment later Ira joined us. He waved a large white envelope in front of my face. "Your new wheels have arrived."

I walked into the living room and glanced out the window in time to see a Pollack Motors panel truck pulling away from the curb. Behind it sat a silver Jetta.

Ira came up beside me and dangled a set of keys in front of my face. "Take it for a test spin. If you're happy, I've got all the paperwork here."

I held out my hand. Instead of dropping the keys into my palm, Ira gently placed them in my hand and folded my fingers over them, holding my hand in his. I pulled away.

Ira followed me into the kitchen. Zack was loading the dishwasher. "Leave that," I said. "Let's go for a ride."

Zack grabbed a towel to dry his hands. We'll be back soon," I said, dashing out the back door.

"I think Ira expected to accompany you on the test drive," said Zack after we settled into the car. "He looked downright crestfallen."

I slipped the key into the ignition and turned it. Unlike the Hyundai which coughed and rattled each time I'd start it up, the Jetta purred. As I pulled away from the curb, I told Zack about the keys-in-hand incident.

"That man has developed a serious crush on you."

"I'm afraid you're right."

"Should I be worried?"

I rolled to a full stop at the corner and turned to him. "You're joking, right?"

He grinned. "You know me so well."

Not really. Nothing Zack said would ever totally convince me he was *just* a photojournalist, but that was an ongoing conversation best left for another time.

"The more I get to know Ira," I said, "the more he creeps me out. Between his obsessive compulsion to please and the way he's raising his kids, I'd really like to distance myself and my family from him and his brats."

"That's not going to be easy with Flora about to marry Lawrence."

"Let's hope Ira's next wife has a father who will replace Lawrence."

"Don't count on it. Ira holds the mortgage on that condo. Lawrence and Flora will be sucking up to Ira for the rest of their lives."

"My worst fear. And exactly why I didn't want to become indebted to Ira for a car." I sped up as the speed limit changed, and the Jetta adjusted without so much as a sputter. "It's a nice car, though, isn't it? Clean. Low mileage. Guaranteed."

"And affordable. You'd never get a deal like that from anyone else."

"That's the problem." I sighed. "I'm not thrilled with the invisible strings attached to this deal. I may only be paying under five thousand dollars for a car worth twice that, but I'm afraid I'll be paying a much steeper price for years to come."

"So what are you going to do?"

"What choice do I have? I'm forced to deal with the devil I know, rather than risking getting stuck with another lemon. I'm just not happy about having to make the choice in the first place."

Yet something else I could blame on my dead louse of a spouse. *Thank you once again, Karl Marx Pollack, from the bottom of my poverty-stricken heart.*

~*~

Ira arranged for several of his mechanics to move Lawrence and Mama on Sunday. I was certain they hadn't given up their day off out of the goodness of their hearts. Ira bought their help the same way he continued to buy his way into our lives.

In that respect he was no different than his half-brother. Karl had manipulated me into believing he was someone he wasn't; Ira tried to manipulate me with his wealth. I couldn't help but wonder about the dearly departed Isidore Pollack. Had he, too, been a manipulator, or did both his sons inherit some long dormant manipulator gene?

As much as it bothered me that Ira was insinuating himself deeper and deeper into my family, I was grateful that I didn't have to spend the day lugging cartons and hauling furniture. I only had to help Mama unpack, sort, and find places for all her belongings.

To my surprise, Lawrence arrived at the apartment with little besides a few suitcases of clothing and a carton of books. "Where are all Lawrence's things?" I asked Mama as we unpacked and washed her china.

Mama screwed up her face. "Cynthia donated all his belongings to charity after she moved him into the McMansion. She didn't even tell him until the Salvation Army had hauled everything away."

"That's awful!"

"That's Cynthia. Lawrence said if he had to do it all over again, he would have raised her with a lot more discipline and a lot less giving in, no matter how much she whined. You know the worst part?"

"What?"

"He sees Ira making the same mistakes."

I glanced into the living room where Ira's kids sat zombie-like on the sofa, watching a movie. They were the only ones not helping unpack the apartment. Ira and Lawrence were in the bedroom, assembling the bed, while Alex placed towels and sheets in the linen closet, Nick filled the hall coat closet, and Zack hung pictures for Mama.

Surely, Ira could have assigned some task to his kids. Even nine and eleven-year-olds are capable of drying dishes or unpacking and shelving books. Instead, the moment he arrived with his kids, Ira set about connecting the television to the cable box to keep Melody, Harmony, and Isaac from dying of boredom.

Is there a Twelve Step Program for over-indulgent parents? I wondered what Ira was like before his first wife became ill and died. Maybe his obsessive need to please came from insecurity and the fear of losing another loved one, not simply from poor parenting skills. Either way, the man needed professional help before his kids turned out like Cynthia. Or worse.

We didn't finish unpacking, assembling, storing, and hanging Mama's possessions until dinnertime. Ira clapped his hands together and said, "Let's all go out for burgers. My treat."

"With them?" asked Melody/Harmony, an expression of disgust directed toward me and my family.

"Do we have to?" asked Isaac.

I'm a non-violent person by nature. I had never spanked my kids when they were little. However, I now found myself fighting an uncontrollable urge to smack the smirks off those kids' faces.

I balled my fists behind my back and bit down on my tongue until the urge passed. After this weekend, I had no desire to spend any more time than necessary with Ira and his kids. Ever. I pasted a smile on my face and lied, "Another time, Ira. I still need to do laundry and run to the supermarket tonight."

Ira turned to Alex and Nick. "Boys? Why don't you come with us?"

"Can't," said Alex. "I still have homework to finish."

"Me, too," said Nick.

"Flora? Dad?"

"Sorry, son," said Lawrence, "Flora and I are bushed. We'll take a rain check."

Poor Ira looked like he'd just been picked last for the team. Again. With a resigned sigh, he told his kids, "I guess it's just the four of us."

"Good," said Harmony/Melody. "Let's go."

"I want a milkshake with my burger," said Melody/Harmony.

"Can we stop at Toys R Us on the way home?" asked Isaac.

"Sure," said Ira.

The rest of us rolled our eyes at his departing back.

SIXTEEN

Monday morning, I almost didn't mind the bumper-to-bumper traffic on Route 287. Thanks to Ira and his need to please, my new (well, new to me) silver Jetta came not only certified for a year but with twenty-four-hour roadside assistance, compliments of Pollack Motors. I no longer had to worry about breaking down in my old rust bucket Hyundai.

Best of all, the air-conditioning hummed along, enveloping me in a cool breeze. Although the calendar claimed we were more than a week into autumn, Mother Nature had apparently missed the memo.

The weekend news made no mention of either progress in Philomena's murder investigation or the discovery of embezzlement at Trimedia. Same for 1010, the all-news radio station I tuned to in the car. However, when I turned down the access road that led to the Trimedia parking lot, I noticed Batswin's unmarked Crown Vic and two Morris County patrol cars parked in front of the walkway leading to the main entrance.

I pulled into the parking lot expecting to find Tino waiting for me in his usual spot. He wasn't.

Two Morris County patrolmen blocked the doors of the main entrance. I recognized them at once. Officers Simmons and Garfinkle had responded to my panicked phone call the night I discovered Marlys Vandenburg's body glue-gunned to my office chair and keyboard.

"Sorry, ma'am, but you can't go inside right now," said Garfinkle. The nearly seven-foot officer had shaved his walrus mustache and gained a few pounds since our last encounter.

I don't think he recognized me. I craned my neck in an attempt to make eye contact. "Why not?"

"Police business, ma'am."

"Did something happen?"

"We're not at liberty to say," said Officer Simmons.

I turned my attention to him. At less than half a foot taller than I am, he didn't cause me neck spasms during a face-to-face conversation. "How long before I can go inside? I have work to do."

Simmons shrugged. "Shouldn't be too long. Step aside, please."

I whipped out my phone and called Cloris as I walked back to my car. She always beat me into work unless she had a morning meeting. With a maximum of six officers, judging from the three county vehicles present, no one stood guard at the other doors. They only opened from the inside outward, but Cloris could open one for me.

When she answered, I explained the situation.

"If something's up, it's very hush-hush," she said. "And definitely not on our floor."

I leaned against my car, keeping an eye on the front door. "I wonder if it has to do with the embezzlement."

"Could be. Are there any reporters milling around?"

"None."

"If this is breaking news, someone forgot to break it to the media."

The front door opened. "Wait a minute. Something's happening." I inched closer to the building. "Two patrolmen are exiting. They each have a handcuffed suspect."

"Who?"

"Hold on. Batswin and Robbins are now coming out, and they're also each leading a suspect. Damn. You're not going to believe this."

"What? What's going on?"

"They've got the entire Human Resources department in handcuffs!"

The first two officers led Catherine Chenko and Sandy Sechrest to one of the patrol cars and settled them into the backseat. Batswin and Robbins ushered Nita Holzer and Gwendolyn Keene into the backseat of the second patrol car. The four patrolmen drove off with their suspects.

"Gotta go," I said to Cloris. "Batswin and Robbins are headed my way."

"Mrs. Pollack," said Batswin, "I want to thank you for the tip."

I smiled. "Happy to help, detective. And it appears your day is off to a busy start. All four of them were in on the embezzlement?"

"The evidence we've uncovered so far suggests so. We'll know more after a forensic accountant audits the books."

"Who was the guy in the black Escalade?"

"Holtzer's husband," said Robbins.

For someone who was such a stickler for rules, the Human

Resources Nazi certainly didn't practice what she preached, writing us up for coming to work ten minutes late while she plunged her greedy fists into the corporate till.

"Are they responsible for Philomena's death?"

"My gut tells me no," said Batswin, "but one of them might surprise us during interrogation, assuming they don't lawyer up before we have a chance to question them."

"My gut agrees with your gut."

She raised her bushy eyebrows. "What else does your gut tell you?"

"Nothing but common sense. Killing Philomena would kill the scam. They'd have nothing to gain and everything to lose. I thought at first maybe Philomena found out about the embezzlement and confronted one of them, but that seems unlikely."

"Why?" asked Robbins.

"Philomena had nothing to do with anyone at Trimedia other than Gruenwald and her staff. *Bling!*'s editorial director didn't know about the bogus employees. So how would Philomena find out? According to the other members of the *Bling!* staff, Philomena rarely showed up at the office, and when she did, she didn't stay long."

"They did all the work, and she got all the credit?" said Batswin.

"Exactly. Which is probably why Gruenwald is convinced the killer is someone at Trimedia. The motive might be jealousy."

"Why do I get the feeling you disagree?" she asked.

"I've spoken to those people. They're all really upset about losing their jobs."

"Why are they losing their jobs?" asked Robbins.

"The magazine is folding. Philomena was *Bling!* Without her, there's no magazine. They knew that. None of those people would kill her for the same reason none of the HR women killed her. No Philomena means no money."

Batswin chuckled. "Very good, Mrs. Pollack. We'll make a detective out of you yet."

With that she and Robbins headed for her Crown Vic, leaving me staring at their retreating backs.

~*~

"Batswin, Robbins, and I certainly have an interesting relationship," I said a few minutes later while relating events to Cloris. We were in the conference room awaiting the start of our monthly planning meeting.

She poured two cups of coffee and handed one to me. "At least they don't suspect you this time."

When we first met, Batswin and Robbins zeroed in on me as the prime suspect in Marlys Vandenburg's murder. Quite a bit of convincing on my part eventually set them straight. I think they now play nice because I'm privy to a secret regarding those illegally borrowed unmarked bills they used in the failed Ricardo sting.

I studied the platter of croissants on the credenza next to the coffee pot, finally settling on one with raspberry cream filling and chocolate drizzle. "No wonder I can't lose weight. What are these, seven gazillion calories each?"

"Only six."

"Diet croissants? Great! I'll take two." I have no willpower when it comes to Cloris confections.

She slapped my hand as I placed a second croissant on my plate. "That was six gazillion, not six calories. You want to give yourself a heart attack?"

I offered her a sheepish grin. "At least my sweet tooth will die satisfied."

Cloris lifted the croissant from my plate and returned it to the tray. "Maybe I should stop sharing vendor samples. I don't want to be charged with accessory to murder."

"Someone else was murdered?" asked Tessa, coming up behind us. "Who? Someone from Trimedia?"

"Me. According to Cloris if I eat another croissant."

Tessa cast a critical eye over my figure. "She has a point. You really should go on a diet, Anastasia. Especially if you hope to have any chance of finding another husband."

The nerve of her! Yes, I could stand to drop a few pounds, but I was by no means heavy. On a good day I could still squeeze into a size eight. Just your typical pear-shaped, middle-aged mother with a slowing metabolism. Hardly a candidate for the Plus Size department. "I'd like to see what you look like twenty years and two kids from now."

Tessa poured herself a cup of coffee, adding neither sugar nor cream. "I'll look exactly the way I look now. I don't intend to let myself go after marriage the way some women do." With that, she flounced her size zero butt over to the conference table and settled into her chair.

"Fashion editors, the bane of my existence," I muttered. The longer Tessa worked at *American Woman*, the nastier she became, especially toward me. "What is it with me and fashion editors? I'm no threat to them."

"You got along with Erica," said Cloris.

"Erica doesn't count. She inherited the position and didn't last long."

"Maybe you send off the wrong vibe, something only fashion

editors pick up on."

"You mean like a noise only dogs can hear?"

Cloris shrugged. "It's a theory. You might have an anti-fashion aura."

"Do I look like I have an anti-fashion aura?"

"Beats me. I don't believe in that woo-woo stuff."

"Woo-woo aside, for once I'd like to see someone put Tessa in her place."

"Shall we get started, ladies?" Cloris and I turned to see that Naomi had entered the conference room and settled into her place at the head of the table. We all quickly took our seats.

"First order of business," said Naomi, "as you can see, we have a couple of empty chairs this morning."

I glanced across the table. Neither Tessa's nor Nicole's assistant was present.

"Trimedia has instituted some cost cutting measures," continued Naomi. "From now on fashion, beauty, and decorating will be sharing an assistant."

"What!" Tessa jumped out of her seat. "This is totally unacceptable. How do you expect us to get our work done with only a third of an assistant each?"

"Five of us on this side of the table share an assistant," I said, "and we all manage."

"You hardly count," said Tessa. "Fashion and beauty carry this magazine."

Naomi nodded to her assistant. "Not according to recent demographic surveys," said Kim. "More people read *American Woman* for the recipes, followed by the health and finance articles, craft projects, and decorating ideas. Travel comes next, then beauty and fashion."

"Which necessitates a change in editorial," said Naomi. "We need to give our readers more of what they buy us for. As it turns out, that's not fashion and beauty. We obviously can't compete with the other monthlies in those areas, so we need to play to our strengths."

"You can't do this," said Tessa.

Nicole said nothing. She obviously had prior knowledge of Naomi's bombshell and had come to terms with it. Nicole was no prima donna.

I made eye contact with Jeanie. She offered me an easy-come/easy-go shrug. Jeanie had often shared her assistant with us bottom-feeders because she preferred the control of doing things on her own. She'd have no problem sharing her assistant with Tessa and Nicole.

"Take it up with Uncle Chessie," suggested Janice.

"That's exactly what I intend to do." Tessa turned and headed for the door.

"Sit down, Tessa," said Naomi. "I'm tired of you storming out of meetings whenever you don't get your way. If you leave now, you can clear out your office."

"You can't fire me!"

"Can and will," said Naomi. "Just try me."

Tessa glared at Naomi. She looked like she was debating calling her bluff, but it was hard to tell, given the numerous Botox injections that had eliminated most of the expression from her face. She'd scored the position thanks to nepotism and had only worked at the magazine a few months. With little experience, the most she could hope for was a job as an assistant at another magazine and only if Naomi gave her a good recommendation—not something I'd stake my future on at the moment. Apparently,

Tessa had enough smarts to realize this and finally returned to her seat.

Naomi had definitely put Tessa Lisbon in her place.

"How'd you do that?" Cloris whispered in my ear.

Damned if I knew, but I hardly had time to gloat. This change in editorial direction meant more work for me. Twice as much per issue, according to the new page distribution Naomi proceeded to lay out before us. Tessa might be out an assistant, but she now had half as much work to do each month. I, on the other hand, now had double the work to cram into my days. *Be careful what you wish for, Anastasia.*

~*~

Tino stopped by my cubicle several hours later. "Has Mr. Gruenwald decided I don't need further protection?" I asked.

He plopped his huge frame down into the spare chair. "No, but I can't be in two places at once."

Tino's normally immaculate appearance looked a bit rough around the edges today. His bespoke suit needed a good pressing, his face a shave. "You look like you were up all night."

He tried to stifle a yawn. "I was."

"Oh?"

"Family matter. All taken care of now."

"That's good. Can I assume you didn't hear what happened earlier this morning?"

Tino perked up. "What? Did the police make an arrest in Philomena's murder?"

"They made *four* arrests but not for the murder. They led all four Human Resources employees away in handcuffs. The guy in the black Escalade was the husband of one of them."

Tino whistled under his breath. "All of them?"

"All. The detectives don't think there's any connection between the embezzling and the murder, though."

"Too bad. That would wrap things up very nicely." Tino yawned again, no longer attempting to cover it up.

"Why don't you go home? Get some sleep."

"Can't. I have a job to do."

"Tino, this is ridiculous. If someone wanted to kill me, he'd make his move when I'm not in the office and protected by you. Nothing has happened. Nothing is going to happen. I'm no threat to Philomena's killer because I don't have a clue who he is. Go home."

He shook his head.

I stood and placed my hands on my hips. "Why are men so stubborn?"

"I'm not stubborn. I take my responsibilities seriously."

"Fine. Be responsible." I stepped out of the office.

He jumped up to follow me. "Where are you going?"

"To get you a cup of coffee."

He smiled and sat back down. "Thanks."

When I returned a few minutes later, Tino was fast asleep, his feet propped up on my worktable, his mouth open. I sat back down at my computer and drank his coffee.

"What's that god-awful noise?" yelled Cloris from across the hall.

"Come take a look," I yelled back.

A moment later Cloris stood at the entrance to my cubicle. "Wow! I didn't think it was possible for anyone to snore louder than my husband. How can you concentrate with that noise?"

"It's not easy."

"How's he protecting you if he's sound asleep?"

"I'll wake him if I see any Ninja assassins lurking in the hall." I related the little I knew of Tino's all-nighter. "He didn't go into detail, but I'm guessing a parent was taken ill and hospitalized. Why else would he be up all night, right?"

"You should make him comfortable."

"He looks pretty comfortable to me. I could never fall asleep in a desk chair."

"At least take his shoes off." Cloris began unlacing one of Tino's shoes while I worked on the other.

The guy was dead to the world. He didn't so much as stir when we removed his shoes. "You'd think someone who saw action in Iraq and Afghanistan would be an extremely light sleeper," I said.

"Is that where he served?"

I thought for a minute. "I guess I just assumed that. Gruenwald said Tino was a former Marine, but he didn't go into detail. For all I know, he never saw combat."

"Which would explain why he didn't jump up and try to kill us just now."

"Yeah, maybe taking his shoes off wasn't the brightest idea."

Cloris examined the shoe in her hand. "Gruenwald must pay Tino well. I had no idea Gucci made sneakers."

Sneakers that looked incredibly like shoes. Maybe they're a special style designed exclusively for bodyguards, the Secret Service, and all the other men in black. Suitable for wearing with six-hundred-dollar suits, yet still allowing for chasing after crooks, assassins, and other assorted bad guys. I wondered if Zack had a pair. "According to Tino, Gruenwald pays him *extremely* well. Unlike us."

"My, my!" Cloris held up the black leather sneaker to show me the sole. "You think Tino's getting it on with Tessa?"

Several small crystals were lodged deep into the treads, the same type of crystals we'd seen on Tessa's Vajazzled nether region. "I hardly think Tessa would lower herself enough to date a chauffeur and bodyguard. Besides, she said the crystals start falling off after a few days. Tino probably stepped in some. Along with something else."

Cloris examined the sole more closely, then scrunched up her nose. "Euww!"

She dropped the sneaker. Tino didn't flinch a muscle.

"It's probably just caked mud."

"Let's hope so. Ever think about what's on the bottom of your shoes?" she asked. "All those germs? And we track them onto our floors and carpets."

"I file that under what-I-don't-think-about-can't-hurt me."

"Maybe we should adopt the Japanese custom of removing our shoes before we enter our homes."

I placed the other sneaker on the floor next to Tino's chair. "That would only work if Mephisto wore paw covers. Do you think Japanese dogs wear booties?"

"Maybe their owners wash their paws after taking them for a walk. Anyway, now that we're both totally grossed out, we'd better get back to work."

"If I can work through all this racket." I held my hands over my ears. "Man, he's loud. I pity whomever he marries."

"I'm popping in ear buds," said Cloris. "I've got a spare pair you can borrow."

~*~

Tino still snored away come quitting time. I shook his shoulder, trying to wake him but had no success. I even tried shouting at him, but I doubt he heard me over the sound of his own snoring.

"Should I leave him?" I asked Cloris.

"Might as well. He'll wake up eventually on his own."

Before leaving, I sent Alex and Nick a text: *Pls put casserole sitting in fridge in 350 oven @5:30.*

I left my desk lamp light on so Tino wouldn't awaken in the dark and become disoriented. I didn't need to arrive at work tomorrow to find him lying unconscious on the floor from having stumbled and hit his head.

Tessa passed us as Cloris and I stood waiting for the elevator. "Stairs are great exercise, Anastasia. You could walk off some of those calories you consumed today." Before she pushed open the door to the stairwell, she tossed me a catty smile over her shoulder.

"Do you believe her?" I asked. "She's getting as bad as Marlys was."

"Comes with the territory," said Cloris. "Ever meet a fashion editor who wasn't all full of herself?"

"Erica wasn't."

"Erica became fashion editor by default and held the position only briefly."

"True. Even if she hadn't entered the Witness Protection Program, she wouldn't have survived the sharks on Seventh Avenue very long."

"My point exactly. Maybe we should nominate Tessa as the next Trimedia victim," said Cloris.

"What do you mean?"

"The way things are going around here lately, there's bound to be another murder at some point."

~*~

On my drive home from work I learned just how prescient a statement that was.

SEVENTEEN

Norma Gene Mortenson was dead. I learned this from a breaking news story on 1010 as I drove home from work. Late this afternoon sanitation workers had discovered her body stuffed into a Dumpster in an alleyway behind a bar in South Philly. The radio gave no further information other than mentioning Norma Gene's relationship to Philomena and Philomena's death a week earlier.

Poor Norma Gene. She must have suspected one of Philomena's old cohorts of her murder and decided to take matters into her own hands. Except along with not preventing Philomena's death, she'd also now failed to prevent her own.

My phone rang. I grabbed it and glanced at the read-out. Cloris. Since I currently sat in bumper-to-bumper rush hour traffic, not even crawling along at ten miles an hour, I answered without fear of being slapped with a ticket. "I'm guessing you heard the news?"

"I'm freaking out. A few minutes ago I say we're due for

another murder, and what happens? We get one."

"Cue the woo-woo music."

"You think she went to Philly to confront someone about Philomena's murder?"

Traffic began to move. I pushed the speakerphone button and placed my cell in the console beverage holder. Not that I'm ungrateful, but my life would be less stressful if Ira had found a Bluetooth enabled car for me. "Probably. I wonder if she told anyone where she was going or whom she planned to see."

"If she suspected someone, she probably told Batswin and Robbins when they questioned her."

"Not if she cared more about revenge than justice."

"I wonder if the detectives have any leads. Do you think they still suspect Gruenwald?"

"I'm guessing he'll remain at the top of their list until they can prove otherwise." My own recent experiences had made me realize that innocent until proven guilty only worked in court cases. The cops believed in a suspect's guilt until they had enough proof to the contrary. "I haven't heard anything one way or the other, though. Not from Batswin and Robbins and not from Tino. And I haven't spoken with Gruenwald since our one and only conversation last week."

"Do you think Norma was on to something?" asked Cloris.

"It sounds logical on the surface—"

"I sense a *but*."

"The *but* involves where we found her body. How would anyone from her old life have access to Trimedia? And not only have access but have enough knowledge of the security cameras to be able to remove them without being seen?"

"But if it's not someone from her gang days, it must be

someone from Trimedia," said Cloris. "Who else would have access to the building and know about the security cameras?"

"Unless that's what the killer wants us to think," I said. "Why would someone connected to Trimedia dump the body back here? That's what puzzles me. If we knew the killer's motive for dumping Philomena's body in our models case, we could probably figure out who did it."

"Oh, is that all?" asked Cloris. "Piece of cake."

"Indubitably."

~*~

I arrived home to find Lawrence's car parked in front of my house. Now that Mama and Lawrence had moved into their own apartment, I was looking forward to a little less chaos at *Casa Pollack*, not to mention lower food bills. Silly me. With the two of them living a mere two miles away, I'd probably now have one more mouth to feed, not one less. Mama had never met a recipe she couldn't burn to a crisp, and Lawrence didn't seem the handy-in-the-kitchen type.

For that matter, Lawrence didn't seem the handy-at-anything type, which made me wonder about his pre-retirement profession. Whatever he'd done, he certainly hadn't saved for his golden years. Or maybe he had and lost it all in bad investments like Mama's last fiancé. I knew next to nothing about Lawrence Tuttnauer. Then again, aside from my own father, I'd known little about any of Mama's husbands. Most hadn't lasted long enough for in-depth back-stories to emerge.

The blended aromas of chicken, broccoli, and cheese wafted through the house, telling me one of my sons had read my text and remembered to pop the casserole in the oven. A baseball game blared from the den. I assumed that's where I'd find Alex, Nick, and Lawrence. Lucille was either camped out in her bedroom or off rabblerousing with her fellow Daughters of the October Revolution.

Mama sat alone at the dining room table, her brow furrowed, a myriad of papers spread haphazardly before her. One glance at the assorted computer printouts of venues and menus told me she'd entered into serious wedding planning mode.

"Have you settled on a date?" I asked.

"Sunday," she mumbled without looking up.

"This Sunday? Six days from now?"

"Of course, dear."

I waved toward the papers on the table. "And you haven't settled on a restaurant yet?"

"We're having the reception at Ira's home. I'm trying to decide on a caterer for the dinner."

Early October had become a huge wedding month for New Jersey brides. How many of these caterers even had an opening for Sunday?

Not my problem, I told myself, tamping down the urge to voice my opinion. Instead, I asked, "Speaking of dinner, are you and Lawrence planning to join us this evening?"

Mama finally looked up from her papers and beamed me a gracious smile. "We'd love to, dear."

Great. I hoped I had enough salad in the crisper or an extra box of rice to stretch a chicken and broccoli casserole for four into one that would feed six.

"Why are you doing this here, Mama? I would have thought you'd be happy for the peace and quiet of your own apartment. No Lucille. No Mephisto. No Ralph."

"We took the boys to be measured for their tuxedos after

school. Besides, I wanted to see you in your dress."

"My dress?"

"It's hanging on your closet door."

"You bought me a dress?" I had served as matron-of-honor for each of Mama's last four weddings, but she'd never picked up the dress tab before. Nor had she paid for tuxedo rentals for her grandsons. Either Mama had robbed a bank or she'd wheedled a credit card out of Mr. Ira Moneybags. I'm not sure which option bothered me more.

"I also wanted to ask Zack if he'd do me the honor of walking me down the aisle, but he's not home."

"Zack?" Alex and Nick had escorted Mama on her last four trips down the aisle. "Why Zack?"

"Why not? I thought I'd mix things up a bit this time. Alex and Nick are old enough to be ushers now."

"Whom will they usher?"

"Why all of the guests, of course."

"What guests?" Mama's previous weddings had been small, intimate affairs with just the immediate family present.

"All of our friends. Plus, Ira's friends and business associates."

"For a wedding this Sunday? When are you planning to invite these people?"

"Heavens, Anastasia! You're so last century. I sent out e-vites this morning. The RSVP's are already pouring in." Her entire face lit up. "We should have quite a crowd."

I never thought I'd live to see the day that Flora Sudberry Periwinkle Ramirez Scoffield Goldberg O'Keefe, a lifelong member of the very proper DAR, would turn her back on her Emily Post sensibilities and send wedding invitations via cyberspace. Then again, I never thought my not-so-dearly departed husband would turn into a dead louse of a spouse. So what did I know?

All of which makes me wonder about my ability to read people. I'm no detective. Part of me felt guilty about taking Alfred Gruenwald's money under false pretenses, even though he'd really left me no choice. Batswin and Robbins would find Philomena's killer long before I came up with a credible suspect. At least I'd uncovered the embezzlement, thus saving Trimedia countless millions, which in turn helped assuage my guilt over taking Gruenwald's money.

Turning my thoughts back to Mama and her gala wedding, I asked, "Who's paying for all these guests?"

"Ira gave me his AmEx card and said not to worry about the expense. I'm sure he's writing part of it off as business entertainment."

That solved one mystery. Mama hadn't robbed a bank. "I doubt he meant for you to charge clothes for your grandsons and me on his card."

Mama sighed. "Why do you have to be so obstinate, Anastasia? Ira has plenty of money, and he enjoys spending it on his family."

"We're not his family."

"Of course we are, dear. Besides, you should be happy."

"How so?"

"You don't have to do anything for the wedding this time. No centerpieces, no bouquet, no decorations. Thanks to Ira's generosity, I've hired professionals to handle everything. All you have to do is show up and enjoy yourself." She reached over and patted my hand. "Now go try on your dress."

I bit my tongue as I headed for my bedroom. Had Mama expected me to craft her a wedding in six days' time, she would have been sorely disappointed. I've been known to pull off a crafting miracle or two but not on such short notice during a work week. I suppose I should be grateful to Ira for not having to deal with a Flora meltdown over a lack of wedding frou-frou.

I stopped dead in my tracks as I entered my bedroom and gaped open-mouthed at the dress hanging on my closet door. I'll say this for Mama, she has exquisite taste. Exquisite but expensive. Oscar de la Renta expensive.

I grabbed the price tag and nearly choked at the numbers staring back at me. The two-thousand-dollar dress, an evergreen sleeveless silk faille, had a ruffled round neckline and bias seams that extended from the bodice to the narrow cocktail length skirt. I'd need to squeeze into seven pairs of Spanx to keep from looking like a stuffed pepper in it.

I turned around and marched back into the dining room. "Are you out of your mind, Mama?"

She looked up from her menus and frowned. "Don't you like it, dear?"

"The dress is gorgeous. What I don't like is the price tag. I will not let you take advantage of Ira in this way."

Mama slammed her hand onto the table. "I am not taking advantage of Ira. He insisted on paying for everything."

"I doubt he expected you to choose a two-thousand-dollar cocktail dress for me. We're returning it after dinner."

"We're doing no such thing. You'll hurt Ira's feelings. He chose that dress for you."

"What?"

"Ira took me shopping today."

"You're kidding!"

"Well, I couldn't exactly have Lawrence drive me. It's bad luck for the groom to see the bride in her dress prior to the wedding."

"What about your dress, Mama?"

Her face lit up at the mention. "Oh, you'll love it, dear! It's Vera Wang, a metallic jacquard sheath with crystal beading around the neckline."

"How much?"

"That's really none of your business, Anastasia."

"How much, Mama?"

We stared each other down for a full minute before Mama finally capitulated. "Twenty-five hundred."

I half expected her to say five thousand. Or more. Still, the total for both dresses came to a staggering forty-five hundred dollars, the equivalent of one third my real estate tax bill for the year or six months of mortgage payments. And Ira thought nothing of throwing that kind of money away on two dresses that would be worn for all of a few hours. I found that obscene.

"This ends with the wedding," I said. "Mr. Moneybags will not be spending another dime on this family after Sunday."

"You can't tell Ira how to spend his money."

"Watch me." With that I headed back to my bedroom to try on a dress that turned my stomach into knots.

It fit like a glove. And with only one pair of Spanx. I stepped into the bathroom. As I stared at my reflection in the full-length mirror that hung on the back of the door, the creepy crawlies skittered up my spine. Had Ira really picked out the dress, or had Mama chosen it and strongly suggested he buy it? I had to admit, I looked stunning. Very stunning and very sexy. And I didn't want my husband's half-brother having those kinds of thoughts about me. Ever.

"You look beautiful, dear." I turned around to find Mama

standing in the middle of my bedroom. "Ira has good taste."

"He really picked out this dress?"

When Mama nodded, the creepy-crawlies traversed another lap up and down my spine. "Ira should spend more time fixing his own problems and less time picking out clothes for me."

Mama frowned. "Don't be so hard on him. He's had a rough time the last few years."

"As opposed to whom? Me?"

"He's trying to help you."

"I don't want his help. Besides, spending two-grand on a dress doesn't help me."

"Honestly, Anastasia, did you expect us to shop at Wal-Mart?"

Mama didn't get it; Mama would never get it. In her world men took care of women.

An awful thought popped into my head at that moment. Had Mama seduced Lawrence because of Ira's money? She'd previously admitted to such a scheme with the recently deceased Lou Beaumont. Was her relationship with Lawrence a case of *déjà vu*? He might not have money, but his son-in-law certainly had plenty. And judging from the way Ira was tossing Franklins at Mama and Lawrence, he seemed to care more about his father-in-law than his soon-to-be ex-wife.

"Well?" asked Mama, hands on hips.

Rather than answer her, I slipped out of the dress, placed it back on its hanger, removed the Spanx, and stepped into a pair of jeans. After tossing on a T-shirt, I headed for the kitchen to start the rice and cut up a salad.

~*~

Lawrence, a diehard Mets fan, suggested eating dinner in the den so he and the boys could continue watching the National League

Wild Card playoff game. When Alex and Nick cast pleading eyes in my direction, I agreed. After all, how often do the Mets make it to the playoffs? Mama, having chosen her caterer and menu, decided to join them. Lucille remained off with her fellow rabble-rousers. I filled my plate and settled into a kitchen chair with only Ralph to keep me company.

"So how was your day?" I asked the bird.

He flapped his wings and squawked. "*Nor night, nor day, no rest. The Winter's Tale.* Act Two, Scene Three."

I stabbed at a piece of broccoli. "Like you have something to complain about. I'm the one who never gets any rest. Make yourself useful, Ralph. Tell me how to deal with Ira."

Instead of offering up further pearls of wisdom, the bird decided to ignore me and preen his feathers. Apparently, Shakespeare never wrote about an Ira problem.

EIGHTEEN

The next morning Tino greeted me as I stepped out of my car. He looked no worse the wear for having slept in my office. No stubble. All tucked and pressed and ex-Marine intimidating. Then again, he may have awakened shortly after I left and spent most of the night in his own bed. Since he didn't mention anything, I decided not to bring up the subject. Tino didn't strike me as the sort of guy who'd take kindly to being reminded he'd fallen asleep on the job—literally.

"Did you hear the news about Norma Gene?" he asked as we headed toward the building entrance.

I nodded. "Do you have any details?"

"Me? Why would I have details?"

"I thought the police might have spoken with Mr. Gruenwald."

Tino stopped short and turned to face me. "You think Mr. G. killed her?"

"No, of course not, but Philomena was murdered, and now

Norma Gene is found dead. There's got to be a connection, right?"

"Maybe. Maybe not." He resumed walking.

"The news report I heard said she was found in a Dumpster but didn't say how she died. If she was severely beaten, it's the same M.O. as Philomena."

Tino shrugged. "People wind up in the wrong place at the wrong time all the time. Shit happens. Especially in certain sections of South Philly."

"You know the area where they found her?"

He opened the door, and we stepped inside. "Driven through it a few times. It's got a seedy rep. Lots of gang activity. Not the sort of place you want to wander around on your own."

Since we were alone in the lobby, I continued the conversation but kept my voice low. "I thought perhaps she had an inkling as to who killed Philomena and decided to take matters into her own hands."

Tino glanced around. Assured that no one could overhear our conversation, he pressed the elevator button, then continued, "That would have been very foolish and totally out of character for Norma Gene."

"How so?" From what I'd observed of Norma Gene, plus our conversation in the ladies' room, I could certainly see her heading down to Philly to confront Philomena's killer, foolish though such an attempt might be.

"The woman was a lover, not a fighter."

"I didn't realize you knew her that well." When he didn't expound on his statement, I continued, "You have another theory?"

"Sure. She went to Philadelphia to help her foster mother make arrangements for the funeral. She was either the victim of random violence or crossed the path of some homophobic thugs. Given the neighborhood, my money's on the thugs. Especially if she was beaten to death."

I had to admit, Tino's theory made perfect sense. "If she fought her attackers, the police might find DNA evidence that will lead to their capture."

"Certainly a possibility if the guy is in the system. If not, it's a dead end." When I raised an eyebrow, he added, "No pun intended."

"What's the likelihood of a thug not being in the system?"

Tino laughed. "Good point."

"Same for Philomena," I continued as the elevator doors opened and we stepped inside. "Maybe the detectives are waiting for the DNA results to come back before they make an arrest. Even if the killer isn't in the system, with DNA evidence they'd know if the same person killed both of them."

Tino stabbed at the button for the third floor. "You should be a detective, Mrs. Pollack."

"Your boss already thinks I am."

He grunted. "Yeah, I know. So where are you on figuring out who killed Philomena?"

I sighed. "Absolutely nowhere as you well know. I'm totally stumped. Nothing makes sense, starting with why her body was dumped at Trimedia. Someone was making a statement, but what was it?"

"The most logical answer would be to frame someone at Trimedia," said Tino.

"But that's totally illogical."

"Why?"

"People who commit murder want to get away with the crime,

not lead the police to their doorstep. If the killer were someone connected to Trimedia, as Mr. Gruenwald believes, the last thing he'd do is transport the body here. Don't you think he'd make it disappear? Dump it in the river or a landfill or bury it in the woods? Isn't that what you'd do?"

Tino raised his hands as if warding off an accusation. "Hey, I didn't kill her!"

"Of course not. I'm not suggesting you did, but think about it. If you were a killer, what would you do with the body?"

Tino grew thoughtful. "I see your point. So you're convinced the killer wasn't connected to Trimedia?"

"Except that doesn't explain the disappearing security cameras. The killer had enough knowledge of the building to know to remove the cameras before bringing the body through the loading dock doors. Not to mention having access to those doors."

"So the killer is either a Trimedia employee, or he isn't. That certainly helps narrow down suspects."

The elevator doors slid open, and we stepped out onto the third floor. "Exactly. And now you know why I'm essentially stumped." And that's when it hit me. I stopped so abruptly Tino's massive chest collided with my back.

I wobbled on my heels, losing my balance. Tino grabbed my arm just in time to yank me upright and keep me from landing face first onto the Terrazzo floor. "Hey! Sorry. You shouldn't stop short like that."

But I hardly acknowledged his save. My mind whirled. Essentially. Essential. *Bear Essentials.*

"You okay?" he asked.

I waved away his concern and continued to roll the thought around in my mind.

"Earth to Mrs. P.!" Tino waved his hand in front of my face. "What's going on?"

I had ruled out any *Bling!* employees as Philomena's killer. Her death meant they all lost their jobs. But what about a disgruntled *former* employee? Someone who lost his job when Gruenwald folded one magazine to make room for another.

There are millions of teddy bear collectors all over the world and only a handful of publications devoted to them. How could *Bear Essentials* not turn a profit, the reason corporate gave for shutting them down?

"I need to speak with Marie," I said and raced down the hall toward my cubicle.

Unfortunately, Marie's voicemail greeted me on the other end of the phone line. I left a message, asking her to call me back as soon as possible.

"So what's your brainstorm?" asked Tino after I hung up the phone.

"Perhaps nothing but let's wait until I talk with Marie. You're welcome to join me."

"Fair enough. You want some coffee?"

"Love some." Tino headed for the break room. I booted up my computer and found a memo from corporate. Trimedia planned to host a memorial tribute to Philomena at Madison Square Garden Saturday. The event would be recorded and broadcast at a later date. All Trimedia employees were expected to attend.

"Did you see this memo?" I called across the hall to Cloris.

"Leave it to Trimedia to make a buck off Philomena's death," she answered. "I wonder how much they're charging for tickets."

"Easy to find out," I said, "but whatever the price of tickets, the real money is in the advertising. You can bet all of Philomena's sponsors will be shelling out big bucks for those commercial slots. One final time to capitalize on her celebrity."

I heard the clickety-clack of computer keys, followed by a long whistle. "Holy guacamole! Tickets range from seventy-five dollars for the nosebleed section up to a thousand dollars for prime locations."

"And that's before the scalpers snap them all up."

"Good thing we don't have to pay for our tickets."

"If you want to bring a guest, you can have mine," I offered.

A moment later she was standing beside me, hands on hips. "Two questions: One—how do you plan on getting out of going? And Two—can I come with you?"

"Ask Mama. She's scheduled her latest trip down the altar for Sunday. I've got the rehearsal and rehearsal dinner Saturday night."

"That was quick. How long has she known this latest guy?"

"Less than three months."

"Think it will last?"

"With Mama's track record?"

Cloris shook her head and sighed. "Poor guy." Then she added, "The concert is at two with the private Trimedia memorial service scheduled for eleven. What time is the rehearsal?"

"Five."

"Plenty of time to put in an appearance. No one will notice if you sneak out early, but Gruenwald will notice if you don't show up for the gathering ahead of the concert. He'll expect you there."

"Why?"

"Checking out suspects, Sherlock. Don't the cops always show up at the funerals of murder victims?"

"Damn, I hate when you're right."

A few minutes later Cloris headed off for a meeting in the city. While I waited for Marie to call back, I turned my attention to the March issue where I was tasked with combining leprechauns and Easter bunnies. Craft-wise St. Patrick's Day and Easter were two of my least favorite holidays. Coming up with ideas that didn't scream *kitsch* and look like they came from the dollar store stretched even my creative brain cells.

None of the other editors faced this problem. Both holidays featured traditional foods for Cloris to tap into. Jeanie would cover spring cleaning. Janice planned an article on dealing with spring allergies. Sheila's column would cover tax tips, Serena would concentrate on planning summer getaways, and the duo of fashion and beauty would deal with spring trends.

I alone struggled with the March issue and dragged my feet to the point that I had no suggestions to offer at yesterday's planning meeting. I needed a proposal on Naomi's desk before leaving the office today.

However, instead of shamrocks and pastel colored eggs, all I could think about were teddy bears. "Why fight it?" I muttered.

"Fight what?" asked Tino, returning with coffee minus any Cloris confections.

I frowned as he handed me a cup. "No muffins?"

"All gone. Fight what?"

"Teddy bears. Soon to be teddy bear leprechauns and teddy bear Easter bunnies."

"You have an interesting job, Mrs. P."

"So that's why you keep hanging around?"

He studied me over the rim of his cup as he sipped his coffee. "It's my job."

And a cushy one at that. But I kept my tongue firmly planted behind my sealed lips. Instead, I grabbed a sheet of paper and a Sharpie and began sketching out my idea.

I could fill my additional editorial pages with full-size patterns. Readers loved full-sized patterns. Every time I included patterns that required enlarging, I received nasty-grams. Now, thanks to Naomi's editorial changes, I could include full-size patterns, which in turn meant I wouldn't have to come up with additional craft projects for each issue. I'd design one teddy bear with accessories that would morph the furry little dude from a St. Patty's teddy into an Easter teddy. Genius!

Two hours later Marie Luscy returned my call as I rooted through plastic tubs of fabric in the closet that housed models and my supplies. "I can spare you a few minutes during my coffee break," she said. "That's all. It's unbelievably chaotic up here today."

"Does that mean you won't be able to do any computer searches for me?"

"Definitely not today."

Marie sounded harried. Or nervous. Maybe both. Something was going on, and I doubted I'd find out what by trekking upstairs. I heard too many voices in the background. The hushed quiet of Gruenwald's inner sanctum was anything but hushed at the moment. "Why don't you come down here for coffee?" I suggested.

"Good idea. I need a break from this place. I'll see you in ten."

With Tino close behind, I headed for the break room to brew a fresh pot of coffee and wait for Marie.

The two previous times I'd met Marie Luscy, she'd given off a consummate executive assistant vibe—capable and businesslike, able to handle anything thrown at her without ever a hair out of place. Not this morning. Marie arrived with her blouse untucked and a leg-length run in her left stocking.

She plopped into one of the molded plastic chairs, let loose a huge sigh, then asked, "Got anything stronger than coffee?"

Tino and I both gaped at her. She of all people should know Trimedia's strict policy against alcohol in the workplace. "What's going on?" I finally asked after shutting the break room door.

"Mr. Gruenwald announced this morning that we're moving back into the city. Today."

"Why?" I asked.

"With Philomena gone and *Bling!* folding, he has no reason to be here."

Not that he ever did since Philomena rarely showed up at *Bling!* and when she did, she never stayed long.

"Anyway," continued Marie, "we're vacating the corn field for a view of the greener pastures of Central Park. I've got the entire janitorial staff packing up his office."

She turned to Tino. "Did you know about this? Because I would have appreciated a bit of warning."

"This is the first I'm hearing about it," he said.

"He expects you to load up his car with cartons, then drive him back into Manhattan."

"When?"

"Soon."

"And leave Mrs. P.?"

"Apparently Anastasia's safety comes second to carton and CEO delivery."

"So nice to know where I stand in the pecking order of Trimedia," I said.

"What did you want to discuss?" she asked me.

I told her and Tino about my *Bear Essentials* light bulb moment. "I really don't pay any attention to what goes on at the other magazines. Were there any threats made by members of the laid-off staff? Anyone with a grudge? Because that would explain the killer bringing Philomena's body back here and knowing about the security cameras."

"No more than the usual," she said. "There are always a few angry people making threats after a layoff. People are scared. They've had their paychecks and security yanked out from under them. They lash out, say things they'll never act on."

"Except when some do," said Tino. "Look at all the workplace shootings that have involved former employees."

"Anything's possible," said Marie. "I don't have time today, but if I get a chance tomorrow, I'll email you the personnel files of all those who were laid off." She stood, coffee in hand. "I'd better get back upstairs."

She paused at the door. "For what it's worth, though, I don't think the police are eyeing Mr. Gruenwald as a suspect any longer. You could probably stop investigating."

"What makes you say that?"

"Mr. Gruenwald said the police corroborated his alibi for the night Philomena was killed. They no longer suspect him."

"He could have hired someone to kill her," said Tino.

"Nothing like having your boss's back," I said.

"Hey," he once again held up his hands in that defensive gesture. "I don't think he had anything to do with her murder. I'm just saying that's the way cops think. After all, Mr. G.'s loaded. Rich guys don't get their hands dirty; they hire out their dirty work."

"So why don't the police think Gruenwald hired himself a hit man?" I asked Marie.

"According to Mr. G., they have another suspect who looks good for the murder."

"He told me he was worried they might suspect Mrs. Gruenwald," I said.

"Why would he say that?" asked Tino.

"A woman scorned is a woman capable of doing anything," I said. "She might have hired someone to kill Philomena."

"What about the divorce?" asked Marie. "Why have Philomena killed if she was divorcing Mr. Gruenwald?"

"The divorce filing may have been a ruse to avoid being considered a suspect. Even Mr. Gruenwald suggested the police might think so."

"That's ridiculous," said Tino. "When did he say that?"

"When he asked me to investigate."

Tino turned to Marie. "Did the cops tell Mr. G. anything about this other suspect?"

"He asked, but they refused to say."

"There's another possibility," I said. "They could just be saying he's no longer a person of interest so that he lets his guard down."

"She's right," said Tino. "Cops lie all the time to trip up suspects."

"How do you know that?" asked Marie.

He offered us a sheepish grin. "TV cop shows."

"Which are so accurate when it comes to factual information," I said. "I suppose you also believe medical examiners run around in four-inch designer stilettos and DNA results arrive before the last commercial break."

He added a shrug to go along with his sheepish grin.

"Mr. Gruenwald paid me to find Philomena's killer," I said.

"That's what I'll continue to do unless the cops find him first or Mr. Gruenwald tells me to stop looking."

"That's very honorable of you," said Tino. "Just make sure you don't stick your nose where it doesn't belong."

"Is that a threat?" His eyes had narrowed, and his face took on a menacing hardness that turned the coffee in my stomach to acid.

"Consider it a warning," he said in dead seriousness. "I'm paid to protect you, and I can't be by your side twenty-four/seven. You get yourself killed, I lose my job."

And once again Anastasia Pollack is shown where she stands in the universe. I inhaled a shaky breath. "Nice to know you care, Tino."

"I'm heading upstairs to see what's going on with Mr. G.," said Tino. "Stay out of trouble while I'm gone."

"I'm off to the closet in search of fake fur for Teddy the Lepre-Bunny-Bear. Unless the killer overheard this conversation and is lurking behind a plastic tub of fabric, you have nothing to worry about."

I didn't mention that I'd previously confronted a killer in that same closet. What Tino didn't know couldn't hurt me.

Before heading down the hall, though, another thought occurred to me. I sat back down at my computer and fired off a quick email to Marie.

NINETEEN

Shortly before the end of the day Tino, pushing a hand truck loaded with heavy-duty document storage boxes, appeared at the entrance to my cubicle. "I'll walk you down to your car if you're ready to leave," he said.

I powered down my computer and grabbed my purse. "I didn't realize you were still here. I thought Mr. Gruenwald wanted you to bring him into the city earlier."

"Already did. This is my second trip."

"Why are you playing moving man?"

"Most of the contents of his office are going by truck. This is stuff of a more delicate nature he didn't want to trust to movers."

I supposed that meant the various framed items and expensive awards that had lined the shelves of Gruenwald's ebony bookcases.

I headed down the hall, Tino at my side. "Did Mr. Gruenwald mention anything about the investigation?" I asked once we were alone in the elevator.

"I told him your latest theory. He thought you might be onto something."

"Don't you think the detectives would have looked into former employees who might have a grudge against the company? I'm probably several steps behind them."

"Or you might uncover something they overlooked. You found the embezzlement, didn't you?"

"Which turned out to have nothing to do with the murder," I reminded him.

"Still, no one else in the company realized what was going on until you looked at those files."

I tilted my head to eye him. "You mean until I stuck my nose where it didn't belong?"

Tino blushed. "I didn't mean for that to come out the way it did. I like you, Mrs. P. I don't want to see anything bad happen to you."

"I don't want to see anything bad happen to me, either, Tino. Thanks for caring."

Tino had parked next to my car. I waited while he popped the Lincoln's trunk and carefully began loading the cartons. As he stooped to hoist the last one off the hand truck, something small and sparkly on the trunk lining caught my attention. I reached in, scooped it off the carpet, and slipped it into my skirt pocket before Tino turned around.

"Are you and Tessa dating?" I asked after he slammed the trunk shut.

His brow furrowed in puzzlement. "Who's Tessa?"

"Our fashion editor."

"Why do you ask?"

"She's made a few comments."

"About the two of us going out?"

"No, about having the hots for you."

Tino's face broke out in a wide grin. "Jealous, Mrs. P.?"

"You're a little young for me, Tino."

"Not the cougar type, huh?"

"Definitely not. And I see you're avoiding answering my question. Should I read something into that?"

He shook his head in denial. "Nothing to read. I'm not even sure who she is, but if she's got the hots for me, I hope you'll introduce me to her."

"Deal." I headed for my car. Tino waited until I pulled out of my parking space before he slipped behind the wheel of the Lincoln.

When traffic on Rt. 287 slowed to its usual rush hour dead stop, I reached into my pocket and pulled out the item I'd pilfered from the trunk of the Lincoln. Just as I suspected, it was a small crystal, the same kind used in Vajazzling, the same kind Cloris and I had noticed wedged into the sole of Tino's shoe. I reached for my phone and called Cloris.

"Are you suggesting Tino killed Philomena?" she asked after I filled her in on the events of the day.

Was I? "He's not dating Tessa," I said. "He didn't even know who she is."

"Doesn't mean he's not dating someone else with a sparkly hoo-ha. But even if he were, how would a Vajazzling crystal get into the trunk of the Lincoln?"

"You mean unless it fell off a dead body? It was only one crystal, though, and the interior of the trunk showed no evidence of having recently transported a body. No stains on the carpet. No odors. Besides, wouldn't the police have searched the car if they suspected Gruenwald of killing Philomena?"

"Maybe they don't have enough evidence for a search warrant yet. And Tino could have cleaned up the trunk after he dumped the body."

"I don't know. The trunk didn't look recently cleaned; it just looked like the interior of a typical trunk belonging to someone who doesn't cart around all sorts of kid paraphernalia and groceries."

"Not particularly dirty but not pristine?"

"Exactly. Plus, even if Tino did clean the trunk, the police would still have ways to find evidence you couldn't see with a naked eye."

"If we can believe what we see on cop shows."

"Maybe the crystal was wedged in the plush of Gruenwald's carpet and stuck to one of the cartons Tino transported earlier in the day."

"Sounds like you're trying to convince yourself of something."

"Maybe I am." I didn't want to think of Tino as a killer. Or even a transporter of dead bodies. I'd come to like the guy. "What if Gruenwald killed Philomena and tasked Tino with cleaning up the mess?"

"You think Tino would do that for Gruenwald?"

"Who knows how far his loyalty goes?" Or what he'd be willing to do for the right price. Tino had made that comment about rich people paying others to do their dirty work. Was he referring to his own relationship with Gruenwald?

"But if Gruenwald killed Philomena, why would he pay you to find her killer?"

"Maybe he paid me to keep me from finding her killer."

"I don't follow you."

"What if Tino was assigned not to protect and help me but to keep me from learning the truth? Gruenwald thinks I've got this incredible Sherlocking ability. Hiring me might have been his answer to keeping tabs on me, making sure I didn't go off on my own to ferret out the truth."

"Okay," said Cloris. "Let's assume you're right. Whether Gruenwald killed Philomena or paid Tino to do his dirty work, why would Tino dump the body back at Trimedia?"

"That's the part of this scenario that makes no sense." And the puzzle piece that I hoped proved Tino wasn't involved in Philomena's murder.

"Are you going to talk to Batswin about this?" asked Cloris.

"She's my next call." For one thing, I didn't even know if Philomena had a Vajazzled vagina at the time of her death. The photos in *Bling!* had been taken months before the issue hit the newsstands.

I hung up from Cloris and dialed Detective Batswin, but my call went directly to her voicemail. I left a message, asking her to call me back as soon as possible.

I arrived home to find Zack's Boxster parked in the driveway and the lights on in the apartment above my garage. Instead of heading into the house, I made my way up the steps on the side of the garage and knocked on the apartment door.

When Zack swung the door open, I gasped. "What happened to you?" His left eye sported a huge shiner. "And don't you dare tell me you walked into a door."

"All right, I won't."

"And?"

He stepped aside, and I entered the apartment. "What? You told me not to tell you."

I studied his sheepish grin and knew I'd get nowhere. "You

realize this just adds to my theory about you and one of the alphabet agencies."

He shrugged. "If I told you what really happened, you'd still cling to your conspiracy theory."

Two points for Zack. I gingerly touched the purple flesh under his swollen eye. "Maybe you need to take a refresher course in ducking. Does it hurt."

"Only when I laugh."

"That's not helping."

"It looks a lot worse than it feels." Zack headed over to the fridge and removed a chilled bottle of Sauvignon Blanc.

"Mama is going to have a fit."

"Why? It'll heal."

I grabbed two glasses from the cabinet and placed them on the counter while he uncorked the wine. "Not before Sunday."

"What's Sunday?"

"She expects you to walk her down the aisle." I laid out Mama's plans as he filled our glasses. "You're going to spoil the wedding album," I said.

"Album?" Zack set down the bottle and calculated on his fingers. "This is her sixth marriage, right?" When I nodded, he continued, "And she still plans to have a wedding album?"

"She's got one for each of her other five weddings."

"I'm sure between your artistic talents and my photographic talents, we can Photoshop out the shiner."

"That may pacify her."

"If not, she can always find someone else to give her away. I'm sure Lucille would be more than happy to do the honors."

"Very funny."

~*~

Detective Batswin didn't return my call until the following morning. "You wanted to speak with me yesterday, Mrs. Pollack?" she asked when I answered my cell.

Unfortunately, Tino was taking up most of the available space in my cubicle. I could hardly discuss the purpose of my call when the possible suspect sat two feet away from me. "Yes, thanks for calling me back, Winnie."

"I didn't realize we'd moved on to a first name basis, Mrs. Pollack, but I much prefer Fred to Winnie."

"Of course, you do, Winnie. I called because I'm doing a holiday teddy bear spread for the March issue and was wondering if you had any new fabrics I might feature. Possibly fake fur or a textured plush. Preferably washable."

"I see. I take it you can't talk right now?"

"Yes, an embossed velveteen might work, depending on the color and pattern."

"Are you presently in danger, Mrs. Pollack?"

I chuckled. "Not at all. At Trimedia we're always happy to showcase advertisers' products in our editorial spreads."

"I can be there in ten minutes."

"Thank you. I'd love to come see the new collection."

"You want to drive here? When?"

"A dozen new lines? Sounds like I'll have a tough time deciding."

"Noon?"

"Sounds great, Winnie."

I flipped my phone closed. "I'll be out for a few hours this afternoon," I said to Tino.

"I'll drive you."

"No need. I'm only heading over to a vendor."

"Mr. Gruenwald would want me to take you. What if someone follows you?"

"Who? The same someone who's followed me home each night? Get real, Tino. I'm no threat to the killer. I have no clue who he is."

"I'm getting paid to keep you safe."

I rolled my eyes, wondering how much Tino had been paid for a week of babysitting duty. Probably more than I made in a month, given his bespoke suit, designer running shoes, and Bulgari shades. He'd done nothing other than shadow my every move. And for what? Why?

The more I thought about it, the more suspicious I became of Gruenwald's motive in hiring me to play detective. Was Tino here to keep me safe or to keep an eye on me? The more I puzzled over the aspects of Philomena's death and its aftermath, the more I believed ulterior motives came into play. If only I could figure out what they were....

"If you want to do something useful," I said, "spend the time I'm gone perusing the *Bear Essentials* employee records. Marie emailed them to me a few minutes ago. I'll forward the files to your phone. What's your email address?"

Tino rattled off a G-mail account, then asked, "What am I looking for?"

"Start with anyone who'd been written up for any work-related infraction."

"And then? What am I supposed to do, call to ask if they killed Philomena?"

"Very funny. If this bodyguard gig dries up, you should consider stand-up."

"I wasn't joking," he deadpanned.

"Could have fooled me. I'd suggest something a bit less direct."

"Like?"

I thought for a moment. "Pretend you're an independent researcher doing a study on corporate layoffs. Ask if they've found another job yet, how they're handling being out of work if they haven't. Let them talk. See what they say."

"You want me to record the conversations?"

"That would be illegal, wouldn't it?"

"Not if I ask permission. For research purposes."

"Great idea."

"Except I think you'd do a much better job of it."

"Why is that?"

"You know, the woman's touch. Women are more sympathetic. They'll open up to you more than they will me."

"I don't—" I stopped short. "Damn! This won't work. We can't call people and pretend we're someone else."

"Why not?"

"*Trimedia* will pop up on their Caller ID."

"Not if you use my phone." Tino waved his iPhone at me.

"Won't your name appear on the display?"

"Thanks to a simple software program, my display reads *Semper Fi.*"

"The Marine's motto?"

"Short for *Semper Fidelis.* Always faithful. You can be Semper Fi Research."

"You make the initial calls. I'll do follow-up. We'll appear more legitimate that way." Why, I didn't know, but Tino bought my argument and grudgingly agreed. I still worried that he might follow me when I left Trimedia. The last thing I needed was for him to discover I'd driven to the Morris County police headquarters instead of some fictitious fabric manufacturer's showroom.

Twenty minutes later I saved and closed the open file on my computer, grabbed my purse, and stood. "I'm heading to the ladies' room."

He grunted his acknowledgment, never looking up from his iPhone.

At the entrance to the ladies' room, I glanced over my shoulder to make sure Tino hadn't stepped out into the hall to watch me. When I didn't see him, I continued down the corridor, rounded the corner, and headed for the stairwell.

Less than five minutes later I was on my way to meet Batswin at police headquarters. Throughout the short trip, I couldn't help but keep glancing in the rearview mirror to make sure no black Lincolns tailed me.

TWENTY

Detective Batswin and her colleagues worked out of the Morris County Courthouse, a building reminiscent of colonial times and possibly as old. Every school kid growing up in New Jersey knows the significance of Morristown in the history of our country. Washington really did sleep here—on multiple occasions.

The courthouse facade offered a stark contrast to the high-tech facility housed within its red brick exterior. However, when I arrived, Detective Batswin ushered me into an interview room straight out of a *Law & Order* episode, the only nod to state-of-the-art being the cameras I noted mounted near the ceiling.

She motioned toward one of two metal chairs facing each other across a battered wooden table. I settled into one chair. Dispensing with any social chitchat, she took the seat across from me and asked, "What's on your mind, Mrs. Pollack?"

I weighed my words carefully. From past experience I knew Batswin turned testy if she thought I was accusing her of not doing her job correctly, and the tight set of her mouth suggested a sour mood. "Can I assume you're in the process of investigating former Trimedia employees?"

"Of course. Anyone in particular you think I should focus attention on?"

"Not that I know of but are you aware that Mr. Gruenwald recently folded *Bear Essentials*, one of the company's other magazines, to make room for *Bling!*?"

"We are, and we've been looking into those former employees." She tapped a pen against a legal pad, signaling that I was wasting her time. "Anything more?"

"I suspect Gruenwald fudged the books to get board approval to fold *Bear Essentials*."

Batswin halted the staccato tap-tap of her pen and raised both eyebrows. "Go on."

I outlined why I didn't believe *Bear Essentials* wasn't making a profit. "The numbers don't add up."

I had asked Marie to check circulation figures and ad revenues for the past two years prior to the demise of *Bear Essentials*. All indicators pointed to a healthy annual profit. If the board folded the magazine because they believed it was bleeding red ink, someone had fudged the books.

"You're suggesting Mr. Gruenwald had some ulterior motive for shutting down the magazine?"

"I do. Of course, I'm not privy to the inner workings of the board, but I suspect they wouldn't approve of adding another publication in this shaky economy. Magazine publishing isn't a growth industry. In order to get approval for *Bling!*, Gruenwald had to argue for replacing one of the other magazines." I suppose I should breathe a sigh of relief that he'd chosen *Bear Essentials* and not *American Woman*.

"Still, that probably has nothing to do with Philomena's murder unless the killer was more motivated by a need to get back at Gruenwald. Kill Philomena, and you kill *Bling!*" And maybe that's why her body was dumped at Trimedia rather than in the Hudson.

"But you don't know of anyone in particular who might harbor a grudge against Gruenwald?"

I flipped my palms upward and shrugged. "I don't even know the people who worked at *Bear Essentials*. Each magazine is fairly autonomous. We generally don't interact with each other, especially magazines headquartered on different floors of our building."

Batswin scowled. "So you really don't have much of anything for me, do you, Mrs. Pollack?"

I hesitated. "There is one other thing. It could be nothing, but—"

"Yes?"

"Did Philomena have a Vajazzle?"

Batswin's brows knit together in puzzlement. "A what?"

I provided a quickie summary of the art of Vajazzling. After which, Batswin muttered something under her breath that sounded suspiciously like, "So that's what it's called."

"Then she did?" I asked.

Batswin returned to cop mode. "I'm afraid I can't divulge anything involving an ongoing investigation. Why are you asking?"

Instead of answering her, I asked another question. "Did you ever search Gruenwald's Lincoln?"

"We don't have enough probable cause for a search warrant. Why?"

"I found something. It's probably nothing, but it seemed odd."

"What did you find?"

I reached into my pocket, removed the crystal, and placed it on the table between us. "This is a Vajazzling crystal. I found it in the Lincoln's trunk."

"What were you doing snooping around Gruenwald's car?"

"I wasn't snooping. Tino was transporting cartons from Mr. Gruenwald's office. I just happened to notice the crystal while we were chatting as he loaded cartons into the trunk. It probably came from the office carpet. Apparently, the crystals start falling off after only a few days, but I thought I should bring it to your attention."

Batswin picked up the crystal with her thumb and forefinger and examined it. "I can't get a search warrant based on this. Did you notice anything else about the contents of the trunk that seemed odd?"

"Like what? Suspicious looking stains?"

"Or anything else out of the ordinary."

"That would be too easy, wouldn't it? No, the trunk wasn't particularly dirty, but it didn't look like it had been cleaned recently, either. Sometimes a trunk is just a trunk."

Batswin didn't get the joke. Instead, she rose and extended her hand to indicate the conclusion of our meeting. "Thank you for stopping in Mrs. Pollack. Now, before you wind up getting yourself killed, stop playing Nancy Drew and let the professionals do their jobs."

Nancy Drew? So much for doing my civic duty. I left police headquarters unconvinced Batswin was any closer to solving Philomena's murder.

~*~

Back at Trimedia I found Tino working the phone. "I'll bet you're really pissed at your former employer," he said.

"Subtle," I mouthed to him as I dropped into my desk chair and powered up my computer.

After commiserating with the caller for a few more minutes, Tino hung up the phone. "Guys don't do subtle, Mrs. P. It's not in our DNA. You want to know what's eating them, you gotta ask, then let 'em rant."

"There were guys working at *Bear Essentials*?" Stereotypes aside, I envisioned only female employees working on a magazine devoted to teddy bear collecting.

"Tough economy," said Tino. "A job's a job."

And those in magazine publishing grew scarcer with every passing day. "So did anyone rant enough to land in the suspects column?"

"Everyone who hasn't found another job yet except for one guy."

"Why not him?"

"He plunked down a dollar for a scratch-off the day he got canned and won half a million bucks."

"Lucky him. How many suspects do we have?"

"I starred the most likely candidates," he said, handing me a pad of paper. "Most of the people didn't object to having their conversations recorded, but I also made notes for the important stuff."

I quickly flipped through the pages. On top of each sheet he'd listed a *Bear Essentials* employee's name. Copious notes regarding the employee's time at Trimedia, as well as details of subsequent job searches and results, filled each page.

Inwardly, I breathed a sigh of relief. Anyone this involved in finding a killer couldn't possibly be the killer. That Vajazzling crystal must have hitched a ride on one of the cartons from Gruenwald's office.

I tore off the three pages with stars. Two men, one woman. I pulled up the computer files Marie had emailed. "I think we can eliminate Christina MacIntyre. She's confined to a wheelchair. I can't see her hoisting Philomena's body into the shipping case, let alone removing the security cameras."

"Unless she had help. Read my notes."

I turned to the dossier on Christina MacIntyre and began reading through Tino's scrawled notations. My eyes bugged out as I scanned a litany of invectives and threats, all directed toward Trimedia in general and Gruenwald specifically. "She actually said these things to you?"

"Not her. Her husband. Paul."

I glanced up from the page. "Huh?"

"He's also out of work. Has been for about two years. His unemployment insurance ran out. Bills are overdue. Her unemployment barely covers food each week for them and their three kids."

"So you did a bit of guy bonding over the phone?"

Tino grinned. "It worked, didn't it? I got him to spill his guts. He's mad as hell, and he blames Gruenwald for their situation. I can see him getting even by offing Philomena. Did you get to the part where he's ex-military? Same for the other two with stars."

"Is that how you bonded with them?"

Tino offered me a sheepish grin. "Hey, *Semper Fi*, Mrs. P. Whatever works."

Gruenwald should have hired Tino to solve Philomena's murder. I never would have gotten MacIntyre to drop his guard and open up to me.

"The killer could be one of these other men," I said, waving the pages listing the two male employees. According to Tino's notes, neither of these men had held back in their conversations with him, either. Both had served in the armed forces, one in the army, the other army reserves, giving them the training necessary to rappel down the side of the Trimedia building to remove the security cameras without being captured on them.

Gruenwald certainly knew how to bring out the worst in people, but I suppose the same could be said for any CEO who lays off employees. Still, most people don't act on their threats. If they did, CEO's would be an endangered species in this country.

"How do you want to proceed?" asked Tino.

"We should turn this information over to Detective Batswin."

Tino scowled. "These guys will lawyer right up. They know the score. The cops won't get jack."

"You have a better idea?"

"You should go talk to them."

"Me? I don't do guy bonding. You should meet with them. Take them out for beers and burgers."

"I'm not the one getting paid to investigate the murder," he reminded me. "You are."

"True." Tino was just getting paid to babysit me. Or keep tabs on me. I pondered my options. Christina MacIntyre might talk to me, but if her husband had hatched the plot to get back at Gruenwald, she might not even know about it.

How many killers confess their sins to their spouses? My husband kept me in the dark throughout our marriage. I had no idea of his gambling addiction, let alone that he stole his mother's life savings and set her apartment building ablaze.

I needed Tino to fill these guys' bellies with enough alcohol that one of them lost his inhibitions and admitted his crime. "We'll both go. We can pretend we're scouting for a new reality TV show about long-term unemployment and its impact on families."

"Clever, Mrs. P. And we're looking for families to star in the show?"

"Exactly. Can you reprogram your cell to bring up a different name on the Caller ID?"

"Sure. Why?"

"I'll phone to set up appointments with these three men, but we'll need something other than *Semper Fi* to show up on their phones. We used that for the research calls."

"You think they'll agree to talk to us?"

"Reality TV stars get paid. They're out of work. Do the math, Tino."

"Right. I read where that little redneck Boo Boo kid and her family make fifty G's a season."

"Good to know." My life didn't allow for much television watching these days. I knew little about current reality TV other than it filled both cable and network programming due to low production costs. "A chance to make fifty thousand dollars plus a bottomless pitcher of beer might catch us a killer."

We decided to meet with all three men the following day, spacing each an hour and a half apart. Since none of the men lived near each other, we needed to factor in half an hour to travel between each location. I tasked Tino with finding a bar in the general vicinity of each man's home. Hopefully, they'd drink enough in an hour's time to loosen their tongues sufficiently.

Investigating Philomena's death had already eaten up too

much of my schedule. Deadlines for multiple issues loomed. I had a photo shoot scheduled for Friday morning, not to mention Lepre-Bunny-Bears to design and craft, and none of these tasks could be palmed off on my overworked, shared assistant.

Given the memorial concert, wedding rehearsal and dinner on Saturday, and Mama's wedding Sunday, catching up over the weekend wasn't an option. I needed to cram about a week's worth of work into the next two days, but I also needed to follow through with this investigation, or Tino might rat me out to Gruenwald. I might not find Philomena's killer, but I had to justify accepting that five-thousand-dollar check.

While Tino searched Google Maps for suitable bars, I jotted some notes for our fictitious television show. I needed a name and a short overview of the series before we could set our charade in motion. "How's this for a show title?" I asked. "*Out of Work, Out of our Minds.*"

"A little wordy, isn't it?"

"It's a work in progress. We can tell them the network hasn't firmed up the title yet."

"Works for me." He handed me a sheet of paper. "These are the bars."

After Tino reprogrammed his phone, I called the three men. All jumped at the chance to become the next reality TV star. I didn't even have to mention the free beer.

~*~

The following morning Tino showed up in a white Ford Focus decked out with a logo for UsTV, a cable network Trimedia had recently purchased—so recently that none of the three men we were about to meet would even know of the acquisition.

I ran my hand over the image. Paint. No slapped on decal.

"Very impressive."

He settled a white UsTV ball cap on my head and handed me a lightweight matching UsTV windbreaker, twins to the ones he wore. "We need to look legit and easy to spot," he said.

We'd be hard to miss. The red and blue UsTV logo covered most of the back of the jacket as well as the upper left quadrant of the front. I slipped the jacket over the blazer I'd pulled from the back of my closet this morning. For the first time since the autumnal equinox two weeks ago, AccuWeather promised fall-like temperatures throughout the day.

I turned my attention back to the car. "Please don't tell me you stole wheels for us."

Tino opened the passenger door for me. "Consider it a perk of working for the CEO. He wants Philomena's killer caught, and he's losing patience with the police."

He slammed the door shut, rounded the car, and with a grunt squeezed his massive physique behind the wheel. Poor Tino wasn't built for a compact car, but apparently the Focus was standard issue for UsTV employees. I wondered if he'd fit after eating three lunches.

"Where to first?" he asked.

I rattled off the address of a bar in Morristown. He programmed the GPS, switched on the ignition, and we headed off to meet Suspect Number One.

I scheduled our first meeting for eleven o'clock, a bit early for lunch, but Suspect Number One didn't seem to mind. The lure of becoming a television star was so great that these guys probably would have agreed to meet at two in the morning in the parking lot of the local Wal-Mart. In their birthday suits.

O'Malley's Irish Pub was a typical working-class bar, short on ambiance, the air thick with the dizzying smells of malt liquor and frying oil. Not the place to order a salad, the only green on the menu most likely the green beer served solely on Saint Patrick's Day.

I was surprised to find the place nearly half full at such an early hour. The other customers turned to take note of the newcomers when we walked through the door but quickly returned to their food, drinks, and the sports network blaring from a flat screen TV above the bar. Tino and I made our way to a booth by the window.

A waitress who looked like she still belonged in school brought us menus, her gaze lingering on Tino as she blindly set paper placemats and napkin-wrapped utensils in front of us. He graced her with a broad smile when she handed him a menu. "We're waiting for one more," he said. "You can start off by bringing us a pitcher of Sam Adams and three glasses."

"Sure thing, doll." She added another place setting and menu to the table on my side, returning shortly with the beer and three frosted mugs.

"I hate beer," I told Tino as he filled the mug in front of me.

"Too bad. Pretend you like it."

A few minutes later a beefy man with micro-dreads and a scraggly blond goatee entered the bar. His jeans, jeans jacket, and the hint of T-shirt peaking from behind the open jacket qualified as Salvation Army rejects. I pegged him as mid-thirties. He scanned the room, zeroed in on us, and headed over. As he approached, I took note of the barbed wire tattoo that encircled his neck.

"Mike Monahan," he said, extending his hand in my direction, a hand covered in scrapes and scratches, the perfect complement to his bruised knuckles, split lip, and fading black eye.

Had we found Philomena's killer?

TWENTY-ONE

Although I paid little attention to the other Trimedia publications, I had no idea whether or not any of these men might recognize me or my name. For that reason, I'd pulled my hair up into a ponytail, donned a pair of large-frame sunglasses, and borrowed the name of one of my favorite authors from back when I had time to read. "Emma Carlyle," I said, shaking Mike Monahan's hand. "And this is Tino Martinelli, my co-producer."

We didn't have to worry about Tino being recognized. He'd started hanging around our building after Gruenwald closed the coffin on *Bear Essentials*.

The men shook hands. Tino squeezed a bit too hard, and Mike grimaced. "Sorry about that. Did you at least win?" Tino asked, grabbing the beer pitcher to fill the remaining frosted mug for Mike.

Mike settled into the booth beside me. "Win what?" With his left hand he raised the mug to his lips and polished off the beer in one long draught.

The guy might be former military, but he didn't come across as the sharpest needle in the pin cushion. With one hand Tino motioned toward the black eye while his other hand refilled Mike's mug. "The fight."

"No fight," he said. His face contorted into a scowl. "Took a header off the roof. We've got a leak, and I can't afford to hire someone to lay new shingles. Lost my footing. Luckily, we live in a rancher—at least until the bank forecloses and we wind up on the street—so it wasn't that far a fall."

"Good thing you didn't break any bones," I said, not believing a word of his story.

Mike's injuries weren't the kind he'd sustain from a fall off a roof. Black eye plus fat lip plus raw knuckles equaled fist fight. Or beating to death a woman who had fought back before she lost the battle. I chanced a quick glance across the table at Tino. His eyes told me he wasn't buying Mike's tale, either.

The waitress returned, and we placed our orders, a steak burger with a large order of cheese fries for Mike, a meatball Parm sub for Tino, and a turkey on rye for me.

After the waitress left, Mike downed half the beer in his mug, then said, "So about this reality show. I sure could use the job, what with one kid and another on the way."

"We're in the early stages of development," I said. "Let's start with you telling us about your former job. You worked for a magazine, right?"

"*Bear Essentials.*" He gulped down the remainder of the beer, then wiped his mouth on the sleeve of his well-worn denim jacket.

"Really?" I feigned surprise. "I used to subscribe to that magazine. I collect teddy bears."

Mike snorted. "When they hired me, I thought I'd be working

on a girlie magazine, not a rag about stuffed animals."

"Yeah, I can see where you'd make that mistake," said Tino. "What did you do there?"

"Circulation. When they folded, I figured I'd just get transferred to one of the other publications. The parent company owns dozens, and circulation is circulation. Doesn't matter, you know? But they canned all of us. Bastards." He grabbed the pitcher and poured himself a third beer. Tino motioned the waitress for another pitcher.

"Which company?" I asked.

"Trimedia."

"Really? Wasn't one of their employees murdered recently?" I asked.

"Some ex-rapper skank Gruenwald was banging."

"Gruenwald?" asked Tino.

"The CEO." Mike sneered. "I heard he gave her a magazine to run and settled her into our office space. Now he's got no hot pussy and no goldmine. Karma. Gotta love it, right?"

"Goldmine?" asked Tino.

"*Bear Essentials*. That rag pulled in huge advertising revenues. Our circulation topped two hundred thousand last year."

"And that's good?" I asked.

"In this economy? It's fabulous."

"So the CEO folded a successful magazine just to have space for his girlfriend?" I asked.

"Can you believe it? Why not fold one of the loser publications?"

"If he planned to start another magazine," I said, "why not keep the *Bear Essentials* staff?"

"The bitch probably wanted to bring in her own people," said

Mike.

The waitress arrived with our meals. After she left, Mike took a huge bite out of his burger and talked around the mouthful, "Seems to me, whoever killed the skank should've killed Gruenwald instead. Now that would've been justice."

We let Mike rant for the remainder of the hour, but the more he drank, the less intelligible information he provided. Tino had set the alarm on his phone to go off at noon. When it did, he signaled the waitress for the check.

"We need to head out to another appointment," I told Mike.

"What about the gig?" he asked. "Do I get it? I can convince my wife to give birth on live TV if it helps. Great for ratings, right?"

I stood to leave. Tino headed over to the bar to settle the tab. "As I said, we're first doing preliminary interviews. We'll be in touch."

He grabbed my hand with both of his. "I'll do whatever you need me to do. Hell, I'll even fall off a roof. I've got experience."

I raised my eyebrows as I extricated my hands and took a step away from the table.

"I'm no fool," he continued. "I know these shows are scripted." Then he pointed to my half-eaten turkey sandwich and barely touched beer. "You gonna finish that?"

"Help yourself."

~*~

"Gut feeling?" Tino asked after we'd settled into the car and headed off to our next bar.

"I hope he isn't going to get behind the wheel of a car any time soon. I've never seen anyone drink so many beers in such a short amount of time."

"He won't." I turned to question him, but before I could say anything, he continued, "I slipped the bartender a twenty to grab Monahan's keys and call his wife to pick him up."

"That makes me feel better."

"Even if he's our killer?"

"I don't think he is, even though I highly doubt he fell off his roof."

"Aside from that," said Tino, "his injuries are too fresh. They didn't come from killing Philomena. Maybe we'll have better luck with the next guy."

~*~

Twenty minutes later we pulled into the parking lot of an Applebee's on Route 10 in East Hanover. Our next interview subject immediately zeroed in on our matching UsTV ball caps and approach as soon as we entered the lobby. He was a stocky man in his forties of average height with a dark complexion, close-cropped midnight black hair and a matching well-trimmed beard. Unlike Mike Monahan's sartorial homage to grunge, he'd dressed in a charcoal gray pinstripe suit with a double-breasted jacket. He reeked of tobacco.

"Borz Kazbek," he said in a thick Eastern European accent, extending his hand toward Tino.

"Tino Martinelli." He nodded in my direction. "And this is my associate Emma Carlyle."

Borz Kazbek didn't offer me his hand, let alone acknowledge my presence beyond stating, "You brought your girl with you?"

This guy needed to be put in his place, and I was just the girl to do it. "I'm not his *girl*, Mr. Kazbek; I'm the senior producer. Tino is *my* assistant." *Take that, you smelly misogynistic cretin!*

If I thought I'd receive an apology, I thought wrong. The guy quirked his mouth in disdain and said nothing. As the hostess led us to a table, Tino grabbed my arm to hold me back and whispered in my ear, "We might get more out of this guy if you let me do the talking."

I nodded, knowing instinctively Kazbek would never open up to me. I was in for some major tongue biting.

As soon as we were seated and handed menus, a waiter appeared. "Can I start you off with drinks? We have a special on our house margarita today."

"Sounds perfect," I said. Anything to help take the edge off what promised to be a very long hour.

"Want to split a pitcher of beer?" Tino asked Kazbek.

"I do not drink alcoholic beverages." Disdain dripped from his words.

So much for loosening the guy's tongue with booze but I suppose we shouldn't have been surprised. When I called to set up the appointment and suggested the bar Tino had picked out, Kazbek countered with the Applebee's down the street.

"Water for me," he told the waiter.

"I'll have a Corona," said Tino.

While we waited for our beverages, Tino began to engage Kazbek in conversation. "As you know, we're interested in doing a reality show that follows a group of out-of-work men on their search to find new employment."

"I will be on your show. Your country has a negative image of my people. They need to learn the truth about us."

"We're in the process of interviewing possible candidates," said Tino. "We'll make our final casting decisions once all the interviews are completed."

Kazbek folded his arms across his chest. "You will need an

ethnic balance to avoid boycotts of your sponsors."

Was that a threat? Good thing we fabricated the show. I glared at him, but he refused to make eye contact with me. To this guy I didn't exist. Only he and Tino shared the table.

"Of course," said Tino, doing his best to suck up. "Why not tell us a bit about yourself. What type of work did you do before you were laid off?"

"I presided over an international magazine with a staff of seventy-five."

Luckily, our drinks hadn't yet arrived, otherwise I might have snorted margarita out my nose. Not only did we already know Borz Kazbek was the production manager at *Bear Essentials*, we also knew the entire former staff consisted of eleven people. No Trimedia magazine had a staff of seventy-five. This guy was full of crap.

"What happened?" asked Tino.

"What do you mean?"

"Why are you out of work?"

"The CEO gave my job to his whore."

Not quite the truth but Borz Kazbek definitely had serious issues with women. I certainly could see him beating Philomena to a pulp to revenge the slight to his honor and manhood. Dumping her body back at Trimedia would also make a statement, but my gut told me, as with Mike Monahan, Borz Kazbek wouldn't have stopped with Philomena. He would also have gone after Gruenwald.

I never thought of myself as biased; I try hard to like everyone with the possible exception of Mafia loan sharks, my dead louse of a spouse, and his curmudgeon mother. However, I was having a hard time controlling my urge to stereotype Borz Kazbek and an even harder time stifling the urge to swing my leg under the table and make hard contact with his shin. And that was before he started spouting his philosophy on women.

"In my country women do not take a man's job," he said. "Women know their place."

"Barefoot, pregnant, and in the kitchen?" I asked.

He made eye contact with me for the first time. "Precisely."

"That's too bad," I said, "because in my country—this country—women can do anything they want, and this woman is making the casting decisions for our new show." I stood and tossed my napkin on the table. "Let's go, Tino. I've heard enough."

Once out in the parking lot, Tino said, "We might have gotten something out of him if you hadn't lost your temper."

"All we were going to get out of that jerk were outrageous lies. He may be our killer, though. He definitely hates women in general and Philomena specifically."

Tino beeped the car locks open and ever the gentleman, held the door for me. "Which is why we should have stayed."

"Waste of time." I settled into my seat, grabbed the seatbelt, and stretched it across my body.

"Which we now have too much of before our next appointment," he said. With that, he slammed the car door.

When he'd rounded the Focus and wedged himself behind the wheel, I asked, "Was that guy really in the U.S. army? He's not American."

"Reserves. And you don't have to be a citizen to enlist, although he might be one. His family moved here from Chechnya in his late teens."

"I suppose that explains his attitude toward women." By the time he'd arrived on American soil, Borz Kazbek's old-world misogynistic philosophy was set in concrete. "I pity his wife. He probably beats her if she burns his morning toast."

"Could be."

"He might be our killer," I repeated.

"Want to go back to ask him?"

"I'll wait in the car. You can have the honors."

"I'll pass."

"Wuss."

Tino and I stared each other down for a moment before he broke the silence with a deep chuckle and shook his head. "You definitely need that margarita before we meet our last suspect, Mrs. P." He started the engine and pulled out of the parking lot.

Tino drove east on Rt. 10 to pick up Rt. 280, which took us to the Garden State Parkway. We then headed south into Union Township, a once middleclass town that had turned working class over the past few decades.

Our appointment with Christina MacIntyre's husband Paul was scheduled for two o'clock. We arrived at the Five Points Tavern on Chestnut Street half an hour early, surprised to find Paul MacIntyre already waiting for us. Given his inebriated state, he'd bellied his massive beer belly up to the bar some time ago. His bloodshot eyes squinted to focus on us the moment we walked through the door.

Apparently sober enough to recognize the logos on our jackets and caps, he waved us over. "Paul MacIntyre," he said. He didn't offer his hand in greeting. Instead, it remained firmly gripped around a glass half-filled with brown liquid. He raised the glass to his lips, drained the contents, and slammed the glass down on the bar. Then he stumbled off the bar stool and lumbered his way to the one vacant table in the room. Tino and I followed.

"You see this guy rappelling down Trimedia's roof?" I whispered to Tino. Paul MacIntyre weighed so much, while seated at the bar, his butt cheeks had spilled over the sides of the bar stool.

"Looks like he packed on a few pounds since his Marine days," he whispered back.

Borz Kazbek looked better and better as prime suspect material. The guy had both the motive and the physique, plus the arrogance to believe he'd get away with murder. I wondered if Batswin had questioned him yet. I'd love to be a spider under the table during that interview.

Once seated, Tino waved over a waitress and ordered a margarita for me and a pitcher of beer for himself and our final suspect, not that MacIntyre, reeking of whiskey, needed any more alcohol. He also told the waitress to bring a platter of nachos for the table even though we'd both already eaten lunch.

As soon as she left with the order, MacIntyre plunged into beg-mode. "I don't care what I have to do on your show; I'll sweep floors. I need a job, any job."

Even though we'd scratched MacIntyre off our list of probably suspects, Tino and I had to maintain our ruse. I parroted my spiel about the early stages of the process and conducting preliminary interviews, ending with, "Why not tell us about your situation?"

He immediately launched into a summary of the trials and tribulations that comprised his life, beginning with a one-car accident that had permanently landed his wife in a wheelchair two years ago and cost him his career.

"What caused the accident?" I asked, suspecting I already knew the answer.

He didn't disappoint. "The cops said I was drunk, but I wasn't. I'd only had four beers that night. They used a faulty

Breathalyzer."

I wondered how often the police heard that excuse.

"We skidded on a patch of black ice," he continued. "The car swerved off the road and slammed into a tree. Christina suffered permanent nerve damage to her legs. I walked away without a scratch."

"Man, that's rough," said Tino.

"Tell me about it. She'd just gone back to work after eighteen months of treatment and therapy when that douche bag Gruenwald fired her."

"Fired?" Tino raised his eyebrows and challenged MacIntyre. "I thought you said on the phone that she was laid off when the magazine she worked for folded?"

"Did I? Fired. Laid off." MacIntyre shrugged. "What's the difference? She's out of work, thanks to him." He continued to whine until the waitress returned with our drinks.

"What about you?" I asked after taking a sip of my margarita. "You said the accident cost you your career. Why? You weren't injured."

"I can thank the cops and their damn false police report for that. According to my employer, I violated their code of conduct, and that's grounds for dismissal."

"What type of work did you do?"

MacIntyre mumbled his answer. "I was a drug counselor for the state corrections bureau."

"I see."

He slammed his hand on the table, knocking over the salt and pepper shakers and sloshing the liquid in our glasses. "No you don't. I'm a big guy. I can handle four beers, dammit! I wasn't drunk."

Like he wasn't drunk now. I'm sure, had he lived for me to learn his secrets, Dead Louse of a Spouse would have denied having a gambling problem. Addiction and denial went hand-in-hand.

The waitress brought out the platter of nachos. Even though I had no appetite, I placed a few on my plate to nibble while I drank, not wanting the tequila to go to my head.

Tino and I were wasting our time with this guy, but I continued to let him rant while I sipped my margarita, nibbled on a few nachos, and allowed my mind to wander. From dealing with Mama and Lucille over the years, I'd perfected the fine art of pretense. With frequent nods of my head and the occasional, "I see" or "Uh-huh," I gave the impression of engaging in the conversation while my mind focused elsewhere. As Paul MacIntyre continued to blame everyone else for his own shortcomings and troubles, I contemplated how few variations of Lepra-Bunny-Bears I could get away with making for the March issue.

After another ten minutes, Tino glanced at his watch. "Look at the time. We've got to hustle to make it to our next appointment on time." He signaled the waitress for the bill, then headed to the bar to pay it.

"Sorry to cut this short," I said to MacIntyre when Tino returned to the table. "We'll be in touch once we've made our decisions."

"I meant what I said; I'll do any job you've got."

"I'll keep that in mind, Mr. MacIntyre. Good luck to you and your wife."

"Luck?" He laughed derisively. "If I had luck, I wouldn't be sitting here begging you for a spot on some stupid reality TV show, would I?"

I decided not to answer. Instead, I turned my back on him and headed for the exit, happy to leave Paul MacIntyre to cry alone into his beer, blaming the world for his woes as he continued to add to them.

As we left the tavern, Tino said, "He drank three double bourbons before we arrived. I gave the bartender money to call a cab for him."

"How do you know about the bourbons?"

"The waitress added them to our bill."

"I'll bet he told her to do that before we arrived."

"No doubt."

"I hope Mr. Gruenwald is reimbursing you."

He shrugged. "Don't worry about it."

I wouldn't have let Paul MacIntyre scam me out of three double bourbons, but people who spend twelve hundred dollars on designer sunglasses don't sweat such trivialities.

~*~

Tino dropped me off at Trimedia shortly after three o'clock. I slipped out of my UsTV windbreaker, removed the ball cap, and undid my ponytail before opening the car door. "You're not coming in?" I asked when he remained seated, the engine running.

"Can't. I have to pick up Mr. G. in the city."

"I'll try not to get myself killed," I said.

"You better not. I don't want your death on my hands."

"Wouldn't dream of it, Tino." I waved good-bye and headed upstairs to cram a day's worth of work into a couple of hours.

"Where have you been all day?" asked Cloris when she caught me ducking into my cubicle. "Off catching bad guys?"

I filled her in on my latest theory regarding *Bear Essentials*. "Of the three most likely suspects, I think we can eliminate two of them."

"And the third?"

I told her about our meeting with Borz Kazbek.

"Aside from being a woman-hating creep, why do you think he's the killer?" she asked.

"Process of elimination." I pulled out my sewing machine from where I stored it under the counter and hoisted it onto a cleared workspace. "If not Kazbek, then whom?"

"You've ruled out your hunky shadow? What about the crystal embedded in the sole of his shoe and the one in the trunk of the car?"

"Coincidence. He probably picked up both in Gruenwald's office. If Philomena and Gruenwald were having an afternoon delight, those crystals could be hiding in the carpet, stuck between the couch cushions, anywhere."

Cloris scrunched up her nose. "TMI. Not to mention what it says about the cleaning staff."

"But logical, right?"

"I suppose. Now what?"

"I mention Borz Kazbek to Detective Batswin, just in case he's not on her radar, then get back to my real job." My Lepra-Bunny-Bear deadline couldn't wait for me to solve Philomena's murder.

For the remainder of the workday, I concentrated on the March issue. Pulling muslin from the storage closet and three sizes of bunny and bear patterns from my files, I constructed a prototype of a Lepra-Bunny-Bear family—mama, papa, and baby Lepra-Bunny-Bear. Once satisfied with the results, I called it a day. It wasn't until I stepped out of my cubicle and headed to the elevator, that I realized I'd totally lost track of time. Quiet filled the halls.

TWENTY-TWO

Ever since last winter when I returned to work after hours and discovered a dead body in my cubicle, silence in the workplace has creeped me out. The lack of click-clacking computer keys, chattering coworkers, and tap-tap-tapping of heels along the corridors reminded me a killer still lurked in our midst. At times like this, I wished the overprotective, imposing hulk of Tino Martinelli stood by my side.

The elevator dinged its arrival. I inhaled a deep calming breath as the doors swished open and stepped inside, pushing the button for the ground floor. I took comfort in knowing that even at seven o'clock in the evening, I wouldn't exit the building into total darkness. Although the days steadily grew darker, the end of Daylight Savings Time wouldn't arrive for several weeks yet.

As expected, the parking lot was empty except for my Jetta. I beeped open the door lock and slipped behind the wheel. After locking the door and fastening my seatbelt, I inhaled another deep breath, but instead of exhaling a sigh of relief, I gasped. A folded piece of paper sat trapped under my windshield wiper.

I sat statue-still for a solid minute, a death grip on my steering wheel, as I stared through the glass at the small white square of folded paper. My mind raced with all sorts of scenarios, none of them good.

Had Borz Kazbek followed Tino and me back to Trimedia and figured out we weren't who we said we were? Was the note a threat? There was only one way to find out, but I first needed to screw up the courage to do so. Part of me—a very large cowardly part of me—wanted to convince myself that ignorance was bliss.

A much smaller part of me knew I had no choice but to open the door and reach around to retrieve the note. First, I started the engine. Then I unbuckled my seatbelt and unlocked the door. As fast as I could, I swung open the door, stepped one foot out onto the blacktop, reached over the door, and grabbed the note. Then I slipped back into the car, slammed and locked the door, and sat trembling with the note in my lap.

I tried a few more calming breaths with limited success. My limbs continued to shake, and my heart continued to beat rapidly. So I ratcheted up my courage as high as possible and unfolded the note.

I WON'T BE IGNORED. I WILL HAVE JUSTICE.

Who won't be ignored? Justice for what? The typewritten note made no sense. It contained no clue as to the sender's identity other than the person probably didn't own a computer. Who uses a typewriter anymore—and an old typewriter, at that, from the looks of the uneven ink and broken J?

Philomena's killer was still on the loose, possibly prowling around Trimedia, but if the note had some connection to the murder, that connection escaped me. I hated word puzzles. I'd dealt with too many of them over the last few months. Between the note I discovered in Lou Beaumont's apartment, the ones sent by Erica Milano's stalker, and the puzzle of Lyndella Wegner's journals, I'd had my fill of cryptic messages. Now this one. I needed an Enigma machine. Or a decoder ring.

Too bad there's never a decryption device around when you need one. In lieu of any code-breaking hardware, I placed a call to Detective Batswin, pushed the button to engage the speaker, and placed my cell in the cup holder.

Never one for unnecessary pleasantries, Batswin answered with, "What can I do for you now, Mrs. Pollack?"

I shifted into Drive, released the brake, and exited the Trimedia parking lot. "I thought you should know about a couple of things that have come up," I said.

"Since we met yesterday?"

"Yes. There's a former employee of *Bear Essentials*, Borz Kazbek, who—"

"Who you went to see today."

"How did you know that?"

"When we picked him up for questioning, he mentioned a meeting with a couple of TV producers. Anyone you know, Mrs. Pollack."

"I'm just doing my job, Detective."

"No, you're doing my job."

"Yes, but—"

"There are no *buts*. Keep your nose out of this investigation. I don't need a killer getting off on a technicality because some overly-nosy civilian decided to play Nancy Drew."

"Does that mean you don't want to know about the note I

found stuck on my car windshield?"

"What note? When?"

"A few minutes ago. It says, "*I won't be ignored. I will have justice.*" All caps. Written on an old typewriter."

"What do you think it means?"

"I don't have a clue. You're the detective."

Batswin's annoyance with me came through loud and clear as she let loose an exasperated exhalation. "You haven't pissed anyone off lately, have you?"

"Other than you? No."

After another loud breath of annoyance, she said, "My life was a lot less complicated before our paths crossed, Mrs. Pollack."

"Mine, too, Detective." What I wouldn't give to turn back the clock and not find a dead body glued to my desk chair. "What do you want me to do with the note?"

"Where are you?"

"On my way home."

"Don't handle the paper any more than you already have. I'll pick it up from you tomorrow." She hung up.

My phone rang a moment later. I flipped it open, quickly glanced at the display, then blindly fumbled with the answer and speaker buttons as I kept my eyes on traffic.

"Good. You're alive," said Zack after I'd said hello. "The natives are restless."

"Which natives? Two-legged, four-legged or winged?"

"All of the above."

"Are you counting yourself among the two-legged variety?"

"Absolutely. I miss you. Coming home soon?"

"I'm about half an hour away. I lost track of time at work. What's going on there?"

"The usual. Lucille's minions have overrun your house. The boys and Ralph are camped out in my apartment. Poor Mephisto wanted to escape with them, but Lucille accused me of attempted dog-napping."

Just another normal day at *Casa Pollack*. If it weren't for a killer on the loose, I'd turn the car around and head back to camp out at the office for the night. Gruenwald's couch looked comfortable enough for sleeping. With any luck, it opened up into a bed. "At least Mama isn't there," I said.

"Oh, did I forget to mention Flora? She and Lawrence are holed up in your basement."

"Doing what?"

"I'm not sure. Concocting something for the wedding, I think."

I groaned. The last time Mama helped herself to my crafting supplies, she nearly left permanent scars on her body from an altercation with my glue gun. Tangling with a killer at Trimedia looked better and better. "She hired a wedding planner and decorator. What could she possibly be doing?"

"Beats me. She wouldn't let anyone down the basement to see."

"If you love me, you'll toss them all out of my house before I arrive home."

"Hey, you don't need a lover; you need a miracle worker."

"So find me Annie Sullivan."

"Good to see you still have your sense of humor."

~*~

Zack apparently had no luck conjuring up the ghost of Annie Sullivan. When I arrived home, I found Harriet Kleinhample's rusted-out circa 1960's orange Volkswagen minibus parked in front of my house. Harriet was the designated driver of the

Daughters of the October Revolution. She looked like the late Estelle Getty, sounded like Don Rickles, and hated my guts.

At least I saw no sign of Lawrence's gold Honda Accord, which meant he and Mama had finished their wedding project and gone home.

Mass chaos greeted me the moment I stepped into my kitchen. Dirty pots and pans littered my kitchen table and counters and filled my sink. From the looks of the empty food packages, someone had raided my refrigerator and freezer. I stormed out of the kitchen in search of the guilty parties.

At the entrance to the den I found the thirteen Daughters of the October Revolution crowded around our forty-eight-inch flat-screen television, the last toy Karl had bought himself before dropping dead on that roulette table in Vegas. The credit card bill with the charge arrived a week after his funeral.

A Russian troika blared at a decibel-shattering level from the wall-mounted surround-sound speakers. Dirty dishes and glasses filled my coffee table, both end tables, and the floor. My mother-in-law held court in the middle of the sofa, a less-than-happy Mephisto trapped on her lap.

"What's going on?" I asked.

No one answered me. With these women, it was hard to tell whether they were ignoring me or didn't hear me. I tried again, louder. "Lucille!"

Twelve heads turned to glare at me and whisper-shouted, "Shh!" in unison.

Without averting her gaze from the screen, my mother-in-law said, "Be quiet, Anastasia. Can't you see we're watching something?"

I turned to the television to see what had them so thoroughly engrossed. A documentary on the glory days of Mother Russia? No. The Commie Cabal's collective rapt attention was glued to *Dancing with the Stars*. "You have got to be kidding me!"

"Shut the hell up!" yelled Harriet Kleinhample, loud enough for half of Westfield to hear her.

I marched across the room, grabbed the remote off the end table, and hit the *off* button. All thirteen commies glared at me as they hurled invectives. No one would ever mistake this bunch for sweet little old ladies.

Ignoring the insults, I said, "You can finish watching your show as soon as you clean up the mess you made here and in my kitchen."

With that I spun around and with the remote firmly clenched in my hand, marched out of the den, out of the house, up the stairs and into Zack's apartment. I found Alex and Nick doing their homework at the kitchen table, Zack sitting on the sofa, reading the newspaper, and Ralph pecking away at a bowl of sunflower seeds.

The boys glanced up from their books, greeted me with, "Hi, Mom," and went back to their homework.

"Did you eat dinner?" I asked them.

"Zack fed us," said Alex.

I hung my head. "I am such a bad mother."

"Yeah, we know," said Nick, "but we love you anyway."

"Thanks. I think." I turned to Zack. "I don't know why you put up with us. I can never repay you for all you do."

Zack planted a kiss on me. "I'll think of something."

"Just wait until we leave," said Alex.

"I'm going to pretend I didn't hear that." Not that Alex and Nick cared that Zack and I had entered into a relationship. My sons started playing matchmaker the moment they met Zack.

I decided to change the subject. "Did you see the mess those women made in my house?" I punctuated my words with a wave of the remote. "And they helped themselves to just about all the food in my freezer!"

"*Who wanteth food, and will not say he wants it, or can conceal his hunger till he famish?*" squawked Ralph. "*Pericles, Prince of Tyre*. Act One, Scene Four."

I glared at the parrot. "No one asked you."

Ralph cocked his head in my direction, flapped his wings, and helped himself to another sunflower seed.

"Why are you holding the TV remote?" asked Zack, removing it from my grip.

When I explained what I'd done, Alex said, "Mom, if they can't figure out how to turn on the TV without the remote, they'll just go into your bedroom to continue watching."

The thought of the entire contingent of thirteen Daughters of the October Revolution sprawled on my bed was more than I could take. I collapsed onto the sofa and groaned. "I didn't think of that."

"Your dinner's warming in the oven," said Zack, bending over to plant another kiss on me. He scooped Ralph into his arms, then turned to the boys, "Let's go, guys."

"Where?" they both asked at once.

"To recapture your home and drive out the Red Menace."

~*~

Zack returned forty minutes later. "What the hell is this?" he asked, waving a piece of paper in front of my face.

TWENTY-THREE

Zack held the paper by one corner, setting it down on the coffee table. "Don't touch it."

I stared at the single typewritten sentence, all in caps, uneven ink, centered on the sheet of white paper: PAY UP OR ELSE.

"Where did you find that?" I asked, panic taking hold of me. Whoever left the note on my car had followed me home. He knew where I lived!

"Taped to your front door. I checked the surveillance cameras."

Zack had installed a state-of-the-art security system in my house and the garage a few months ago. He claimed he needed to protect his expensive camera equipment, especially after Ricardo broke into my house several times, stealing anything not nailed down. I didn't argue with him. After all, at the time a Mafioso threatened me and my family.

"And?" I asked.

"Someone left the note about an hour ago. Tall guy. Over six feet. Dressed all in black and wearing a ski mask."

"What about a car?"

"He didn't park near enough to the house for the cameras to capture one. Does this have anything to do with that murder at Trimedia?"

Did it? I honestly didn't know. I shook my head. "I don't think so, but—"

He headed for the kitchen area of the large room, opened a cabinet, and pulled out a box of plastic Ziploc bags. Removing one, he returned to slip the note inside the bag. "But you can't be sure?"

"No. It doesn't make any sense, though." I told him about the first note. "I called Detective Batswin. She's meeting me tomorrow morning."

"Ricardo didn't escape from prison, did he?"

"Wouldn't someone have notified me?"

"Probably but who knows? Maybe someone was paid off not to notify you. Or he's still in prison and someone on the outside took over his collections."

My husband had died owing fifty thousand dollars to Ricardo Ferrara, a Mafia loan shark who worked for Joey Milano. Both Ricardo and Joey now called a maximum security prison home, but that didn't mean either had given up the life. Many crime bosses continued business as usual from behind penitentiary walls.

Zack headed for his bedroom. A minute later he returned, a gun in his hand. An eye-popping, scary-as-hell, bad-ass gun. The kind of gun used by alphabet guys in the movies and on television. "What are you doing with that?"

"Protecting you and the boys. Until we figure out who sent those notes and why, you're not staying alone in the house."

My hero. But he'd added more fuel to my spy theory. "Why

does a photo-journalist need a Glock or Beretta or whatever that thing is?"

"It's a Sig Sauer, and I need it for protection."

"Against meerkats and monkeys?"

"Against poachers and drug lords."

Did I believe him? I decided not to think about whatever secrets Zack kept from me. Right now, a kick-ass guy, who may or may not be a spy, stood before me, a semi-automatic pistol clenched in his hand, ready to protect me and my sons. He'd get no argument from me. At least not tonight.

Leading the way, his Sig at the ready, Zack escorted me back to the house. We entered into a spotless kitchen. "Who cleaned up?"

"Call it a collaborative effort."

"Yeah, said Alex, strolling into the kitchen. "Grandmother Lucille and her groupies did a half-ass job, and we—" His eyes grew wide as he spied the gun in Zack's hand. "Holy crap!"

Zack tucked the gun into his waistband. "Get your brother."

"What about Lucille?" I asked.

"She went to bed," said Alex.

"Let's keep her in the dark as long as possible," said Zack.

"Works for me." What's one more secret to keep from my mother-in-law?

When Alex returned with Nick, we sat around the kitchen table, and I explain about the threatening notes. I finished by saying, "Until we find out who's sending the notes and why, I don't want either of you alone. Zack will escort you to and from school tomorrow."

"What about you, Mom?" asked Nick.

"Yeah, who's going to protect you?"

"I can take care of myself."

"I'll be taking your mother to work tomorrow," said Zack.

"That's not necessary," I said. "The police in Morristown know about the first note, and I'm going to call the Westfield police now."

"It's absolutely necessary," said Zack in a voice that warned me not to argument with him.

I didn't.

~*~

Half an hour later, Officers Harley and Fogarty, my two favorite Westfield cops, showed up. "We checked. Ricardo Ferrara is still locked away. Joey Milano, too," said Harley.

"They could have someone working on the outside for them, though," said Fogarty. "We'll keep an eye on you and the boys until we clear this up." He held up the bagged note. "Maybe someone got sloppy and left us a fingerprint."

"That's what we're hoping," said Zack.

"What about the other note?" asked Harley. "Still have that one?"

"I was going to give it to Detective Batswin tomorrow morning."

"We'll take both of them," said Harley.

I knew this would piss off Batswin, but she and the Morris County police could fight out jurisdiction issues with the Westfield police. I didn't care who investigated as long as someone caught this creep before he confronted me or my kids.

Even though I took comfort in having Zack snuggled in bed beside me, his weapon within easy reach on the nightstand, I never fell asleep. Neither did he. As I lie awake, holding my breath at every nocturnal sound—a breeze rustling the leaves, a car driving down the street, the rumble of a freight train half a mile away—I sensed him equally alert. I marked time by the grandfather clock announcing the passage of each quarter hour and heard each one from the moment I crawled into bed until the alarm went off hours later.

~*~

The next morning Zack and I dropped the boys off at the high school and waited until they'd safely entered the building before we headed to Trimedia. I didn't worry about leaving Lucille alone in the house. Creepy Note Guy would know I'd be at work today.

"You don't have to stay," I told Zack when we arrived. "I've got my Tino Shadow to protect me." I indicated with a tilt of my head to where Tino stood half-hidden in the shadows of the building at the edge of the parking lot.

"If you don't mind, I want a good look at your Tino Shadow before I hand you off to him." He parked the car and took me by the arm to escort me across the parking lot.

I dug in my heels and spun around to face him. "You don't think Tino—"

Zack stared over my shoulder. "Just making sure."

I pivoted to watch Tino out of the corner of my eye. He stepped from the shadows and headed toward us.

"It's not him," said Zack, now able to get a better look.

I breathed a sigh of relief. Even though circumstantial evidence kept cropping up to indicate otherwise, I desperately wanted Tino to be one of the good guys in my life. "You're positive? You said you couldn't see the features of the guy who left the note."

"No, but I did get a good view of his build as he approached the house and as he walked away. Your friend's about the same height, but the guy at the door didn't have his Conan the Barbarian bulk."

"Everything okay, Mrs. P.?" asked Tino as he quickly covered the remaining distance between us.

"Yes, thank you. This is Zack Barnes."

"Her boyfriend," said Zack, offering his hand to Tino.

The two men clasped hands as their latent caveman Y chromosomes performed the time-honored ritual of sizing up each other's testosterone levels. No matter how advanced a society we become, some things will probably never change.

I cleared my throat to break up the stare-off. "If you gentlemen want to continue your male bonding, go right ahead. I have work to do."

Zack dropped Tino's hand and kissed me good-bye. Then he turned to Tino and added, "I'm holding you responsible if anything happens to her."

"She's my top priority," he told Zack. Then, as we walked toward the Trimedia entrance, Tino asked me, "Something I should know about?"

"I received two threatening notes yesterday. One was on my car when I left work, the other taped to my front door last night."

"You think they're from the killer?"

"I don't know. The messages were very cryptic." I told Tino what both notes said. I also told him about how Detective Batswin knew we'd spoken with Borz Kazbek. "And she wasn't happy. She's going to be even less happy when she shows up for that first note this morning, and I don't have it."

"What did you do with it?"

"I handed it over to the Westfield police, along with the second note."

"I didn't notice anyone suspicious tailing us, but I suppose Kazbek could have followed us back here yesterday, then followed you home." Tino mulled things over as we waited for the elevator, then said. "Doesn't make sense. Those notes sound more like blackmail threats. A killer would leave notes saying 'Back off if you know what's good for you.' or 'Keep your nose out of things.'"

"I agree."

The elevator arrived, and we stepped inside. Tino pushed the floor button. "You have any enemies I should know about, Mrs. P.? Anyone trying to shake you down?"

"You mean aside from the Mafia loan shark and the head of one of the Five Families I helped put behind bars?"

"Not funny, Mrs. P."

I craned my neck to look Tino straight in the eyes. "I'm not joking."

"Holy shit! Why didn't you tell me?"

"I thought you knew."

"How?"

"From Gruenwald."

He shook his head. "I know about your involvement in the murder here last winter and the one at the TV studio in the spring, but he never mentioned a word about any Mafia connection."

As we stepped out of the elevator and walked to my cubicle, I quickly filled Tino in on Ricardo and the possibility that he'd handed over the collection of Karl's debt to one of his cronies.

"I don't buy it," said Tino. "The Mafia ain't that subtle. If someone had taken over this Ricardo dude's accounts, he'd be in your face demanding payment, not leaving you anonymous notes."

"You know a lot about organized crime?"

"Enough."

"You're full of surprises, Tino."

"So are you, Mrs. P."

The more I thought about Tino's theory, the more it made sense to me. Nothing in my dealings with Ricardo indicated that he or his associates would resort to leaving cryptic notes. These guys got their points across by breaking kneecaps, not hammering out their thoughts on an old typewriter.

Once we arrived at my cubicle, I gathered up the projects and props for my photo shoot and headed back downstairs to our in-house photo studio, located on the first floor around the corner from the lobby. Tino didn't leave my side.

Since photography for most of my editorial spreads didn't involve live models, my sessions never took very long. Today we were photographing projects for the January issue, which would hit newsstands December first and be replaced by the February issue on January first. Magazine publishing doesn't conform to the calendar like the rest of the world. Upon completion of photography, our production staff would digitally insert the craft projects into wintry settings.

Tino stood off to the side, watching the proceedings. Because budget cuts last year had eliminated our in-house stylist, I acted as the photographer's assistant, arranging each project with various props. He first took a series of group shots, then the step-by-steps and individual photos of each project from multiple angles. We finished in less than an hour. I gathered up the crafts and props, and Tino and I left the studio.

As we headed toward the elevator, we heard shouting coming from the direction of the lobby. We rounded the corner and found a woman who reminded me of the Wicked Witch of the West, minus the green complexion, arguing with the receptionist.

"What's going on here?" asked Tino.

The woman turned toward us. Her eyes narrowed, the sharp

planes of her face grew more pronounced, and her leathery complexion reddened as she pointed a bony index finger at me, and yelled, "That's her, Henry!"

The man by her side spun around and rushed toward me, his arm extended. Tino stepped between us, grabbed the guy's arm, twisted it behind his back and pinned him to the wall. Although they matched each other in height, the rail-thin man was no match for Tino's body-builder physique.

"Take your hands off my husband!" yelled the woman. She rushed at Tino and started pounding his back with her fists and kicking at his legs. Tino ignored her and kept hold of Henry.

Seconds later Detectives Batswin and Robbins burst through the front door. "Police. Freeze!" they shouted in unison, guns drawn and trained on Tino.

Everyone froze in place.

"What the hell's going on here?" asked Batswin.

The woman pointed her finger at me once more. Seething hatred as she forcefully uttered each word, she said. "She owes me money."

Batswin holstered her gun and turned to me. "Care to fill me in, Mrs. Pollack?"

I shrugged. "I have no idea who she is or what she's talking about."

"I'm Josephine Holmes, and you owe me money for my dentist bill." Josephine raised her leg and stamped down hard on Tino's instep. "I said, take your hands off my husband."

"Sonofabitch," muttered Tino, but he continued to pin Henry against the wall.

Josephine whacked Tino with her purse and said, "I want this man arrested for assaulting my husband."

"If anyone's getting arrested for assault, lady, it's you and your husband," said Tino.

Robbins pulled Josephine away from Tino. "Release him," he said.

Tino spun Henry around and handed him over to Detective Robbins.

"While you're charging them with assault," I said, "you can add harassment, stalking, and extortion." I waved toward Henry and Josephine. "Meet my anonymous note writers."

TWENTY-FOUR

Batswin and Robbins carted Henry and Josephine off to police headquarters. Tino and I followed them to give our statements.

Once we returned to Trimedia, I called Zack to let him know I'd solved the mystery surrounding the threatening notes and that he needn't worry about my safety.

"The moment Josephine mentioned her dental bill, I figured everything out," I told him. "She broke a molar trying to open a bottle of glue with her teeth and claimed I was responsible."

"That makes no sense," said Zack.

"She was making one of the craft projects from our magazine."

"And the directions said to open the bottle with your teeth?"

"Of course not."

"Then how are you responsible for her own stupidity?"

"I'm not, but these nuisance complaints happen all the time."

"Are you really going to press charges against some misguided elderly woman?"

"I already have."

"Seems kind of harsh, doesn't it?"

"You won't think so when you hear the rest of the story." At first I had planned to file charges, then drop them. Maybe Josephine and Henry lived on a small fixed income and couldn't afford the cost of the dental repair work. "I only wanted to scare them enough that they never tried to pull another stunt like this on anyone else."

"What changed your mind?" asked Zack.

"Batswin searched her handy-dandy police database and discovered those two have operated as shakedown artists for the past ten years."

Josephine and Henry Holmes ran an extortion ring that included a medical doctor, a physical therapist, and an attorney—all willing to write bogus prescriptions and reports and file nuisance lawsuits for a cut of the take. Over the years they'd collected millions. "She probably never even broke a tooth. Most likely, the dental X-ray belonged to someone else."

Zack laughed.

"What's so funny?"

"You have to admit, it's a rather ingenious way to fund retirement, a real Golden Fleecing."

"If you don't mind spending your golden years in prison."

"But they got away with it for ten years. Who knows how long their scam might have continued if not for making the mistake of trying to shake down Anastasia Pollack?"

Now I laughed. "Hey, the Mafia tried to shake me down and failed. Do you really think I'm going to let a geriatric Bonnie and Clyde get the best of me?"

"Still, it seems odd none of their victims ever pressed charges."

"Probably because they didn't realize they were victims of a scam. Batswin said this type of extortion works so well because most insurance companies are willing to settle out of court rather than risk a David versus Goliath trial where the jury could turn around and award the plaintiffs far more than they asked for in the original lawsuit."

"You were never served with papers, were you?"

"No, but it was only a matter of time after ignoring their initial letter demanding payment." I didn't know if Josephine and Henry had heard from the Trimedia sharks yet. Either way, they may have decided on a little one-on-one intimidation, hoping I'd cave and write a check. Little did they know, they picked on the wrong patsy this time. Had they run a credit report on me, they never would have bothered.

~*~

On the way home from work later that day Zack turned the conversation to another mystery. "Did you ever find out what Flora and Lawrence were cooking up down in your basement yesterday?"

I closed my eyes and groaned. "I forgot all about that. They were gone by the time I came home."

After tangling with the dance-crazed commies last night, I had headed straight for Zack's apartment, never checking out what sort of mess Mama had created in the basement. "Since she didn't burn down the house by leaving my glue gun plugged in, maybe ignorance is bliss."

"You're not curious?"

"I'm too tired for curious." Still, it did seem odd. Not only was Mama craft-challenged, she'd hired a wedding planner and decorator for her latest nuptials. "All the same, I suppose I'd better check out the state of my basement when we arrive home."

~*~

Half an hour later Zack and I stood in the middle of the aftermath of Hurricane Flora. Every storage container of craft supplies had been pulled from the metal shelving units, rifled through, and left open on all available horizontal surfaces. Ribbons, fabric, buttons, sequins, and pompoms lay strewn across my work table. Glitter dusted the floor. An open bottle of decoupage glue with a brush now firmly cemented inside it, sat on a stool next to the table.

I slammed a container of pompoms closed and shoved it back on the shelf. "I'm thinking this qualifies as justifiable matricide. Do you think the jury will buy it?"

"If you have a good lawyer and they have mothers like Flora?" Zack shrugged. "Slam dunk." He pointed to a bare section of the table. "What do you suppose she was making?"

The empty area of the table was rectangular in shape, roughly two-and-a-half by three-and-a-half feet. I headed across the room to where I stored sheets of foam core board. I had recently purchased a package of six sheets. Torn shrink-wrap now lay on the floor beneath a shelf holding five sheets of foam core board.

Mama had some 'splaining to do. I picked up the phone and called her, hitting the speaker button so Zack could hear our conversation.

She answered on the second ring. "Hello, dear."

"Hi, Mama. I see you got crafty yesterday."

"Oh, yes, dear! Lawrence had the most brilliant idea, a collage of both families for the reception, and since I knew how busy you are—"

"You decided to tackle the project yourself?"

"I knew you wouldn't mind."

"No, Mama, I don't mind. What I do mind is that you didn't

bother to clean up after yourselves."

"What are you talking about, Anastasia? Of course we cleaned up."

"Really? It certainly doesn't look that way to me. The basement is a mess."

"Well, don't look at me. That pinko probably messed things up after we left."

"You know Lucille can't navigate the basement stairs."

"She probably had her minions do her dirty work for her."

"Why?"

"To get me in trouble, of course. You know how they are, dear. And speaking of trouble, what happened to Zack's eye?"

I glanced at the shiner that had turned from black and blue to yellow and green. "He walked into a door."

"What am I going to do about the wedding pictures? They'll be ruined. How can he be so clumsy?"

At least one Pollack woman bought into his flimsy excuse. "You can always have the boys walk you down the aisle the way they always do."

"And ruin my plans? No, he'll have to wear pancake makeup."

Zack snorted as I hung up the phone.

"She could be telling the truth about Lucille," I said. "I wouldn't put anything past my mother-in-law and her zealots." Since I hadn't gone down the basement last night, I had no way of knowing if Mama and Lawrence had cleaned up or not. "The Daughters of the October Revolution may have created this mess today, especially since they knew Mama and Lawrence were here working yesterday."

"Your Sherlocking skills need honing, Sweetheart. Take a look at the evidence." He pointed to the bare spot in the middle of the table.

Duh! I smacked my forehead. If Lucille and company had tried to pull a fast one, the craft supplies would cover the entire table, leaving no delineated bare spot. "Told you I was tired."

TWENTY-FIVE

Sleep or clean underwear? I stared down at the overflowing hamper later that night and realized as much as I would have loved to sleep in Saturday, I needed to rise early and tackle a few loads of laundry prior to leaving for the city.

By the time I heard the boys getting up at eight the next morning, folded piles of clean clothes covered my bed, and a mushroom and cheese breakfast frittata, compliments of Zack's culinary prowess, baked in the oven.

"I'll be home in plenty of time for the church rehearsal," I said after giving Alex, Nick, and Zack my schedule for the day.

"That floozy's getting married again?" asked Lucille. She shuffled into the kitchen and flopped into a chair at the table. "No accounting for some people's taste, I suppose."

Too bad we couldn't find a geriatric commie with bad enough taste to sweep Lucille off her feet. Although, with my luck, he'd move in instead of moving her out.

I chose to ignore her as I started serving breakfast and

continued to speak to my sons. "I need you boys showered, dressed, and ready to leave by four-thirty."

"That's going to be cutting things close," said Nick. "We've got an away game today."

"Where?"

"Phillipsburg," said Alex.

I stared at my sons. "Are you serious?" Several counties and an hour's drive separated Westfield from Phillipsburg. "Why on earth is Phillipsburg on your team schedule?"

Nick shrugged. "Beats me."

"They better not," said Alex.

"What if I pick you up after the game?" suggested Zack.

"Coach will have a cow," said Nick. "We'll miss the post-game analysis."

"Mama will have a cow if we're late," I said.

Nick, a born athlete, had a shot at a football scholarship. Only a sophomore, he'd made the varsity team this year as their starting kicker. His coach had an in with college recruiters. When scouts came in search of prospects, we needed Nick to be high on his coach's list. My son's future far outweighed Mama's sixth wedding rehearsal.

"It's not like we don't know what to do," said Alex. "This is Grandma's fourth wedding in twelve years."

"Same church, same minister," said Nick. "I don't even know why she has to have a rehearsal."

"Tradition," I said. "Plus, the minister requires a rehearsal to make sure the ceremony runs smoothly. Do your best, guys. I'll call her later. She'll have to understand."

She didn't.

"You know how important this is to me, Anastasia. I don't see why Nick can't miss the game. They have other players, don't they?"

"That's not the point, Mama."

"The point is my grandsons are putting a football game before their grandmother's wedding. How do you think that makes me feel?"

"It's only the rehearsal, Mama, and I didn't say they wouldn't be there, just that they might be late."

"Which will throw everything off schedule."

"We can adjust. Call the restaurant and push back the dinner reservation by half an hour."

"On a Saturday night? What makes you think they can do that?"

"Try, Mama."

She sighed heavily. "I'm not happy about this, Anastasia. It's a bad omen. You know what terrible luck I have when it comes to husbands. I want this marriage to last."

"We're talking scheduling conflict, not bad juju."

"What's the difference? Something awful will happen now. I just know it."

"Nothing's going to happen, Mama." At least, I hoped not. Given Mama's track record with husbands, the odds were already stacked against her.

~*~

Trimedia had booked the theater at Madison Square Garden for Philomena's private memorial service, with the tribute concert taking place afterwards in the arena. I took the escalator up from Penn Station and made my way toward the theater. In the lobby I found Cloris and Jeanie queued up at the end of a snaking line for the ladies' room.

"If we're lucky," said Cloris, "the service will be over by the time we get to pee."

"I don't see why we all have to give up a Saturday for this," said Jeanie. "I never even met the woman."

"What about the consumer show?" asked Cloris.

"Were any of us introduced? I'd hardly call that a meeting. It was more like a dissing."

"At least we now get comp days for things like this," said Cloris. She nodded in my direction. "Thanks to Anastasia."

Thanks to Naomi, actually. However, our editorial director had sworn me to secrecy last spring concerning her role in negotiating a settlement over my threatened lawsuit against Trimedia. I never planned to sue after another Trimedia employee tried to kill me, but when Cloris suggested to Naomi that I might, Naomi used the threat to leverage a sizeable check for me and better benefits for her entire staff.

Unfortunately, inching our way toward the stalls only took about fifteen minutes, and we made it into the theater with several minutes to spare. Even more unfortunately, we couldn't slip into seats near the back. Each Trimedia holding had a designated section.

"The better to see who doesn't show up," muttered Cloris after an usher handed us programs and led us down the steps to the seats reserved for *American Woman* staff members.

"You think they'll take attendance?" asked Jeanie.

"No need," I said. "Big Brother is probably capturing us all on video as we arrive." I looked around and saw the rest of our editors minus one. "I don't see Tessa."

"Maybe they'll fire her for not showing up," said Jeanie as we filed into the row with the other *American Woman* editors. I took a seat next to Janice with Cloris on my right and Jeanie to her right.

"Be careful what you wish for," said Cloris. "We could wind up with another Marlys."

"Tessa is morphing into Marlys," I said.

"She's surpassed Marlys," said Janice. "Check out the stage."

The three of us turned toward the stage. To the left sat Sue Evens and the entire, soon-to-be-laid-off *Bling!* staff. Gruenwald, his wife, Tessa, and a dozen Trimedia head honchos sat on the opposite side of the stage. "What's she doing up there?" I asked.

"According to the program," said Janice, "she's giving one of the eulogies."

"For a woman she hated?" asked Cloris.

"Maybe Uncle Chessie owed her," I said. "I'm more surprised to see Sylvia Gruenwald up there."

"Looks like she and hubby are back together," said Jeanie. "Why else would she come?"

Why indeed?

"Maybe your hunky bodyguard stud knows something," said Cloris.

Speaking of Tino, I scanned the front of the theater but didn't see him. When the lights began to dim, I was forced to halt my visual search.

"Wake me when it's over," said Janice. She slumped down in her seat and closed her eyes.

The service dragged on forever. One by one members of the Trimedia board and the *Bling!* staff praised Philomena and spoke of the terrible loss of someone so talented, taken from the world too soon.

"A loss to the bottom line," mumbled Cloris. "How many of

them even knew her?"

"Not many. Sue Evens and her staff did all the work. Philomena strutted around the *Bling!* offices like some *prima donna*, looking down her nose at the hoi polloi."

Jeanie laughed. "*Hoi polloi?* I'll bet she didn't even know what the term means."

"Shh," said Cloris. "Tessa's about to speak."

Our jaws dropped as we listened to Tessa, all teary-eyed, speak of her *good friend* and fellow fashionista, how the two of them bonded over a shared common vision of fashion.

"What a load of crap!" said Jeanie.

"She sounds like she's applying for Philomena's job," said Cloris. "Doesn't she know Trimedia's folding the magazine?"

"Apparently not," I said, "but it doesn't matter. Check out the expressions of the board members." Each and every one of them broadcast their displeasure with their narrowed eyes and downturned mouths. Tessa's Uncle Chessie sported the angriest frown of all.

"Looks like Jeanie might get her wish," said Cloris. "Tessa's ploy to take over *Bling!* may have landed her a spot on the unemployment line."

Gruenwald spoke last. By the time he finished, we had less than fifteen minutes to head over to the arena for the tribute concert. "They're not going to feed us?" asked Cloris.

"Apparently not," I said.

"Who holds a memorial service without serving food afterwards?" asked Jeanie.

"I'm starving," said Janice.

"We'll have to grab something at the arena," said Cloris.

"The hell with that," said Jeanie. "I'm not paying ten dollars for an overcooked hot dog."

"What do you suggest?" I asked her.

"We pop into one of the delis on Eighth Avenue and buy some sandwiches. No one will notice if we slip into the arena a little late."

"They won't let us bring outside food into The Garden," said Janice.

Jeanie grinned. "Ladies, we're all wearing coats with pockets. Security only glances into handbags. They won't pat us down."

"Even for a concert to honor a rap star?" I asked. I expected extremely tight security to prevent any of Philomena's homies showing up with weapons.

"They'll use metal detector wands like they do at the ballparks," she said.

Half an hour later we slipped into our seats. While the darkened arena pulsated with laser lights and the deafening beat of rap music, and three dozen scantily clad dancers gyrated on the stage, I wolfed down my half of the corned beef special on rye I shared with Cloris.

There's nothing like a New York deli corned beef special, but they're hard to eat without something to wash them down. We hadn't bought beverages at the deli, knowing they'd be too hard to conceal. "I'm going for a Coke," I told Cloris. "Want something?"

"Same," she said.

I squeezed past the others in our aisle and headed up the stairs to the concession area. The lines snaked back and forth through roped-off areas in front of each stand. I glanced around. At least twenty people stood waiting in each line. Too thirsty to wait, I decided to find a water fountain before buying the sodas.

Knowing water fountains are usually located near restrooms, I checked the overhead signs and began walking, only to find the water fountain out of order when I arrived. Rather than continuing to walk around the stadium, I headed for the stairwell off to the left of the restrooms, figuring the stadium had been designed with the restrooms on each floor situated one above another.

I began to descend the stairs when I stopped short at the sound of angry voices floating up from below me. Maybe they thought no one would hear them because of all the noise coming from the arena, but the acoustics of the stairwell amplified their voices to the point where I heard them as clearly as if they stood before me. And one of those voices sounded very familiar.

"You're crazy if you think I'm going to do that for you," said Tino.

"You've already proven you'll do anything if the price is high enough."

"Not that."

"You'll do it, or I'll go to the police and tell them you killed those two women."

"I didn't kill anyone. You did. I only cleaned up your mess."

The woman laughed. "And who do you think they're going to believe?"

I inched forward to peek over the railing to the landing below and spied Sylvia Gruenwald. Unfortunately, at that moment she glanced up and saw me. "Get her!" she yelled.

Tino turned, and for a split second our eyes met before I spun around and raced back up the stairs.

TWENTY-SIX

Sylvia Gruenwald killed both Philomena and Norma Gene? And Tino disposed of the bodies for her? For money? I processed this information as I raced through the Madison Square Garden concourse. In heels never meant for anything besides walking, I quickly dodged around various sized crowds, unsure whether or not Tino followed close behind me. Even though I risked turning an ankle, I didn't dare slow my pace. After exiting the stairwell, I had turned left. A fifty-fifty chance meant Tino may have turned in the opposite direction, but Lady Luck and I rarely traveled in the same circles.

Rather than running blindly, I needed to figure out my next move. I spotted a ladies' room up ahead and pushed my way through the line at the door, ignoring the snarky comments.

"Sorry. Just need a sink," I said by way of apology. Once inside, I took a few deep breaths and waited for my heart to stop pounding, but abject fear kept it at a rapid beat.

From the very beginning various signs had pointed to Tino,

but all the evidence was circumstantial and easily explained away. At least Tino hadn't killed Philomena and Norma Gene, but he was responsible for a cover-up, and that could send him to prison for an extremely long time. If he caught up with me, what would he do to keep me from spilling his secret?

Did Gruenwald know about Tino's involvement in Philomena's death? Was that why he wanted Tino keeping an eye on me? To protect his wife by steering me in a different direction if I began to snoop? That had been one of my early theories.

But why would Sylvia have Tino dump Philomena's body at Trimedia? To implicate her husband in the murder? Did she decide not to settle for half his wealth when she could have it all while he rotted in prison? Or had she planned to kill Philomena all along and the divorce was merely a ploy to fend off suspicion? Gruenwald himself had suggested that as a possible police theory.

I pulled out my cell to place a call to Detective Batswin, but I couldn't get a signal. "Damn!"

"I can never get cell service in this place," said a woman standing next to me. "You need to head over to one of the exits."

"Thanks."

Before leaving the ladies' room, I cupped a few handfuls of sink water into my mouth. All that running had increased my thirst by parching my throat. I yearned for a large bottle of ice water but didn't dare stop to buy one.

Stepping out of the ladies' room, I scanned the crowd. No Tino. No Sylvia. I made my way toward the nearest exit sign. My best course of action, I decided, would be to head back to Penn Station and hop on a train. I'd call Batswin once the train pulled out of the station.

I ran as fast as I could toward Penn Station, still fearful of looking over my shoulder. No one paid attention to me. Everyone always runs to catch trains and subways in New York.

Once inside the station concourse, I thought about stopping one of the transit police but quickly dismissed the idea. What if the cop brushed off my concerns? Didn't believe me? I'd be safer on a train heading back to New Jersey. I checked the departures board. Any NJ Transit train would do. They all stopped in Newark where I needed to switch to the Raritan Valley Line to continue home. Seeing that a train was currently boarding at Gate Three, I hurried down the steps.

Seconds later I leaped up into a train car and collapsed onto the first available seat. I lowered my head onto my trembling knees and forced air into my lungs while trying to convince my corned beef special on rye to remain in my stomach. I had my doubts the sandwich would cooperate. A sheen of perspiration covered my clammy flesh, and my body tingled but not in a good way. The last thing I needed was to toss my cookies on the train.

Someone dropped into the seat beside me as the train lurched and began to pull out of the station. After a few additional deep breaths, both the nausea and the tingle began to recede. I slowly lifted my head, glanced to my right and found myself staring at Tino's profile. I gasped. So much for my grand plan. I was trapped.

He placed a hand on my arm and spoke softly. "Relax, Mrs. P. I just want to talk."

I glanced around. Only a few other passengers shared the train car with us, and all wore ear buds. Even if I screamed, chances were no one would hear me. "I know what you did," I said.

"Yeah, I figured you heard."

"I've called the police. They know you're after me." Tino had no way of knowing I hadn't called Batswin yet.

"I'm not going to hurt you," he said.

"Under the circumstances, you'll forgive me if I don't believe you."

"You can trust me."

"Really? And why is that?"

He tilted his head and grinned. "Because I like you?"

"Said the spider to the fly."

"The cops already know I'm with you. They can hear us. I'm wearing a wire."

"Prove it."

He unbuttoned several buttons on his shirt and spread the front placket apart to expose a wire taped to his abs. "I turned myself in and cut a deal with the prosecutor."

"To incriminate Sylvia Gruenwald?"

"She killed Philomena and Norma Gene."

"You helped her get away with it. For money. What made you change your mind?"

Tino sighed. "Money never had anything to do with it."

I raised an eyebrow. "That's not what she said."

"She paid me, but I didn't keep the money. I handed it over to the cops."

"What made you get involved?"

"Philomena came to Sylvia's apartment and threatened her. Sylvia has a violent temper, worse than Philomena's. When Philomena got in her face, Sylvia grabbed a vase off the table and smashed it over Philomena's head, knocking her out."

"Tickets!" The conductor entered the opposite end of the car and began walking toward us, collecting tickets as he approached. Tino clammed up. I pulled out my ticket. He pulled out his wallet.

"Where to?" the conductor asked Tino when he arrived at our

seats.

"Newark."

"Ten bucks. There's a five-dollar surcharge for not buying your ticket at the station."

Tino whipped out a ten-dollar bill and handed it to him just as my phone rang. I flipped it open, looked at the display, and groaned. Cloris! "Hi," I said.

"Where the hell are you?"

"On a train heading to Newark."

"What? Are you all right?"

"Yes, but it's a long story, and I haven't heard all of it yet. I'll call you later."

"I guess I'm not getting my Coke?"

"Not today. I owe you."

"I'll hold your coat ransom until you deliver."

My coat? I glanced down at my lap. I was so overheated from running that I didn't realize I'd left my coat on my seat in the arena. Then again, I'd only left my seat to buy sodas. Why would I have taken my coat?

I hung up from Cloris after promising again to call her as soon as possible. Once the conductor exited the car, I picked up the conversation where Tino and I had left off. "Philomena sustained more than a head injury. I saw the body."

"Sylvia panicked, and like I said, she's got a temper. She grabbed one of Mr. G's golf clubs from the closet and...well, you saw the results. When she realized what she'd done, she called me."

"Why would you cover up such a crime for her?"

"She's my mother."

I stared at Tino. "Your mother?"

"She got pregnant as a teenager. Her folks sent her away to

some place for unwed mothers and put the baby up for adoption. She said she'd been searching for me her entire adult life. A few years ago, she finally tracked me down."

"Does Mr. Gruenwald know?"

Tino shook his head. "She was afraid to tell him. I had just ended my last tour of duty and was looking for a job. She got Mr. G. to hire me by telling him I was the son of a former housekeeper who'd worked for her parents."

I suppose I could understand that Tino acted out of some misguided sense of familial loyalty, but the puzzle was still shy too many key pieces. "Why dump Philomena's body at Trimedia?"

Tino grimaced. "Stupid, wasn't it? I tried to talk her out of that, but she insisted. The whole woman scorned thing. She wanted to make Mr. G. suffer for taking up with that skank."

"If you dumped the body in the river or a landfill, he'd never know what really happened to Philomena."

"Exactly."

"But what about Norma Gene?"

"Poor Norma Gene." Tino shook his head. "I don't know if she somehow figured out that Sylvia killed Philomena or not. Maybe she just wanted to talk to Sylvia. Either way, she never should have confronted her. Sylvia snapped."

"And you transported Norma Gene's body down to Philadelphia to make it look like a member of Philomena's old gang killed her?"

"I rolled her up in a rug and slipped out the service entrance of the condo."

"That's why you were so tired the other day."

Tino nodded.

It also explained the Vajazzling crystals imbedded in the sole of Tino's shoe and the one I discovered in the trunk of the Lincoln. Norma Gene must have had a Vajazzle.

"Afterwards," he continued, "Sylvia started talking about getting rid of Mr. G., too. Making it look like a suicide. She couldn't forgive him for cheating on her."

"Yet she broke up his first marriage."

This time Tino raised an eyebrow. "Really?"

"You didn't know?"

"No one ever mentioned a first Mrs. G. Those two fought like they'd been married forever."

"Twenty years." Tino's view of marriage spoke volumes and made me wonder about his life with his adoptive parents. "You do realize Mr. Gruenwald is old enough to be Sylvia's father? And Philomena's grandfather?"

Tino shrugged. "Some men like younger women."

I'd had enough of delving into Gruenwald's sex life. "Getting back to the staged suicide?"

"Right. Anyway, Sylvia planned it all out. She'd force him to write a suicide note, showing remorse for the killings, and I'd stage his death to look like he hanged himself."

"What made her think you'd go along with such a diabolical plan?"

"She thought because I killed for my country in Iraq and Afghanistan, I'd have no problem killing for her."

"But you were a Marine. You killed to protect us from terrorists."

"Exactly. And believe me, even then it's not easy to look someone in the eye and pull the trigger." He shifted to face me more completely. "Don't get me wrong. I'd do it again in a split second, but you never get over taking a life. You live with it for the rest of your life. No way was I killing for Sylvia. Even if she was my mother."

"She was using you, Tino. A loving mother would never ask her son to kill for her."

"I know."

"And that's when you went to the police?"

"Yeah. I admitted my part in disposing of both bodies. I was willing to take whatever punishment the D.A. doled out, but they offered me a deal. Get Sylvia on tape, and they wouldn't press charges against me."

"What about me, Tino? Where do I fit into all this?"

"What do you mean?"

"Why did Mr. Gruenwald offer to pay me to find Philomena's killer?"

"I don't know why, but he genuinely believed the killer was someone working at Trimedia. He knew the cops considered him and Sylvia prime suspects. Since he hadn't killed Philomena, and he couldn't conceive of Sylvia killing her, he needed someone on his side to figure out what really happened."

"He isn't going to like the truth."

"Yeah, I know."

"Do you also realize he's responsible for everything that happened?"

Tino knit his brows together. "How do you figure that?"

"All actions have consequences. Gruenwald set the first domino in motion by cheating on Sylvia. When that first domino toppled, it created a chain reaction."

"Cheating isn't a crime."

"No, but he'll have to live the rest of his life knowing his libido ultimately resulted in two murders and his wife's incarceration.

Philomena and Norma Gene are dead because Gruenwald couldn't keep his fly zipped."

"He can't be held accountable for Sylvia's actions."

"Unfortunately, the law probably agrees with you, but what about his other actions?"

"Besides taking up with Philomena? Like what?"

"He manipulated *Bear Essentials* out of existence in order to give Philomena the magazine she wanted. How many people are out of work and about to lose their homes, thanks to Alfred Gruenwald?"

"I see what you mean."

"Good, because even if he can't be charged with any crime, he at least deserves to lose his job."

I'd worked myself into a rage, probably because the adrenaline surging through my body over the last half hour needed some outlet of escape. I leaned my head back against the seat, closed my eyes, and took a deep breath as the train slowed to pull into Newark Penn Station.

"I'm sorry," I said. "I didn't mean to blow up at you, but that man's been a thorn in my side ever since he orchestrated the hostile takeover of our magazines. Just once I'd like to see justice win out over greed."

Tino rose and stepped into the aisle. I followed. "You just might get your wish," he said.

"Something else you're not telling me, Tino?"

"Not my place to say, Mrs. P." Then he winked at me.

"What happens now?" I asked as we stepped onto the platform.

"I'm heading back into the city. By now the cops have picked up Mrs. G."

We headed downstairs together. "So I guess this is it? We probably won't see each other again."

He bent down and kissed my cheek. "You never know, Mrs. P. You stay safe, hear?"

"You, too, Tino."

"Count on it." He headed for the door to Platform One to catch the train back into the city, and I headed for the nearest food stand to buy a bottle of water before making my way to Platform Five for the train to Westfield.

~*~

Once settled into a seat on a Westfield bound train and sufficiently rehydrated, I called Cloris to explain why I'd gone AWOL.

"Park Avenue matron Sylvia Gruenwald, a cold-blooded killer? Who would've guessed?"

"In a way, I did. One of my first theories was that Gruenwald was covering for his wife."

"But he wasn't?"

"No. That man is in for a rude awakening when he learns she not only killed his mistress and her girlfriend but was plotting his murder."

"If he wasn't such a scumbag, I might feel sorry for him."

"My feelings, exactly." I sighed heavily into the phone.

"You sound exhausted."

"I am. The last thing I want to do this evening is deal with Ira, his bratty kids, and Mama drama."

"I don't suppose you can get out of the rehearsal and dinner?"

I laughed. "Only if Tino had turned out to be the killer and got to me before I got away. And even then, Mama would probably be pissed with me."

Cloris gasped. "Don't even joke about such a thing!"

"At least we get half a comp day out of today's extravaganza. I'll get through the weekend somehow, then take Monday morning off."

"Sounds like an excellent plan. Hopefully, tonight and tomorrow will go smoothly for you."

I laughed again. "We're talking Mama here. How likely is that?"

~*~

By the time I trudged the several blocks from the train station to my home, only the late afternoon sun winking through the autumn leaves could convince me it was really half-past four in the afternoon and not in the morning. The adrenaline rush that carried me through the events of the last couple of hours had long since dissipated, leaving every fiber of my body numb, every muscle screaming from exhaustion.

Only the crisp breeze kept me from collapsing onto the nearest lawn. I hugged my arms around my body, quickened my steps, and cursed not having my coat.

Like a Siren's call, my bed beckoned from my house down the street, but unfortunately, we were due at the church in thirty minutes. Far too many hours loomed ahead before tonight's threesome rendezvous between me, my pillow, and my mattress.

Yelling coming from inside the house greeted me as I approached the front door. I recognized the two screaming banshees immediately: Mama and Lucille. Coward that I am, for a split second, I considered not entering the house. What if I turned around, got into my car, and drove straight to Tahiti? Then I laughed. With my brain suffering from sheer exhaustion, my thoughts made little sense. No bridge across the Pacific, I reminded myself.

I shook the absurd idea from my head, took a deep breath, and stepped into the house, nearly tripping over one of Mama's suitcases.

TWENTY-SEVEN

I found Mama and Lucille standing nose-to-nose in the living room, both shouting at each other, spittle and venom spewing forth. I slammed the door to grab their attention. "What in the world is going on?"

Lucille jabbed a finger at Mama. "This harlot is not moving back into my room! I forbid it."

"Your room?" screamed Mama, swatting at Lucille's hand. "This is my daughter's home, not yours, and if I want to spend the night, you have no say in the matter, you socialist freeloader."

Just what I needed. If it's not one thing, it's my mother. Or my mother-in-law. Dealing with murder obviously wasn't enough drama for one day, not in my life.

I stepped between the two of them, pushing each back an arm's length from me. "Enough! Both of you shut up!"

Lucille shoved my arm away. "You can't speak to me like that."

"I can and I will. Now what's this all about?"

They both began yammering and pointing fingers at each

other.

"Stop!" I glared at my mother-in-law. "I understand that you're upset about sharing a bedroom." I turned to Mama. "Why are you here with a suitcase? Have you decided to cancel your wedding?"

"Of course not!"

I crossed my arms over my chest and waited for a further explanation.

"I can't stay at the condo tonight."

"And why not?"

"Really, dear, everyone knows it's bad luck for the groom to see the bride before the wedding."

"Superstitious nonsense," said Lucille, "but I wouldn't expect any less from a silly twit like you."

Given the fates of Mama's last four husbands and one fiancé, I understood why she didn't want to take any chances. She needed all the good luck she could get for her latest trip down the aisle. "It's only one night, Lucille."

My mother-in-law crossed her arms over her voluminous sagging breasts, set her jaw, and narrowed her eyes. "I don't care if it's only one hour. I don't want her in my room."

"You're living in my home," I reminded her.

"So there!" said Mama, emphasizing her statement by sticking out her tongue.

"Enough!" I said. "Act like adults, or you'll both find yourselves out on the sidewalk." With that, I marched down the hall to my bedroom, slammed the door behind me, and collapsed onto my bed.

Big mistake.

Twenty minutes later Mama was shaking me awake. "For

heaven's sake, Anastasia, what are you doing napping? We're due at the church in ten minutes!"

Sometimes I think the last nine months have all been a bad dream. Then I wake up and realize the dream is my new reality. At which point I want to pull my quilt over my head and go back to sleep.

Unfortunately, Mama had whipped the quilt off my body. "You're not even dressed yet!" she said. "What is the matter with you?"

For a split second I toyed with the idea of telling her but bit my tongue. Literally. Not only didn't I have the energy, Mama is too self-absorbed to accept any excuse that throws a monkey wrench into her perfectly orchestrated works. She and Lucille have much more in common than either of them would ever admit. Each thinks the world revolves around her.

"Give me five minutes," I mumbled. I dragged myself off the bed and headed into the bathroom to splash cold water on my face and run a comb through my hair.

Two minutes later I found Mama, the boys, and Zack waiting for me in the living room, Lucille nowhere in sight. Mama looked pissed; the boys looked uncomfortable; Zack looked concerned. He crossed the room, draped his arm around my shoulders, and planted a kiss on my temple. "You look beat. Everything okay?" he whispered.

I nodded.

"Why don't I believe you?"

"Because you know me so well?"

He raised both eyebrows. "Now you really have me worried."

"I'm fine, but it's a long story. We'll talk later. Let's get through this evening first."

Mama clapped her hands together to interrupt us. "We need to leave. Now. We're already late."

~*~

We needn't have rushed. Lawrence and the minister greeted us at the church, but Ira and his kids were nowhere in sight.

"Ira's running late," said Lawrence.

Mama threw her arms up in the air. "Of course, he is! Why should I expect anything to go as planned?" She pulled out her cell phone and called the restaurant to push back our dinner reservation a second time.

Ira finally arrived—*sans* brats—an hour later. "I'm so sorry," he said, hurrying down the aisle to the front pew where we all sat.

"Where are the children?" asked Lawrence.

Ira offered up a chagrined expression accompanied by a shrug. "They refused to come. I finally called a babysitter and left them at home."

I wondered if they'd dare pull a similar stunt tomorrow for the wedding. Not my problem, I told myself as we began to go through the motions of the rehearsal.

Without Ira's three belligerent offspring to cause problems, we finished quickly and were soon on our way to the restaurant for the rehearsal dinner. The remainder of the evening went by without any problems, although Ira seemed subdued and a bit distracted throughout the evening.

"Is everything all right?" I asked him at one point between courses.

He smiled weakly. "Sorry. Just a lot on my mind."

Perhaps he'd finally come to the unpleasant conclusion that he needed to do something about his children. I chose not to pursue the topic.

We arrived back at the house by nine o'clock. "If you'll excuse me," said Mama, "I need my beauty sleep." She headed toward the bedroom she used to share with Lucille. A moment later we heard them arguing.

"I'm not sure how much sleep—beauty or otherwise—she's going to get tonight," I said.

The boys took off for the den. A moment later a baseball play-by-play drowned out their grandmothers' bickering. "A person can't hear herself think in this house," I said.

"We don't have to stay." Zack entwined his fingers through mine and led me out the back door and up the steps to his apartment.

"Alone at least," he said, once inside. He grabbed a chilled bottle of Sauvignon Blanc from the refrigerator and two glasses from the cabinet. We settled onto the sofa, and he poured the wine. After handing me a glass, he said, "Now suppose you tell me what happened today."

~*~

I woke up the next morning in Zack's bed with no idea how I'd gotten there. The last I remembered, I was relating how Sylvia Gruenwald killed Philomena and Norma Gene and planned to rid herself of her husband.

The aroma of brewing coffee wafted into the bedroom. I slipped into Zack's discarded shirt and padded barefoot into the main room to find him whipping up an omelet. He stopped to pour me a cup of coffee. "Good morning. Sleep well?"

"Hmm. Did I at least enjoy myself?"

He laughed. "Sweetheart, you were out before your head hit the pillow."

"Oh. So I guess you didn't enjoy yourself, either?"

He grinned. "I didn't say that."

I swatted his arm.

~*~

As I stood at the altar watching Mama and Lawrence take their vows, I sent up a silent prayer that this time my mother would find long-lasting happiness. Along with some financial security. I had my doubts about the latter, though, given that Lawrence seemed content to sponge off Ira, a man soon to be his *ex*-son-in-law. How long would Ira continue to foot the bills for a man no longer his relative?

Poor Ira. He thought he could buy love. Had he always been this way or only since his first wife's death? Either way, all that money he tossed around certainly wasn't buying him any happiness. Or respect. He'd married a gold-digger, and his kids alternated between using him as a personal ATM and a doormat. Even though he swam in Benjamins and I was stuck with both Karl's debts and his curmudgeon of a mother, I'd never trade places with Ira Pollack.

I glanced over to where he sat sandwiched between his twins and his son and wondered what he'd promised them to show up today. Apparently, not enough to keep them from slumping in their seats, scowls plastered on their faces, chips the size of two-by-fours on their shoulders.

After last night, Mama came to her senses and decided to forego including twin flower girls and a ring bearer in the ceremony. No woman wants to be upstaged at her own wedding by a three-pronged adolescent plot to sabotage the event. Ira tried to convince us his kids would behave, but I voiced my doubts, and for once Mama agreed with me.

After the *I do*'s we posed for photos in the church. No matter how much Ira cajoled them, his kids refused to cooperate with the photographer.

"They're doing this on purpose," I whispered to Zack. "I'm going to put a stop to their manipulative behavior."

I took a step in the direction of Ira's kids, but Zack reached for my hand to stop me. "Allow me."

He stepped between the photographer and Ira's three brats. One by one he whispered something into each child's ear. One by one their eyes grew wide with fear before each nodded, then plastered on a smile.

Zack returned to my side. "That should do the trick."

"What did you say to them?"

He winked at me. "You don't want to know."

Translation: Zack had threatened them with whichever alphabet agency he really worked for. It must have been a whopper of a threat because once we arrived at Ira's home for the outdoor reception, his kids holed themselves up in the house, not even showing up for the catered luncheon.

Unfortunately, several others made an unwelcome appearance.

Ira had just finished a toast to Mama and Lawrence when two men in dark suits entered the tent and headed straight toward him. Given all my dealings with the police over the last few months, I easily made them for detectives, a suspicion confirmed when I spotted them flashing badges. Ira nodded and followed them out of the tent.

I followed Ira. He and the two men made their way to the patio. I stopped at the entrance to the tent. The men stood with their backs to me, Ira facing me. From my vantage point I couldn't hear their words over the conversations and music going on behind me, but I saw the color drained from Ira's face. He shook his head violently and yelled, "No!" loud enough for me to hear.

I rushed across the lawn to the patio and placed my hand on his arm. His entire body trembled. "Ira, what's wrong?"

"Cynthia," he said in a shaky whisper. "They found her body floating in the canal."

THE ART OF DECOUPAGE

Decoupage is a method of laminating paper to surfaces. The craft dates back to the seventeenth century where it was first used to decorate furniture. The term comes from the French *découper*, "to cut out." Decoupage appears complicated but is actually a very simple craft. All you really need to know how to do is cut and paste.

Basic Decoupage Directions

Decoupage will work on just about any surface—glass, wood, plastic, metal, ceramic, clay, terra cotta, slate, leather, plastic, plastic foam, paper, cardboard, and fabric. To begin, clean the item you want to decoupage. Wood should be smooth and dust free. Wipe down glass surfaces with rubbing alcohol or vinegar. Metal surfaces must be coated with rust-resistant sealer. Lightly sand very smooth plastic surfaces before decoupaging.

Choose the images you want to decoupage onto the surface. You can work with photographs, pictures from magazines, fabric, greeting cards, wallpaper, wrapping paper, ribbons, doilies, dried flowers, postcards, decorative napkins, or clip art images from a computer.

All-in-one decoupage medium is the easiest to use as it works as a glue, sealer, and finish. Some mediums require an acrylic sealer to be applied as the final coat. Check the directions on the medium you purchase.

Materials: Item to decoupage, images for decoupaging, rubber brayer or wooden craft stick (optional,) foam brush, scissors, decoupage medium, tweezers (optional)

Carefully cut out the images to decoupage. Using the foam brush, apply decoupage medium to the wrong side of the image. Position the image on the item being decoupaged. If using small images, a tweezers aids in placement. Eliminate wrinkles, air bubbles, and excess medium by gently pushing down on the image with your fingers, the brayer, or craft stick and working from the center outward. Remove any excess medium with a damp cloth. If using multiple images, glue each in place in the same manner. Allow decoupage to dry completely. Once dry, apply several coats of decoupage medium to the entire surface, allowing each coat to dry completely before applying the next coat.

Tips

Patience is key when it comes to decoupage. Always allow plenty of time for the medium to dry completely between coats.

If using images from your computer, print with a laser printer. Images printed from an inkjet printer will smear when the medium is applied.

For flimsy papers, apply a layer of medium to the back and allow to dry before cutting out the image.

If you're decoupaging a curved surface, place the print face up on a damp sponge to moisten the paper first.

For papers that are printed on both sides, apply a coat of white acrylic paint to the reverse side to prevent the image from showing through to the front once it's decoupaged.

Experiment with tearing paper instead of cutting it to create a deckled-edge look.

Eliminate any stubborn air bubbles by pricking them with a pin and pressing down firmly with your fingers.

The more finish coats of medium you apply, the more the paper images will recede into the surface, making them look like they were painted on.

Potichomanie Decoupage

Potichomanie Decoupage originated in Victorian England. The technique was developed to simulate the look of Chinese vases, a popular decorative element in wealthy Victorian homes. Potichomanie Decoupage created a convincing, inexpensive substitute for those who couldn't afford real Chinese vases. Potichomanie literally means "pot crazy" and is derived from the French words *potiche*, meaning large vase and *manie*, a fad.

In Potichomanie, a print is decoupaged to the inside of a glass container, and the interior of the glass is painted with latex or acrylic paint to produce a porcelain-like finish. Choose a clear glass container with a wide mouth, such as a bowl, vase, or brandy snifter and a print or prints that will fit within the container.

Carefully cut out the image to decoupage. Place the printed image face up on a damp sponge to moisten the paper. Once the paper is damp, apply decoupage medium to the right side of the image. Position the print inside the glass. Press on the paper to mold it to the curve of the glass, working from the center outward to remove any air bubbles. Allow the decoupage image to dry completely. Once dry, paint the interior of the glass with a latex or acrylic paint.

Illuminated Decoupage

Illuminated Decoupage is a marriage of the decoupage print and paper foil to create a play of light within the decoupage item.

Using a craft knife, carefully cut away areas of the print you've chosen to illuminate, such as the windowpanes of a country cottage. Cut out pieces of paper foil slightly larger than the cut-out portion of the print. Apply decoupage medium to the foil and place behind the cut-out area of the print. Apply decoupage medium to the back of the print. Finish the project by following the Basic Decoupage Directions.

Embossed Decoupage

Embossing will give a three-dimensional look to decoupage. The easiest way to create this effect is by choosing to decoupage prints that are already embossed. If you can't find any, it's easy enough to emboss the prints yourself. It's best to choose images printed on heavyweight paper or card stock for this technique.

Don't trim the edges of the print. Place the print against a window with the back facing you. Using a pencil, outline those areas of the print you wish to emboss. Place the print face down on several layers of felt. Using the handle of a spoon or rounded paint brush, press down on the areas you've outlined. Gently continue to work the paper until you've created a slight depression in the paper. Don't press too hard; you'll tear the paper.

Once you've achieved the desired effect, follow the Basic Decoupage Directions for applying the print to the item you've chosen to decoupage, but don't press down on the embossed areas of the print as you're smoothing it, or you'll flatten the embossing.

Repoussé Decoupage

Repoussé Decoupage is a technique that adds an even greater three-dimensional quality to decoupage by incorporating papier-mâché. The technique works best when used on rounded objects and requires two sets of identical prints and dry papier-mâché (available at craft stores.)

Cut out the first print. Place the image face up on a damp sponge to moisten the paper. Apply decoupage medium to the back of the print. Position the print on the item chosen to decorate, pressing the paper to mold it to the curve and working from the center outward to remove any air bubbles.

From the second print, cut out the areas you want raised. Place the image face up on a damp sponge to moisten the paper.

Follow the manufacturer's directions for mixing the papier-mâché. The consistency should resemble dough. Apply a small amount of papier-mâché to the back of each cut-out shape, leaving 1/8"-1/4" around the cut edge of each shape. Apply decoupage medium and position in place over the identical area of the first print, carefully pressing down the edges of the cut-out shape. As the papier-mâché begins to set up, use the handle of a small paint brush to form indentations to define the raised areas.

Allow the repoussé to dry completely (several days) before finishing the project by following the Basic Decoupage Directions.

ABOUT THE AUTHOR

USA Today bestselling and award-winning author Lois Winston writes mystery, romance, romantic suspense, chick lit, women's fiction, children's chapter books, and nonfiction under her own name and her Emma Carlyle pen name. *Kirkus Reviews* dubbed her critically acclaimed Anastasia Pollack Crafting Mystery series, "North Jersey's more mature answer to Stephanie Plum." In addition, Lois is an award-winning craft and needlework designer who often draws much of her source material for both her characters and plots from her experiences in the crafts industry.

Connect with Lois at the following sites:
Email: lois@loiswinston.com
Website: http://www.loiswinston.com
Killer Crafts & Crafty Killers Blog:
http://www.anastasiapollack.blogspot.com
Pinterest: http://www.pinterest.com/anasleuth
Twitter: https://twitter.com/Anasleuth
Bookbub: https://www.bookbub.com/authors/lois-winston

Sign up for Lois's newsletter at:
https://app.mailerlite.com/webforms/landing/z1z1u5